A WAKE OF BUZZARDS

The Third Jess O'Malley Mystery

JINNY ALEXANDER

Copyright © Jinny Alexander 2023

Jinny Alexander has asserted her right to be identified as the author of this Work in accordance with the Copyright, Designs and Patents Act 1988

All rights reserved.

No part of this publication may be reproduced, distributed, or transmitted in any form or by any means, including photocopying, recording, or other electronic or mechanical methods, without the prior written permission of the publisher, except as permitted by copyright law.

This story is a product of the author's imagination and as such, all characters, settings, and events are fictitious. Any resemblance to real persons, living or dead, is purely coincidental.

ISBN Paperback: 978-1-916814-04-2

ISBN ebook: 978-1-916814-05-9

Cover Design: Wicked Good Book Covers

Map of Ballyfortnum: Jinny Alexander and Dewi Hargreaves

Visit www.jinnyalexander.com

www.OverSpilledInk.com

This book is dedicated to my village - my friends and neighbours and all who live here. A note in the acknowledgements explains why.

Also: in autumn 2023, I ran a contest through my newsletter in which the winner was granted a cameo role in this book. You will, therefore, meet Cindy and her husband Walt within these pages. Thank you, Cindy, it's been a real joy to include you.

A note to my American-English readers

I'm so glad you're here! I'm a British author, living in the Republic of Ireland, and all my books are set in Ireland or the UK. As such, I use British English in my writing so you'll notice different spellings and a few extra letters – **U**s after **O**s, for instance, and **L**s that come in pairs. I make up for these extras by using fewer **Z**s…

I hope you'll enjoy my natural English voice and immerse yourselves fully into my UK and Irish settings and characters, but if you're still not convinced, I recommend a nice cup of tea.

Over here, a nice cup of tea fixes *almost* everything.

Love, Jinny xx

PRONUNCIATION GUIDE TO IRISH NAMES IN THE BOOK

In *A Wake of Buzzards*, many new characters are introduced to the series. Many of them have Irish names. It's not always obvious how these names are pronounced, so I hope this pronunciation guide will help.
Please note, there are variations of many of these pronunciations. I've given the one that represents how I hear that character's name in my own head while I write

SURNAMES:
Geraghty = geh-ruh-tee
Docherty = DOK-uh-tee
Shaughnessy = SHAW-nuh-see

FIRST NAMES:
Aoife = EE-fa
Ciara = KEE-ra
Colm = Cuh-lum
Deiric = Derek
Kieran = KEER-uhn
Seamus = SHAY-mus
Siobhan = Shuh-vawn

(Some of these names only get a passing mention in this book, but you never know when they may reappear later in the series!)

IRISH WORDS AND PHRASES

CÉAD MÍLE FÁILTE (Kay-od mee-leh foyle-cha):
A hundred thousand welcomes.

SLÁINTE (slawn-che): Cheers!

BAILE (boll-ya) = Town. The English names of many Irish towns begin with Bally because it's the Anglicised version of the Irish word.

BALLYFORTNUM

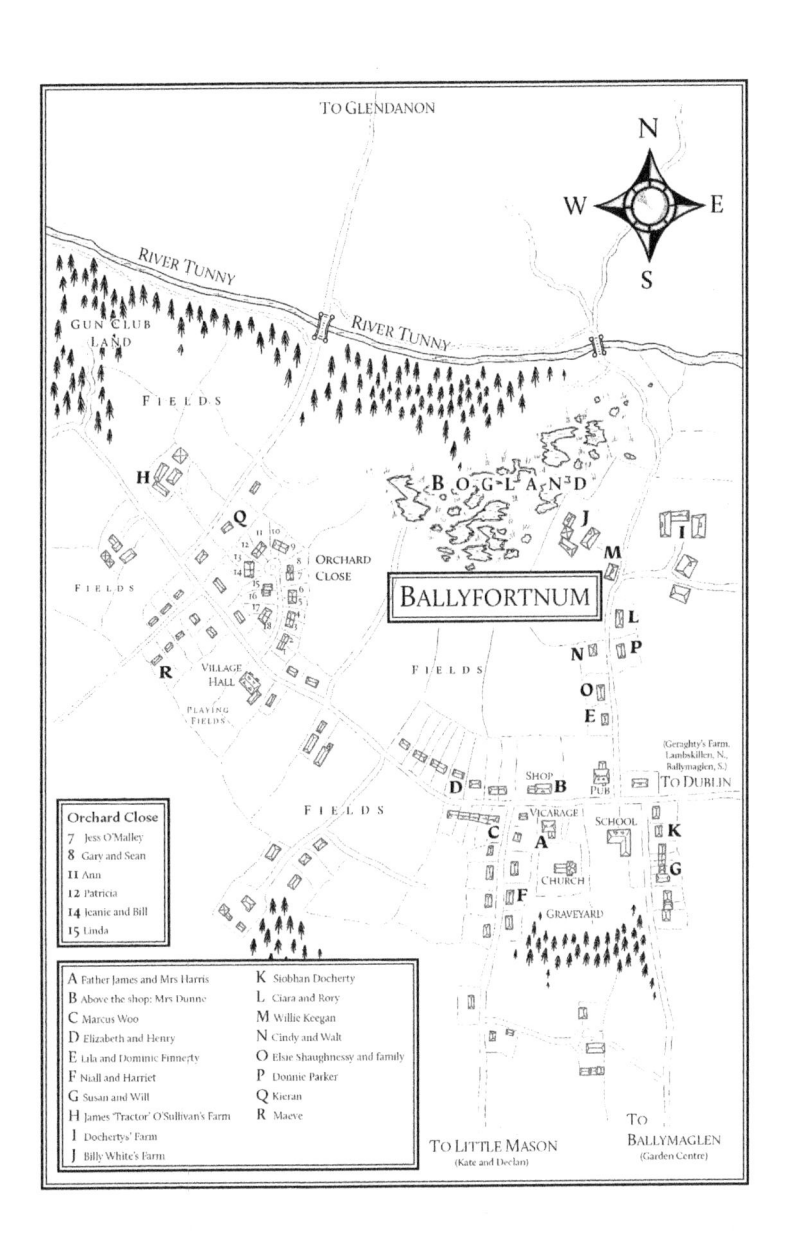

To Glendanon

River Tunny

Gun Club Land

Fields

Bogland

Orchard Close

Village Hall

Playing Fields

Fields

Shop
Vicarage
Church
Graveyard
Pub
School

(Geraghty's Farm, Lambskillen, N., Ballymaglen, S.)
To Dublin

Orchard Close
- 7 Jess O'Malley
- 8 Gary and Sean
- 11 Ann
- 12 Patricia
- 14 Jeanie and Bill
- 15 Linda

- A Father James and Mrs Harris
- B Above the shop: Mrs Dunne
- C Marcus Woo
- D Elizabeth and Henry
- E Lila and Dominic Finnerty
- F Niall and Harriet
- G Susan and Will
- H James 'Tractor' O'Sullivan's Farm
- I Docherty's' Farm
- J Billy White's Farm
- K Siobhan Docherty
- L Ciara and Rory
- M Willie Keegan
- N Cindy and Walt
- O Elsie Shaughnessy and family
- P Donnie Parker
- Q Kieran
- R Maeve

To Little Mason (Kate and Declan)

To Ballymaglen (Garden Centre)

Chapter One

Jessica O'Malley pulled her phone from her pocket and texted Marcus.

Found a body

She hit SEND with a smile tugging at her mouth, although it wasn't really funny at all, and prodded gingerly at the corpse with the toe of her boot. Definitely dead.

She squatted beside it and studied it more closely. No blood. No obvious signs of injury. No sign of a scuffle. It was if it had simply dropped from the sky. Weird.

Fletcher gave it a cursory sniff, and Jess tugged him away by his collar. "Leave it," she told her Labrador, in her firmest voice.

Fletch gave her his most sorrowful chocolate-eyed look, wagged his tail, and ran off into the field beside the track, nose to the ground, to follow a new trail, his fur as black as the peaty land that stretched out all around them.

Snowflake bounced along behind his larger friend, doing his best to keep up on his short West Highland legs.

Jess looked around, wondering what to do, and was saved from making any immediate decision by the phone ringing. "Hello," she said to Marcus, trying to restrain the laughter that threatened to spill from her. "How're you?"

She couldn't decide whether he sounded more annoyed with her or more concerned, as he asked her to explain herself; where she was; who was with her, and what the hell she thought she was doing, stumbling over yet another death.

"Okay, okay!" she conceded, after letting him alternate between worry and bewilderment for a little longer. "It's a bird. A buzzard, I think."

He said nothing, and she pictured him glaring into the phone, his face crumpled into a frown.

"Sorry. I couldn't resist. But I'm not sure if I'm supposed to do something about it? Report it to someone, I mean. Since it's a bird of prey? Aren't they protected? Thought you might know."

"Hold on," he said, and she heard him speaking to someone in a muffled voice, his hand presumably over the mouthpiece while he consulted one of his colleagues in Lambskillen Garda Station.

"Yes," he said, when he returned his attention to her. "I'm texting a number through now. National Parks and Wildlife Services. Give them a call. And Jess?"

"Yes?"

"Do not, I repeat, do not, do that to me again."

"Yes, Detective Woo. Or do I mean no, Detective Woo?" She laughed properly now, no longer trying to contain her amusement. "We're just out for a walk up the track by the pub. Found it on the side of the lane, up where the farmland meets the bog. I see they've been cutting down trees again; there's another stretch of woodland been felled. Can't you do anything to stop it? No wonder this poor guy is dead; he's probably been knocked out of his home."

"Mm hmm." Marcus, having listened to Jess moan about the destruction of the woodlands before, was non-committal. "I'll be finishing in about half an hour. Did you walk there, or drive?"

Jess, having left her car outside the pub, agreed to meet him at his little cottage in the village centre in about an hour, rather than drive Snowflake back to her house for Marcus to collect. Marcus's cottage was only a hundred yards or so away from the pub, on the opposite side of the road. If she got there first, she'd sit in her car and wait, or get herself an early drink and wait at one of the picnic tables on the pavement in front of the pub, since the late March afternoon was dry and bright for the first time in days.

After Marcus hung up, first promising he'd cook them something for dinner, Jess retrieved the number he'd sent, and dialled it.

The phone rang for what seemed like ages, then went to voicemail. Jess left a garbled message and her name and number, and disconnected the call. As she slipped the phone back into her pocket and called to the dogs, it rang again.

A harried-sounding woman spoke rapidly, bringing to mind the bursts of gunfire Jess sometimes heard across the farmland in shooting season. "I haven't listened to your message," the voice said. "Just missed the call and returned it straight away. What's up?" The woman panted a little as if she might be running a marathon or climbing a tree somewhere.

"Are you Parks and Wildlife?" Jess said. "I was given your number by the Gards. I found a dead buzzard. Thought you'd like to know. Well, not like to, but ... you know ..."

The woman laughed, sounding immediately younger, lighter, and a good deal friendlier than she had at first. "Oh thank God. I thought you'd be someone else calling to moan about something. I'm just about done for the day and trying to wrap up and get home and some tosser keeps calling about a leaking water pipe in the town park and I keep telling him it's not my job, and he won't take no." She paused for a breath. "Sorry. What did you say your name was? I can't get to you today. Unless you're in the Chinese takeaway in Glendanon in about thirty minutes, because after that, I'll be in my pyjamas with Netflix on."

"Glendanon?" Jess said, surprise making her voice shrill. "Glendanon near Ballyfortnum?"

"That's it. You know it? Feck it. I'm not supposed to let on where I live, in case people turn nasty. Happens, sometimes, in this job. You nearby then?" The question held a hint of panic, and there was a moment of silence. "I was joking. I don't really want a dead buzzard in lieu of my Chinese, to be honest with you. But ..." She sighed deeply into the phone. "I suppose I could meet you on my way home. If you *are* nearby?"

"Well," Jess said, "what do you think? I'm in Ballyfortnum, so close enough, but I've two dogs with me and nothing to pick the bird up with, and ... What *am* I meant to do with it?"

"Can you take photos? Mark where it is? And look around—is there something you can wrap it in to carry it, so you don't damage it? Your coat, perhaps?"

Jess ignored the hope in the woman's voice. "I am not wrapping my coat around a dead bird, however lovely it might have been before it died. Hang on ..." She squinted up and down the track and across the fields as if some well-prepared farmer might have left a handy wheelbarrow parked there for her.

The woman was talking again. "If you can put it somewhere safe—the boot of your car, perhaps? Somewhere cool. A fridge is best, of course—"

"No. I'm not putting it in my fridge, even if I could pick it up. I'll find something, but I might be a while. I guess I can go get something and then drive back and collect it, but I'm a good half hour away from my car, and then ..." Jess tailed off, as the other woman was speaking again.

A few minutes later, having agreed to do just that, and then call the woman back once she'd done so, Jess hung up, took a series of photos of the buzzard as instructed, and stuck a couple of thick twigs upright into the soil in a makeshift tipi to mark the spot in case something dragged the bird away—a fox, perhaps, delighted to find an easy supper. That done, she called the dogs to her again, and set off towards the village.

She'd not gone far when she found a grubby white coal sack caught in the base of the hedgerow. People were up and down this track all summer long to cut turf from the bog, and these kind of bags were well-used to transport the dried turf bricks home. She was forever finding them flapping in bushes or trodden into the ground by boots or tractors, adding to the rubbish frequently dumped in Ireland's quiet country lanes and boglands. Easing the coal bag from its thorny hold, she returned to the buzzard, picked it up with the sack, making sure not to touch it with her bare hands, and lay it out on the open path to wrap it more securely. It was surprisingly heavy; a magnificent, beautiful bird, with creamy-coloured feathers on its underside and tawny brown along its back, darkening to almost black towards its wingtips. The wing that had been under it where it lay was a little ruffled, but otherwise, as Jess had first thought, it bore no obvious signs of injury. She touched its chest gently with her fingertip, stroking the downy feathers, then wrapped the bag around it and picked it up.

Chapter Two

With the dogs racing ahead, Jess carried the awkward bundle along the track towards the village, her car, and Marcus's cottage.

As she'd noted on her way out, one side of the track was smothered in the golden yellow of dandelions, bright against the long spring grass. On this verge, the grass was fresh and lush, although elsewhere across the bog, it was still lank and brown from the winter. Where the dandelions left space, daisies lay like dropped confetti, their pink-tinged delicate petals a contrast to the vibrant yellows of the other flowers. Further from the track, where the bank was a little raised against the base of the hawthorn hedgerow, the paler yellow of the primroses took over. She was sure there were more than ever, but she was also sure she'd thought the same last year. And the year before.

On the opposite side, to her left as she walked homewards, the verge was a less cheerful sight. The grass had been cut short; the hedgerow hacked almost to ground level. A smattering of dandelions tried their best, and a few stray daisies dotted the shorn grass, but the bare, broken shards of hawthorn and willow were as unfriendly as a barbed wire fence.

Jess averted her eyes and focused on the righthand side, shifting the bulky weight of the dead buzzard as she strolled along. It wouldn't be long now until the hawthorn leafed up, followed later in the spring by its veil of white blossom. By May, most of the fields in Ballyfortnum would be edged with hawthorn flowers; a bright white outline marking the boundaries as clearly as a chalk outline around a body. She smiled at the comparison; where had *that* come from?

As she passed the gateway to the first farmhouse, she shifted the buzzard once more, tucking it snugly under her arm so she could clip Fletcher's and Snowflake's leads to their collars. Holding both leads in one hand and the bird clamped to her side with her other, they stepped onto the verge to allow a mud-splattered pickup truck to pass.

Jess didn't really know the farmers from this lane—she didn't often come up here as it was just a bit too far to walk from her home on the western edge of the village. She'd only decided to come this way today as, not five minutes after she'd arrived home from her college course, she'd realised she needed to run to the shop for bread and milk. Fletcher's mournful eyes when she'd told him to stay at home had guilted her into changing her mind. Besides, the two dogs were in desperate need of a good walk after being left at home for hours. Dead bird aside, she'd been glad of the change—it was a lovely walk, with the open bog stretching for miles at the end of the track, and had she not found the buzzard, they would have gone much further.

The driver of the truck raised a hand in greeting and beeped his horn as he passed.

Billy White, Jess thought, from the farm she'd just passed. His family had the imposing, double-storeyed stone farmhouse at the end of a long straight driveway bordered by an elegant avenue of mature trees and grassy fields, behind the dandelion-strewn verge and tangled hawthorn hedge. A cousin of the O'Sullivans, she thought, although she knew little more about him than that, and wasn't even entirely sure if it was him in the pickup or not.

The O'Sullivans owned almost all the farmland at her end of the village—the west side of Ballyfortnum—and also much of the land that stretched out towards Little Mason, the hamlet that lay to the south, beyond the church. To the east, much was owned by the Geraghtys and Harrises, and beyond that, the Flannery land was up for sale, their bungalow empty and abandoned, and likely to be either demolished or left to fall derelict. Tucked amongst these bigger parcels of farmland sat a couple of smaller farms: the ones with no more than fifty acres or so. Those farmers usually worked other jobs too, to support their farms.

Jess nodded in return to Billy White, or whoever it was, relaxed her taut grip on the dogs' leads, and hopped down from the verge.

At the first cottage beyond the farm driveway, the owner was in the garden, tinkering under the bonnet of a rust-flecked car. He raised his balding head from the depths of the engine and called a cheery hello.

"Lovely day," she called, tipping her head in lieu of a wave.

Opposite the cottage, the drive to the other of the lane's farmhouses snaked through an open gate, beyond which the driveway curved towards the bogland end of the track, and into a wide yard edged with huge steel sheds. The house stood starkly in open land at the front of the yard; another old two-storey, but this one painted white. Smoke wisped from one of its chimneys, and drifted away into the air. Somewhere in the distance, the lowing of cows suggested it may be milking time in the huge sheds beyond the house. Dochertys' land, she knew, although she didn't know which of them lived in the house.

She passed the last handful of houses and joined the road, turning right towards the pub and her car. As she juggled the buzzard and the dogs to fumble in her pocket for her car keys, a dark grey car pulled up alongside, and the driver rolled down his window.

Snowflake's and Fletcher's wagging tails and frantic tugging towards the car would have told Jess it was Marcus even if she hadn't recognised his car.

"Hang on," he said. "I'll park, and come and rescue you. That the bird?" He nodded to the bundle under Jess's arm, as it began to slide from her grip and its coal-bag wrapper.

"Shite, yes, hang on." Yanking the dogs closer to her, she nudged the badly-wrapped parcel back into place to stop it falling. "Stop it you two! Sit down!" she told the dogs, in a firm, no-nonsense voice that Fletcher ignored.

Snowflake, ever the policeman's dog, sat obediently at her feet.

Fletcher scrabbled at Marcus's car door; paws up on the open window.

Marcus eased his car closer to the pavement, pulled on the handbrake, and opened the door.

The package slipped from under Jess's arm; Fletcher threw himself at Marcus, and Snowflake jumped into the car.

With a skill she'd expect on the rugby field, not from a man being tackled by a Labrador, Marcus shoved Fletcher aside and caught the coal-bag, stamped his foot down onto Fletcher's lead, and ducked his head towards Jess to plant a kiss on her cheek.

"Hello," he said, straight-faced bar the minuscule twitch of his mouth that told her he was trying his best not to laugh.

"Right," she said, pretending to glare at him. "You can have the dead bird. And my bloody dog, if you want him. I'll meet you at your house in a minute." And with that, she turned on her heel and strode to her car, her shoulders shaking with laughter as she left him standing there juggling the same assortment of animals, dead and alive, that she'd been dealing with a moment earlier.

Chapter Three

Before crossing the road to meet Marcus at his door, Jess slid into her car, pulled up the call log, and texted the Parks woman: *I have it. What next?*

That done, she started the engine, shunted the car around in a neat three-point turn in front of the pub, and pulled up on the road in front of Marcus's little worker's cottage almost opposite. Lazy, perhaps, but it would be dark by the time she left, and the pub busy with its evening trade. Not that the pub ever got particularly busy on a Monday night, but still ...

Marcus had let the dogs out of his car and they galloped around his garden like a pair of March hares, leaping, ducking, boxing.

She'd not seen any hares yet this year on her walks, now that she thought about it, although if she were a hare, she'd not pop up anywhere near to Fletcher either. There was a certain thrill about spotting those huge, loping creatures—often the size of a small muntjac deer, and easily as big as Snowflake. Not that she ever saw muntjac deer around here either, although now and then locals reported sightings of red deer in fields around the village. She'd have to get up a lot earlier, and walk without Fletcher, for any chance of seeing one herself.

Marcus opened the door and stood back to let her enter first. "Kettle? Would you?" he said. "I need to get changed, won't be a minute. Help yourself." He disappeared through a door to the right of the narrow hallway, and Jess obligingly went to the kitchen and filled the kettle.

She'd become increasingly comfortable in Marcus's house over the last few months, and easily located mugs, tea, and milk. As she snooped in his fridge for an idea as to what he might offer to cook, her phone buzzed in her pocket. The caller ID showed only a number, and she stared at it for a second before realising it must be the Parks and Wildlife woman calling her back.

The caller didn't bother with a greeting or pleasantries, but launched straight in as if their earlier conversation had continued uninterrupted. "Can it wait till tomorrow? I'm bushed, and it's not like I can do anything tonight now anyway? Ballyfortnum, you said, so I can come that way on my way into work. Nine o'clock suit you? What's your Eircode?"

Jess said nothing for a minute, trying to keep up with the barrage of words the woman was throwing at her and simultaneously process the information. Was she home tomorrow? What day was it? Twice a week, Jess drove to Kildare, where she attended a college course on horticulture. On Thursday and Friday afternoons, she worked at the garden centre in Ballymaglen. *Today's Monday,* she decided. She'd been in Kildare today. *Tomorrow's Tuesday.* "Yes," she said, eventually. "I'll be home. Should I meet you somewhere?"

Insisting it was no bother to come to Jess's house in Orchard Close, the woman hung up with a breezy, "I've a takeaway to bond with, must go! See you in the morning, bye!"

"Does this woman only ever speak in exclamations and questions?" Jess mused, splashing hot water onto teabags as Marcus emerged from his bedroom, now wearing blue jeans, an open-necked shirt, and bare feet.

As he entered the kitchen, Jess turned to meet him, and he wrapped her into a hug. "Hi," he said, pulling back to look into her eyes. "How was your day?"

"Dead bird, remember?" She laughed, kissed him, and turned back to the tea. "Come on." She nodded towards the bright, south-facing conservatory at the back of Marcus's little cottage. "Let's sit? I walked miles, and I went to college today. All you've done is sit at a desk and drink tea, I'll bet."

He threw a disparaging glare over his shoulder and dropped onto the wicker sofa looking out across the garden. Outside, Fletcher mooched among the still-bare flower beds, and Snowflake lay half-on, half-off the path, his head on his neat white paws, watching his friend. "Been busy enough, actually, O'Malley. Pass me that tea?"

"Where'd you put the buzzard?"

"Left it in the boot. Seemed as good a place as any for now."

"I need to take it home. She'll collect it in the morning. That woman whose number you gave me. Nine-ish. She says they'll run some tests, could be poison if there's no wounds." Jess shrugged. "Shame though. I used to see so many of them about. There aren't so many lately. That bloody farmer up there keeps ripping out woodland. He's barely a single tree left on his land now. Can't be good for the wildlife. Don't think he'd know wildlife if it crept up on him and bit his arse, to be honest."

Marcus laughed, the lines around his dark eyes crinkling as they always did when he smiled.

"What've you been up to then, Detective Woo?"

Marcus, it turned out, had been engaged on a similar theme—there was to be a protest in Lambskillen Park at the weekend, about the prohibition of farming turf.

Jess didn't know much about this rural tradition of cutting turf to heat homes, having spent much of her childhood in the UK. Even after her parents returned to Ireland, they'd settled in Dublin until retiring to Ballyfortnum less than ten years ago.

"Me either." Marcus sighed and drained his tea. "I've spent most of the day reading up on it."

A ban on turf-cutting had been introduced way back in 2011, he explained, but the centuries-old practice of cutting and burning turf harvested from the boglands still persisted nationwide, with many householders ignoring the new regulations. Many rural families held rights to cutting and removing strips of turf—the black, peaty earth characteristic to the bogs—in a long-established system known as Turbary rights. These rights allowed home-owners to harvest their allocated strips of turf for the heating of their dwelling, and stemmed from the days of large estate owners granting their tenants the right and ability to warm themselves against Ireland's damp climate.

Jess's eyes glazed over as she tried to keep up with the spiel of information he'd learned. She stifled a yawn and he smirked.

"Am I boring you?"

"No, go on. Well, a bit, but it's interesting too."

Marcus gestured towards his rarely-used living room at the front of the house. "The people I bought this place from had a stack of turf left in the shed, but once I get through the last of it, I think I'll block the chimney. It's so draughty; the house'll be warmer without a fire, I'd guess."

Jess's house, newer-built, had no open fires—despite a dummy chimney perched on its roof for 'aesthetic reasons'—for which she was grateful. Who had the energy to lug in firewood or turf every day, especially on the cold, damp days you'd need it most? Not her. Nor the will to clean out the ashes every morning. "So what's the protest about?"

"Think it'll bring both sides out. That's why we want a Garda presence. The environmentalists will be out in force, but so will the bog-workers. They're worried about their jobs, which is understandable."

There'd been a lot of talk about reusing the bog land for other purposes, and in some areas, this was being successfully implemented, but elsewhere, it had caused controversy and uproar. Just over the county border, a few miles on from Ballymaglen, several hectares of bog previously farmed for garden peat was earmarked for a windfarm, and many of the residents were firmly against the idea. "Wind power is great, but not in my backyard," seemed to be the common refrain. "We're all for wind power, but put it somewhere else."

"The bogs should be preserved, though," Jess said, staring into Marcus's tired eyes. While she mightn't know much about the rights or wrongs of turf-cutting, she loved walking out across those endless miles of heather-covered black land, and knew this was a habitat unique to Ireland, and that the peat bogs supported many endangered species of native fauna and flora. "We should protect them, before it's too late."

"Mmm." Marcus sighed again and got to his feet. "Food? Noodles? Chicken?"

Jess stood, offering to help, but he waved her back into her seat.

"It's definitely my turn. Stay there."

Jess and Marcus had only known each other for little over a year, having first met last February after Jess's elderly neighbour died. They'd quickly become friends, and when Marcus had let slip that he may need to rehome the little dog he loved so much, Jess had stepped in. Since last spring, she'd minded Snowflake while Marcus worked his long shifts at the Garda station, but now she was at college twice a week on her horticultural course, and the arrangement had become more complicated. They'd enlisted Jess's widowed neighbour to help, and Jess and Linda were equally determined that Marcus would be able to keep the young Westie. Snowflake, he'd said in a rare moment of despair, was almost all he had left of his young daughter since her mother had taken off for the States with another man, taking Lily with her.

Jess and Marcus, since that first meeting after Linda's husband's wake, had become easy friends, but within just a few months she'd realised her feelings for Marcus were deeper than that, and his the same for her. Since he'd kissed her in a supermarket carpark six months ago, their relationship had grown beyond 'just good friends'. Nonetheless, they were happy to take things slowly, mindful of past baggage and a nearly-ten-year age gap between her thirty-five years and his forty-four, and wary of jeopardising their easy friendship for a fling that could fizzle out.

The rest of the evening slipped by comfortably, with a delicious bowl of *Lo Mein* and a glass of wine—just the one, as Jess had to drive home and Marcus had another long day shift ahead of him tomorrow—before, with one final, lingering kiss, Jess retrieved the coal-bagged corpse from the boot of Marcus's car, and set off home to Orchard Close with Fletcher curled up beside her on the passenger seat.

Chapter Four

Jess was up early on Tuesday morning, ready first for Marcus to deposit Snowflake with her for the day, and then to hand over the buzzard at nine.

She'd left the dead bird in the boot of her car overnight, not wanting to bring it into the house, but even so, the thought of its stiffened, lifeless body kept her awake long into the night.

Marcus had been in a hurry, and sent Snowflake trotting into Jess's home with barely time for a quick hello on the doorstep. "I'll make it up to you later, I promise," he'd said quietly as he slid back into his car, blew her a kiss, and drove away.

Jess hugged her arms around herself as she watched him leave. "Can't wait," she whispered to the departing car. "See you later." She'd yearned to pull him close to her for a moment on the doorstep, but their blossoming romance was too new to broadcast to all the neighbours, although some of them, of course, already knew.

Directly opposite Jess's house, the front door of Number 15 opened, and Linda, in a pale floral dressing gown, stepped out. "Hello Jess, love," she called across the street.

Jess nudged her own front door shut to contain the two dogs, and skipped over the road to give her elderly neighbour and close friend a peck on the cheek.

The two made small talk for a few minutes until Linda ducked back inside her house, returning a moment later bearing a plastic tub. "Gingerbread," she said, as she pushed it into Jess's hands. "Share it with Marcus, won't you."

Linda, closer to Jess than Jess was to her own absent mother, was both unsurprised and delighted by the romance between her young neighbour and "that lovely Garda". Since her husband's death last February, she and Jess had become even closer than before, and Linda had come to share Jess's newfound love of gardening. As she'd encouraged Jess to take up the course in Kildare, she now helped out by minding Fletcher and Snowflake on the days that Marcus's work pattern clashed with Jess's college days, an arrangement that was working far better than Jess had anticipated.

With a promise to collect Linda a few groceries later in the day, and the tub of gingerbread in her hands, Jess retreated to Number 7 for a hurried breakfast before the Parks woman arrived for the buzzard.

A few minutes before nine, Fletcher flung himself up on the back of the sofa to rest his paws on the windowsill, barking frantically, before spinning around, leaping to the floor, and charging to the front door, still barking as if his life depended on rousing the entire street.

Snowflake let out a single yap, and chased the Labrador into the hall.

Jess shooed the dogs back into the living room and shut the door, then swung open her front door to reveal a petite brunette with a mass of short curls, a sprinkling of freckles, a phone to her ear, and a frown on her face. As Jess stepped forward, the woman muttered something into the phone that sounded like "you fecking eejit", glared at it for a second, tucked it into her jacket pocket and thrust forward her hand.

"You're Jess? Yes? Who called yesterday about the bird? I'm Peggy, sorry, I don't think I said yesterday. Busy day." She broke off with an abbreviated half-laugh. "They are *all* busy. Not even nine o'clock, and here I am, already on the job and already dealing with *feckers*. Where's the bird then?"

Jess, not often lost for words, took a step backwards. How could anyone have this much energy so early in the morning? "Er ... hang on... it's in the car. I'll just get some shoes on. Do you want to come in? You look like you could use some coffee?"

The woman—Peggy—pulled out her phone again, lit up the screen, frowned, and then said, "Oh what the heck, go on then. You can tell me where you found it, and all that." Decision made, her shoulders dropped and she smiled broadly, changing her whole demeanour from harassed-and-hurried to friendly-and-cheerful. "Introduce me to those dogs, before they have the door down?"

Jess ushered her in, closed the front door, and put her hand on the living room door handle. "He'll jump," she warned. "You okay with that? He's friendly, but he's a bad-mannered idiot. The Lab, I mean. The other one is very good. He's not mine." She gave an apologetic shrug, and pushed open the door.

True to form, Fletcher launched himself at their guest, and she staggered backwards into Jess, before dropping to her knees and giving Fletch's ears a hearty rub.

"He's lovely, aren't you? What's your name? Aren't you a gorgeous boy?" She extracted herself from the Labrador's slobbery licks, stood up, and stepped into the living room to greet Snowflake.

"Come on through." Jess waved her on into the kitchen, persuaded the dogs into the garden, and shut the French doors behind them. "Tea or coffee?"

As she made Peggy a cup of "Strong, black, one big sugar, thanks a mill," Jess relayed how she'd stumbled across the dead buzzard on yesterday's walk. "I used to see loads of them flying around here, but there don't seem to be so many about, now," Jess mused, stirring milk into her tea. "It's a bit early, but do you want some gingerbread? My neighbour just gave it to me this morning. She's a great baker; it'll be delicious."

Peggy didn't need much enticing, and accepted a plate bearing a large chunk of the gooey cake, and a second cup of coffee, while Jess told her how she'd also noticed how many trees were being felled on the land at the far end of that farm track, and how the farmer seemed to be systematically reclaiming the bog, digging new drains, adding rubble tracks, and turning it over to grazing, bit by certain bit.

"Is he even *allowed* to do that?" Jess asked through a mouthful of crumbs.

Peggy glanced up her. "Maybe. I'll check the land registry. If he owns the land, he can."

Jess swallowed the gingerbread and looked up; her mouth open. "Really? I thought the bogs were protected?"

Peggy sighed, reminding Jess of how Marcus had responded last night over the same topic.

Jess regaled the conversation she and Marcus had shared about the protests, and how the 2011 changes to the law didn't seem to have actually changed anything.

Peggy nodded in agreement. "He's not wrong there." She got to her feet. "Now, show me this bird. If it's been shot at, we may have a prosecution on our hands. They're protected, you know?"

Jess retrieved the coal-bag-wrapped buzzard from her car boot and handed it to Peggy, who immediately peeled back the bag and peered at the bird.

"Hang on." Balancing the package in one arm, she tugged open the back door of her van, emblazoned with the NPWS logo. She shoved aside a crate and laid the bird on the van's floor. Standing slightly skewed, so Jess could see, Peggy gently parted the birds feathers. "Look, see here? Pellet holes."

Jess squinted closer, not really sure what she was looking at, but morbidly fascinated at being so close to a gunshot wound.

Peggy turned the bird over, and pulled open its wings. "It's quite young. A bit underweight. The wing's a bit battered, but that could be from where it fell. We'll run tests. Those pellet-marks aren't new, so I doubt that's what killed it. Might have got hold of poison as well."

"How would someone poison a buzzard?" Jess asked. "And why?"

"Mightn't be deliberate. It could have got hold of mice, rats, that had ingested poison, something like that. We'll know more once the lab reports are back. I'll drop it in this afternoon. Will take a week or so, usually."

"Will you let me know?"

"Sure." Peggy transferred the bird from its makeshift shroud into a lidded container, and handed the coal sack to Jess. "Thanks for calling it in. Helps us to monitor them. Good to know. Thanks for the coffee, too." She smiled a wide smile, her eyes sparkling with fun entirely at odds with her earlier brusque demeanour. "And the gingerbread. Maybe I'll call round in person, with the results." She patted her tummy, swung herself into her van, and drove off, giving Jess a cheerful wave as she shunted the van around in the end of the *cul de sac*, and still waving as she passed by again on her way out.

Chapter Five

After the early start, Jess's Tuesday eased into a lazy day of catching up with chores and walking the dogs down to the shop to collect a few necessities for Linda, in reward for a cup of tea and another chunk of that delicious gingerbread.

Wednesday was a rush of dropping the dogs to Marcus en route to Kildare and her college course; collecting them as she passed through the village on her way home, so Marcus could get off to his night shift, and collapsing, exhausted, in front of the television for the evening.

Before she knew it, Thursday arrived, and by five minutes to one, she was pulling into the car park in the Ballymaglen garden centre, to work her afternoon shift.

As Jess stashed her car keys and phone under the till and did a quick skim of the note Shay had left stuck to the cash drawer, Jack appeared from between the shelving, laden with an armful of pots.

"Seen Shay?" he asked, as gnomelike as ever as he peered comically over the towering plant pots, his eyes almost hidden by deep wrinkles and his thick, white beard and hair.

"Only just got here," she answered, relieving him of some of his load and setting them down on a wooden garden table.

"He was looking for you, a minute ago."

Leaving Jack in charge of the shop floor, Jess headed out through the sliding doors at the rear of the shop, into the covered yard where the plants were displayed for sale. Beyond the rows of tables, stood the polytunnels where most of the growing was done and seedlings sown and nurtured. Two portacabins nestled between the covered space and the nearest tunnel, and it was to the smaller of these that Jess went first.

Shay sat behind a cluttered desk, chewing the end of his pen and scowling at the page open in front of him and the flickering blue light of his laptop screen.

"You're looking for me?" Jess said, from the doorway.

"Always," he said with a wide smile.

Jess laughed, the guilt at having rejected his romantic intent back in the summer when she'd realised it was Marcus who made her heart beat a little faster, not Shay, having finally subsided. Lovely, kind Shay, who for a brief few weeks she had thought she could get involved with. Lovely, kind Shay, who had encouraged her and helped her get onto her course, and given her a job in his garden centre, and who still wanted to be her friend after she'd led him on and let him down.

"I'm here now," she said, sinking onto the chair opposite him, the desk between them. "What's up?"

To her delight, he gave her instructions to spend the afternoon in one of the polytunnels, to plant out as many trays of spring bedding plants as she could manage in the few hours until her shift finished, as long as Jack didn't need her in the shop.

"He'll shout if it gets busy, but it's been quiet so far this week for some reason," Shay said. "I'll be out in a bit to help you. I'll bring tea."

She flashed a smile and left him to his paperwork.

For the next two hours, Jess worked steadily through the seedlings, content in the quiet warmth of the furthest tunnel; her hands stained brown from the crumbly potting compost.

Shay looked in on her once or twice, delivering the promised cup of tea but not the help, and then, a little after four, came to find her to help with a sudden rush in the shop. "Can you sort out this bulk load of glyphosate? There's enough; I ordered it in specially." Shay pushed a printed invoice into her hands. "Sorry, I'd do it myself, but a rep just arrived, and Jack's tied up with another order."

"No problem. In the shed?" Jess followed Shay from the tunnel and gestured towards the locked shed at the rear of the office portacabin, where all large quantities of weedkiller were stored for safety. They only kept the smallest amounts on the shop floor. "Who's it for?" She glanced at the invoice. "Oh, he's from Ballyfortnum. I think I was on his land on Monday."

Jess retrieved the shed key from behind Shay's desk, and lugged the required number of twenty-litre containers onto one of the larger trolleys, locked the shed, pocketed the key, hauled the trolley to just inside the yard gates, and went in search of the farmer, not sure if she'd recognise him or not.

Beside the counter, a wideset, fair-haired man of around the same age as Jess flicked through a brochure about ride-on mowers, but closed it and dropped it back onto the garden table with its companions as Jess approached.

"Thomas?" she asked, deciding that firstly, he was vaguely familiar, and secondly, why else would he be loitering there idly if not waiting for his order?

"That's me." He held out a hand, rough and weathered, for Jess to shake. "Haven't seen you in here before, have I?"

"I'm Jess. I live in Ballyfortnum too, actually. I think I've seen you around—I walked my dog up your way earlier this week. I only do a couple of afternoons here. You parked in the car park?"

The man nodded, and she led him to where she'd left the trolley, slid the bolts across to open the yard gate, and began to manoeuvre the bulky load to his jeep.

"Let me." Thomas Docherty took over the trolley, steering it with ease while she trotted beside him.

"That's a lot of weedkiller," she said, helping him stash the bottles into the load bed of the jeep.

"Lot of weeds," he replied with a grin.

"Not wildflowers?" Jess asked, trying hard to keep her voice light and unaccusing.

"Cows need grass." He shrugged, lifted the last two containers into the jeep, and closed the tailgate. "And I've got a lot of cows." He smiled at her again. "See you around, Jess. Nice to meet you." He opened the driver's door, clambered in, and started the engine, his door still open as he bade her goodbye.

"You too," she said, the response automatically polite, although she wasn't entirely sure she meant it. He seemed pleasant enough, but there was something about his attitude that she couldn't warm too. Surely a few wildflowers couldn't be that bad a thing, could they? She remembered the shorn grass on the roadside as she'd walked along the track the other day, and the regimented squares of paddock, each one divided by a single strand of electric fencing, with a shared water trough bridging every two sections. There were no hedgerows, no trees, no shelter for the cattle. Although, thinking about it, she'd also seen no cows in any of those grassy squares.

Thomas Docherty slammed his door, nodded, and drove away.

Jess dragged the trolley back to the yard; locked the gates, and ambled into the shop, where Jack was dealing with a queue of half a dozen or so customers. She slipped behind the counter and called the next person over to her so she could ring up their purchase of several trays of bright spring primulas and a bucket of bird seed.

The shop stayed busy for the next forty minutes, and Jess and Jack worked side by side with both tills open until at last the surge of customers left. Turning to each other, they both spoke at once:

"Thank God that's over; was a bit mad there for a while."

"Tea, then?"

Jess laughed, nodded, and set off to put the kettle on, leaving Jack to tidy the shelves and drag in the display items from the front of the shop.

Shay met her in the yard, where he'd been restocking the empty spaces on the plant tables. "Bit rushed there for a minute," he said, echoing Jess's words of moments before. "Tea?"

As she waited for the kettle to boil, she stuck her head out of the portacabin door and called across the yard to Shay. "Why would a farmer buy that much weedkiller from us? I mean, isn't it cheaper to get that sort of thing from a farm supplier? Not that I'm trying to lose you business, but I just wondered ..."

"They do, usually, but I set up an agreement with the suppliers and several of the local farmers a few years back. Gave them an incentive to support a local business, made it work for all of us. You'd be surprised how many of them were happy enough to get it from me, once I made sure they didn't pay more for it. Wish I hadn't, to be honest … Can't say I like what it's doing to the environment, now we know more about the long-term effects." He gave her a wry smile. "Be careful what you wish for, isn't that what they say? I got the orders and kept the customers, but now I'm aiding and abetting the destruction of the world."

Jess chuckled at his dramatics, and he threw a clod of earth at her, matted into a clump of grass he'd pulled from a potted shrub. She ducked, and it hit the doorframe with a thud and slithered to the ground. "Kettle's boiled," she told him, and went back in to make them all tea, thinking about the fair-haired farmer and his gallons of poison.

Chapter Six

Arriving home a little after six, Jess slid a ready-made pizza in the oven and set the automatic timer so she'd have half an hour to walk the dogs before her dinner started to cook.

"Come on lads, let's go."

Snowflake sat patiently on his haunches while Jess sank onto the bottom stair in the narrow hall of her little semi-detached house to pull on her walking boots, and Fletcher, as usual when he knew it was time for a walk, bounced around like a child's rubber ball.

At the entrance to Orchard Close, they turned right, away from the village centre, intending to walk past the old farmhouse that had belonged to Tractor O'Sullivan, and onwards towards the river. Tractor's old stone house was now lived in by one of his many relations—a cousin, she thought, but there were so many of the O'Sullivans around here it was hard to keep track. It could've been anyone, for all she knew. She wouldn't want to live there herself, not after what had happened at the end of last summer. She shuddered, and walked on past the turn-off, deciding not to go towards the river after all. Instead, she continued along the road that wrapped around the south-westerly edge of Tractor's farm. She rarely walked along this stretch of the road, with its nasty blind bend and steep hill. For much of the year, the growth on the hedges made visibility poor and the road dangerous to walkers, but in early spring, with the hedges cut back during their dormant winter months, and the leaves not yet out, it was easier to see and hear oncoming traffic.

At the bottom of the hill, a quiet, grassy farm track bordered the back of Tractor's land, making the short stretch on the dodgy bend worthwhile. Wide enough for a vehicle, but not tarmacked, the track was closed in on both sides by cultivated pines set on mossy-edged banks, and green all year round. A couple of streams ran through the trees, tunnelling under the path in pipes, and spreading every now and then into algae-speckled pools, creating a magical, fairytale scene. At this time of year, the edges of the path were dotted with primroses, and the trees were trilling with birdsong. In autumn, the track would be edged with hundreds of mystical toadstools in every shade of brown.

A few paces along the track, safely away from the road, Jess unclipped the dogs' leads, and they bounded off the path and into the trees, darting out of the undergrowth at random places on the path ahead only to promptly disappear into the next cluster of shrubbery.

The idyllic forest track ended less prettily, after about half a mile, at a farm gate bearing a LANDS PRESERVED sign, and under that, in equally loud capitals: NO SHOOTING. Cable-tied below that: BGER WILDLIFE CLUB.

Ballyfortnum, Glendanon, Ennisbaile and Rathdowney. The four neighbouring parishes this side of Ballyfortnum. This sign always made Jess smile in bewilderment, as this patch of land was also the Gun Club land.

How it was possible, or even legal, to call a Gun Club a Wildlife Club, was incongruous to say the least, ridiculous and misleading at best. And as for that NO SHOOTING sign ...

What it really meant, her dad had explained several years ago when he'd first walked Jess down here with his also-now-deceased little Scottie dog, was that the lands were *managed*. The local wildlife club had breeding cages set up on the land for game birds, and at certain times of the year, long after that year's new hatches were released into the wild, there would then be the necessary culls, to ensure stocks were managed.

Jess had not quite followed the logic.

The Gun Club also met here for clay pigeon shoots, and general jollies. Several of the local landowners gathered here regularly, and as often as once a week through the late autumn and winter, the sound of gunshots would fill the air for an hour or two as the men gathered with dogs and shotguns. Jess imagined them in tweed caps, swigging from hip-flasks and calling to each other in a mix of pure Irish country-boy accents and upper-class landowner voices, many of which, in her mind, were English-accented. A throwback to the old days of rich English landowners and the famine, no doubt. Her history of this time was somewhat clouded, as she'd attended school in England for several years before her dad had been transferred back to Dublin, midway through Jess's secondary school years. Funny how the two versions of the same period of tumultuous Irish history were portrayed so differently on either side of the Irish Sea. She tended to keep quiet anytime the issue arose, wary of causing unintended offence.

As Jess rounded the final bend, three tatty vehicles were parked one behind the other in front of the gate, hiding the signs from view. Shooting season was in the autumn, and if there was a clay pigeon meet, she'd have heard about it long before now—and cars would be nose-to-bumper for the length of the track—so she continued, undaunted, towards the gate.

The first of the vehicles was a battered, black pickup truck, covered in mud splatters, and looking as if it had driven through a swamp. It was similar to the one she'd seen on Monday, but then weren't they all? Most of the farmers had some kind of similar four-wheel drive utility vehicle: a jeep-type thing like a Land Rover, or, more commonly, this kind of multi-purpose pickup truck. Something versatile and tough, with a decent load space for lugging around whatever it was that farmers lugged around. Seed. Feed. Lambs. Hay ... She shrugged. *Who cares?* The other two cars were more of the same—dirty, dented, old-looking but with newish number plates. They must face a lot of wear and tear; farmers' cars never looked new for long.

On the other side of the gate, four men stood huddled around a chicken-wired cage. Inside the cage, a couple of pheasants scrabbled at the ground.

Fletcher let out a low bark, and the men turned to look.

A pair of border collies and a black Labrador, sleeker and stockier than Fletcher, moseyed around the men's feet, so Jess clipped Fletcher's lead to his collar before he got any notions of bounding off to join them. She caught Snowflake too, although he was unlikely to go running off, and, dogs restrained, she stepped up to the gate to see what the men were at.

One broke away from the group, and strode towards her. As he neared, she recognised him as the same man she'd waved at on her walk on Monday afternoon—the one in the battered pickup.

"Hello," he called cheerfully as he reached the gate. "You're George O'Malley's daughter, isn't that right? Billy. Billy White." He smiled in greeting, his weathered face open and friendly, but not, contradictory to what Jess had first thought when she'd passed him on Monday, much older than her.

Jess wrapped Fletcher's lead around her hand, pulling him close so he couldn't scrabble through the rails to jump at the man. She rested her other hand—the one loosely holding Snowflake's lead—on the top of the gate, and her foot on the bottom bar. "Yes, I'm Jess. Nice to meet you. You knew my dad?" This wasn't really a surprise—the longer Jess lived in Ballyfortnum, the more she realised just how popular and well-known her dad had become in the few years he'd lived in Orchard Close between his retirement and his death. She didn't wait for the man to answer. "What are all the birds?" She nodded towards the cages, where she recognised pheasants but not the birds in the cages alongside.

"Those?" He followed her gaze. "Red grouse, in that one. Not too many of them around here. We're trying to build stocks. Government scheme." As he spoke, he was already turning back towards his friends. "Thomas, Colm, Matty."

The three men lifted hands or inclined heads in greeting but didn't come closer. One of them, seemingly a good bit older than his fellow Wildlife or Gun Club members, leaned on the cage roof as if he needed it to hold him up. After acknowledging Jess, all three resumed staring intently into the enclosure, where a group of young birds darted back and forth along the fencing.

Billy shrugged. "Best get on. Need to patch a hole. Keep your dog out, yeah? We've a lot of chicks around at this time of year. Lost a few to crows and mink already. Vermin." He spat the word with venom. "Nice to meet you Jess. Enjoy your walk." Already striding away, he threw the words over his shoulder with a smile.

Fletcher scrabbled at the base of the gate, but was too big to get under the narrow gap. Jess pulled him away, and they started back along the trail towards home and pizza. Once they'd passed the parked cars, she unclipped the leads and the dogs charged ahead, racing down the track and dashing in and out of the trees once more. As Jess rounded a curve in the track, Fletcher darted from the undergrowth and bounded out of sight down the path.

"Dammit," Jess muttered. Had he seen a rabbit? "Fletch!" she yelled, and Snowflake appeared at her side. "What's he after?" Jess asked the Westie.

Snowflake's small pink tongue lolled from his mouth in a doggy grin, but he said nothing.

"Fletcher!" Jess yelled again. "Come on!" She picked up pace and rounded the bend, to find Fletcher and a handsome Dalmatian circling and sniffing at each other. She'd met the spotted dog once or twice before, but only in passing and always on its lead, so she wasn't sure how friendly it might or might not be. As she tried in vain to get Fletcher to pay attention and return to her side, the Dalmatian's owner ruffled Fletcher's head and caught him by his collar.

"Someone's looking for you," he told the dog. "Hello," he said to Jess. "How're you? Here you go."

Jess clipped Fletcher's lead back on, and pulled him away. "Thanks. He's so disobedient sometimes, sorry."

"Aren't they all?" The man laughed, and patted the Dalmatian's spotted head.

"You in the Gun Club too?"

He shrugged. "I am, but I'm not the most active member to tell the truth. It's a nice walk for Sidney here. We live round the corner." He nodded towards the village.

"Oh! Yes! I've seen you in the garden. Opposite Tractor's gates? I'm Jess, by the way."

"Kieran."

Jess shuffled Fletcher's and Snowflake's leads into her left hand and returned Kieran's proffered handshake. They chatted for a moment about nothing in particular, then parted ways, dogs on leads and two of the three straining towards each other in protest at being separated. Snowflake, of course, walked demurely and sensibly, leaving Fletcher to the job of trying to unfoot his mistress by getting under her feet.

By the time they got home, Marcus was parked outside Jess's house, and the pizza was burned at the edges.

Chapter Seven

J ess sat up in panic, woken by the ringing of her phone. A quick glance at the screen told her it was only eight-thirty on Friday morning and far too early for anyone to be phoning her, although definitely time for her to be out of bed and not still dozing in that fuggy state between having a bit of a lie-in and getting up to let Marcus and Snowflake in.

"Hello?"

"Well, you were right to call it in. We got the results back; I put a rush on it with the lab and …"

Peggy. Parks and Wildlife. At this ungodly hour of the morning. Jess sat up straighter, shuffled backwards against the pillows, and tried to focus on the spill of words.

"Hang on a sec. Start again. I'm only just up."

Downstairs, Fletcher let out a single low bark and ran to the front door, feet scrabbling on the wooden laminate.

Clamping the phone to her ear, Jess swung herself off the bed and across to the window.

Peggy was still talking. "... pellets ... poison ... system ... have a look ... feckers ..."

Jess tapped on the window, and below her, Marcus looked up. She held up her fingers. *Five minutes, hang on.*

"Tell me that again, Peggy? In idiot's terms?"

Obligingly, Peggy repeated the news. The postmortem had found pellet wounds, shot, and traces of poison in the poor bird. The combination, she explained, had killed it. The shots seemed to be from two separate occasions, one burst causing only minimal damage to a wing. "A lucky miss, really," she said. "The second lot, a bit worse. Would have impaired its mobility, slowed it down." Unable to hunt so effectively, it could have been driven to scrounging around for already-dead or wounded prey. "Vermin loaded up with poison. Perhaps. Hard to tell. Bit of a guess, really, but the poison was the kind you'd use for mice, rats ..."

Jess switched the phone to loud-speaker and shimmied into her jeans. She pulled a T-shirt over her head, picked up the phone and turned the speaker off as she ran down to let Marcus in. "Sorry," she mouthed, waving him through to the living room. "Kettle?"

"... take a look around the area, see if there's any sign of other problems ... hard to prosecute without more evidence ... could be anyone ..."

Jess followed Marcus to the kitchen and plucked mugs from the draining board, turned them the right way up, and dropped a teabag in each.

Marcus opened the French doors and shooed the dogs into the garden, shutting the door behind them to dull the noise of their yappy chase.

"Oh, call coming in, gotta go. Keep in touch. Keep you posted!" Peggy finally cut the call and Jess breathed a sigh of relief.

"I thought she'd talk forever," she said to Marcus, as she splashed boiling water over the tea bags. "Pass the milk? Sorry, I'm not up yet. She woke me, and has been talking ever since." She hoped it would sound like she'd been caught up on the phone for hours, instead of only awake for ten minutes. "You in a rush?"

He nodded. "'fraid so. Was that about your dead bird?"

She rooted in the cupboard for cereal, poured herself a bowl of muesli, and sprinkled a handful of blueberries over the top. "Yes. It had been shot. And poisoned. The poison might be accidental, from it eating poisoned mice or suchlike. Shooting's no accident though, is it?" She spooned muesli into her mouth and looked at him, eyebrows raised in question, although she needed no answer.

Marcus leaned back against the kitchen counter and took a gulp of the too-hot tea.

"She said they'll go and have a search around the area to see if there are any signs of anything else, but it's unlikely they'd find anything, as, well, birds fly, don't they?" Jess shrugged, and gave him a half-smile. "I told her about all the land-clearing that's going on down there, but she doesn't think they can do anything, as it's all private land, until you get way out onto the bog." She spooned in another mouthful of breakfast, still talking. "It sounds like all the bits that have been destroyed are on farmland, or bog that is legally owned by the farmers, at least. Nothing they can do, she said. How is that possible?" Jess stopped, spoon midway to her mouth, to glare at Marcus as if he would have the answers.

He ran a splash of cold water into his tea, drained the cup, and set it down on the counter. "Private land. They can do as they like with it." He twisted his mouth into a grimace. "I'll be late."

Jess sighed, set down her spoon, and shoved back her chair. She stood, and wrapped her arms around his waist. "See if you can find out anything. There must be a way to stop it. You said yourself there are laws?"

He said nothing, holding her close for a moment before gently untangling himself and heading for the door.

"Marcus?" Jess put on a wheedling voice, and he turned. She held his gaze. "It's not right."

He nodded. "I'll ask around. It's not really a matter for the Gards, though. Civil. Not criminal. I doubt there's anything we can do. Unless a crime is committed."

Before he opened the door, he bent and kissed her. "We'll talk later. I'll see you back here. We'll get a takeaway, shall we? Anything will be better than burnt pizza."

Jess swiped at him, but he ducked out of the door, pulled it closed, and left her standing in her hallway with a daft grin on her face and a longing for him to hurry back.

By nine-thirty, Jess had got herself sorted out, and had the two dogs in the car and her walking boots on. She had time enough to bring the dogs for a run before heading to work, and while she hadn't planned to venture far from Orchard Close this morning, Peggy's news had changed her mind. She started the engine and set off towards the village centre, aiming for the lane beside the pub where she'd found the dead bird.

With time pressure on her mind, she turned into the lane and drove along it until the cottages and hedgerow gave way to the open vista of the bog. To the righthand side, the butchered hedge she'd noticed on Monday was gone, and in its place, a ridge of turned earth and a single strand of wire, strung between evenly-spaced wooden posts.

"Oh!" she said aloud to the ravaged land, or the dogs on the seat behind her. "Oh."

Her heart thudded with a feeling she couldn't quite identify—Rage? Disappointment? Sorrow?—Why would someone rip out hundreds of yards of hedging and replace it with a wire fence? And in nesting season, too. That *had* to be illegal. Marcus would *have* to act now. Annoyance tumbled in her chest as she drove on until the track widened into a rough patch of gravel, giving vehicle access onto the farmed part of the bog and providing space enough to leave her car.

She parked haphazardly across the gravelled ground, got out, and slammed her door shut with a bang that reverberated off the open land.

The dogs leaped from the back seat as she tugged open the back door, and within seconds, they were racing across the peaty land, bouncing in and out of patches of still-brown heather, and over the narrow drains. Fletcher cleared these ditches with ease, but Snowflake, more hesitant, ran alongside the drains until he found a place narrow enough or shallow enough to suit his little legs, and then took tentative steps forward, followed by a courageous leap. More than once, he would fall just short of the opposite bank and need to scramble frantically at the soft earth until he climbed to firmer ground. By the time they got home, the white dog, usually the colour of freshly-fallen snow, would be black from the tips of his paws to halfway up his coat. Fletcher, being black to start with, would look no different from usual, but his fur would hold the scent of wet mud for the rest of the day.

As the dogs gambolled like new lambs, Jess ambled more slowly across the bog. Behind her, the sun rose steadily, already bringing some warmth to the day. In the distance, a pair of buzzards looped across the sky. *Not dead yet*, Jess thought, with a pang of sadness for the changing landscape and the bird she'd handed over to Peggy earlier in the week. This pair in flight were the first she'd seen in a while. In the far distance, the sky darkened to the colour of wet tarmac. March, in the Irish midlands, was as unpredictable as the path of an excited Labrador on an off-lead run. Today, it seemed, would be another mixed day, with bursts of sun and showers, less settled than the warmth of the past few days. The forecast for the weekend promised strong winds and icy rain. Jess shivered and pulled her coat tighter around her, then rooted in her pocket to text her new contact in Parks and Wildlife about the demise of the hedgerow, just in case anyone cared.

Peggy, it seemed, did care. She texted back immediately. *Feckers. Can't chat, in meeting. Will look into it.*

Alone with the dogs under a rapidly greying sky, Jess felt suddenly small and lonely; a feeling that threatened to engulf her, and one she'd not felt for a while. When her dad had died, and she'd first found herself living alone in his house in Orchard Close, she'd sunk into depression, and all her days had blurred into one long stretch of dark gloom. Only for the kindness of her neighbours and endless long, long walks through the countryside with Fletcher, had she climbed out of it, and on the whole, she was content with her life, especially now she'd found a new focus in her gardening course, and a rekindled friendship with her sister. And also, Marcus. Unsure where this sudden bolt of sadness had come from, she groped in her pocket for her phone once more.

She turned it over in her hands, wondering who to call.

She texted Alice. *You busy?*

Meetings. U OK? Call U later?

Marcus, then? No, he'd be busy at work.

Kate. She hadn't seen her friend in a few weeks, and they were long-overdue a catch up.

Hey. You about this week? How's my favourite baby?

Teething I think. The message ended with a crying face emoji and a baby emoji.

Jess grimaced and selected a sad face to respond with. Before she'd hit SEND, a second message from Kate arrived.

Catch up Tues? You're home on Tuesdays still?

Sure. Come over in the morn, stay for lunch?

Feeling marginally better for those few moments of communication, Jess squared her shoulders, turned her back on the rolling clouds, and set back towards the car, the sky still bright in that direction. She gave herself a mental shake. She'd cheer up once she was at work, anyway. The focus of working at the garden centre always cleared her mind. "Come on lads!" she called to the dogs. "Let's go get lunch before it rains."

As she drove past the savaged farmland, fresh anger bubbled in her. "It's not right," she told Fletcher, meeting his eyes in the rearview mirror as he sat upright on the back seat beside a curled-up and gently snoring Snowflake. "I'm going to make a fuss about it. He shouldn't be able to get away with it."

A familiar, dark-coloured pickup truck approached on the narrow, single-lane road, so she pulled into a gateway to allow it to pass.

As it drew level, the driver wound down his window and raised a hand. Billy White, again. Funny how she hardly knew the man and had seen him three times in the last four days. She opened her own window and called a hello.

"You again," the farmer said, with a smile. "Going to be a good shower." He gestured to the sky.

"I think we just missed it," Jess agreed. "What happened to the hedge?" She pointed back the way she'd come from, indicating the land on the Dochertys' side of the lane.

Billy White's face reddened. "Fecking lunatic. He pulled out a stretch last year an' the year before that too, and my land's been wetter ever since. No sense. Grass on every inch and nothing left to draw the water from the land, not since he felled the trees and all."

"Why?" Jess asked. "I mean, what's the sense in doing that? He doesn't have any cows out in the fields, so they aren't even eating the grass anyway?"

"Aye. Silage. He's the cows in the sheds and uses the grass for silage to feed them. Puts them out now an' again, he does, but not all that regular."

"Isn't it nesting season? I thought you couldn't cut hedges at this time of year."

"Aye," Billy said again. "One rule for him, another for the rest of us. Someone'll shoot the fecker one of these days. Thinks he's above us all, now he's gone into dairy. Used t' be a fine bit of land, that. Might as well put down that plastoturf stuff, for all the good he's doing to the soil." Billy laughed and thumped a calloused hand onto his steering wheel. "He'll get what's coming, you see if he doesn't." He lifted his hand in a half wave, and let the pickup roll slowly forwards. "Mind yourself now."

The thought of a farm covered in astroturf brought a quick smile to Jess's face. *Plastoturf. Great name for it. Plastic farm, that's turning into.* Thoughts of the little plastic farm figures she'd played with as a child marched through her mind. She pictured the empty green fields of Dochertys' farm filled with identical plastic Friesians; a row of plastic ducks set onto a rigid green plastic base, and a bewildered-looking plastic milkmaid standing beside a flat, blue plastic pond, her arms permanently outstretched and unbending, despite the weight of the two brown plastic pails she balanced each side of her body.

They'd spent hours playing with that farm set; Jess and her brother.

She'd call him later, too, check he was still coming to Ballyfortnum for the Easter weekend, with his wife and their two young daughters: shy, quiet, six-year-old Clara, and the exuberant livewire that was eight-year-old Bryony. If anyone could snap her out of a threatening lapse into the melancholy she'd sunk into when her father died, it would be Bryony and Clara.

Chapter Eight

The afternoon passed in an even balance of pottering quietly in the polytunnels and chatting to customers in the plant yard or shop. Ella, not often in at the same times as Jess unless it was really busy, had been roped in to cover for Shay, who was off on some jaunt buying new ranges of garden furniture in anticipation of a burst of sales leading up to the Easter weekend. As the shop settled into a mid-afternoon lull, Jess dropped onto a garden bench beside the counter, cupping her hands around a steaming mug of tea. Jack perched on a stack of compost bags, and Ella leaned against the counter, her long, straight hair hanging in a highlighted sheet down her back, and a can of Coke in her hands.

"Ye going to the protest tomorrow?" she asked, directing the question at Jess.

Jess glanced up at Ella. Although Marcus had mentioned the protest earlier in the week, Jess had forgotten about it. "Are you?" she asked. "Is it your kind of thing, then?" She lowered her mug and studied Ella for a moment. She wouldn't have put her down as someone who'd care much about turf-cutting.

Ella tossed her hair back and laughed. "No chance. Just heard it might be a massive turnout. Something to talk about! Finn reckons there could be trouble, like. His da will be along. He works for *Bord na Móna*. Job's on the line, innit." She shrugged and took a slurp of her Coke.

"Locally?" Jess asked. There were a few places in the area where *Bord na Móna* still farmed the bogs, although operations had been cut back over the last few years. Set up decades ago to manage the extraction of turf from the peatlands, the national company was one of many having to rapidly adjust to climate challenges. Mostly, as far as Jess could tell, *Bord na Móna* just managed and oversaw and scratched their heads about what to do with the bogs, but to the southeast of Ballymaglen there was still a large plant for harvesting garden peat. The plant employed a fair few workers from the surrounding villages, and supplied a lot of the garden centres across the neighbouring counties, including the Ballymaglen garden centre. If the plant closed, they'd need a new supplier, she supposed. Or a different product. That was really the point, wasn't it?

Ella nodded. "Yeah. They're threatening closure. Or redeployment. Or something. Finn's da's right worried. Says he's too old to learn something new. Poor fecker."

Jack, silently listening, now grunted his agreement. "Lot o' folks in same boat, so there is." He drained his mug and stood. "Best crack on, eh."

Ella crumpled her coke can and leaned over the counter to drop it in the bin behind the tills. "Bit of a worry. Not mine though." She threw Jess a cheery smirk, smoothed her hair back over her shoulder, and took up her place at the till.

Jess scooped up Jack's empty mug, flashed a smile at Ella, and went to deposit the mugs in the office before returning to the potting table in the nearest polytunnel. Maybe she'd go along to Lambskillen tomorrow; see what the fuss was about. She'd never been to a protest before. Might be interesting. She'd ask Marcus about it later, over that promised takeaway.

On her way home, Jess pulled up in front of Ballyfortnum's village shop. She cut the engine and ran inside, finding Mrs Dunne pulling down the shutters on the front window, just minutes from closing.

"Sorry! Just milk, if you're not closed? Forgot to get it in town. Sorry."

Mrs Dunne nodded towards the fridge and stood aside to let Jess pass. "You'll pay it next time, so. Till's off. Go on with you."

Jess ducked around the shopkeeper and grabbed the nearest carton.

"Heard you found a buzzard."

Jess, partway back to the door, stopped in her tracks. "Blimey, Mrs Dunne. Is there anything you don't know?"

"Had some young one in earlier. Could've talked for Ireland, so she could. One of them from the Wildlife services, said she was. Wanted a drink and a bar of something. Took her nearly half an hour, so it did, time she'd told me her life story."

Jess couldn't hold back a burst of laughter. There weren't many around here who could out-talk Mrs Dunne. Sounded like she'd met her match in Peggy. "Must've been Peggy? She does like to talk. She told you it was me, did she?" Jess was surprised by this breach of what she'd assume should be a confidence. She'd felt uncomfortable enough reporting the buzzard to start with, in case anyone thought she was interfering.

"Ah no, not really. I guessed that part from what she said. Couldn' think of anyone else who'd be bothering, besides you. Plus, she said your dog had found it; and there's only one other big black Lab round here, and he belongs to a fella, so had to be you, I said. She quietened up after that; left in a bit of a rush."

"Guess she realised she'd said too much!" Jess laughed again. "But yes, I did, and you're meant to report birds of prey, Marcus said." An edge of defensiveness crept into her voice, and she eased around Mrs Dunne's bulk and put her hand on the door handle.

Mrs Dunne harrumphed and raised her eyebrows. "Don't mean anyone else would, does it now? Lads round here been shooting birds all their lives. Foxes. Deer. Crows. It's part of farming life, you know?"

Jess wasn't sure if the heat that rushed to her face was guilt or the feeling reminiscent of having been reprimanded by her old school principal. "I'll let you finish closing up. Goodnight, Mrs Dunne." She stepped around the door and let it swing shut behind her.

As she drove the short way home, Mrs Dunne's words played in her mind. Mrs Dunne, gossip that she was, would probably have told half the village by now, and everyone would know that Jess had potentially caused trouble for one of the locals. Dammit. She switched on the indicator, swung into Orchard Close, and wondered what else Peggy and her colleagues had discovered during their visit to Ballyfortnum that day.

Fletcher welcomed her home with a wagging tail and barrage of licks. She flung open the French doors, let him and Snowflake into the garden, flicked on the kettle, and pulled out her phone to fire off a text: *Hi Peggy, hear you came to Ballyfortnum today. Any news? Jess O'Malley.*

The reply pinged in seconds later. Peggy must type as fast as she talk, Jess thought with a wry chuckle.

Land not protected so we can't stop the tree cutting. Too late anyway – not many left!! Can't prove who killed the bird, although all fingers pointing at one of the farmers. He's a right fecker, that one with all the grass? Know much about him, do you? He's fecked over the land alright. Could be anyone with a gun, tho. Kid taking potshots, even. Police'd soon step in if that's the case. No signs of any other dead, but that's no surprise – they could end up anywhere! Saw one in the air, so that was a plus point. Peg

Blimey. Even by text she didn't half talk. Surely she wasn't supposed to let on who they were suspicious of though? Jess smiled to herself, thinking of her friend Kate and her attempts to keep her Get Slim clients' details confidential. She'd soon shared everything when it came to catching a killer, though. Confidences; confidence ... something else Kate and Peggy seemed to share in abundance. That aside, Peggy and Kate were polar opposites, what with Peggy in her grubby jeans and stubby fingernails, her hair a frizz of unruly curls. Jess's hair would be a similar froth if she ever cut it short enough to take the weight off, and the exact reason she never did. Scraping it back into a ponytail was easier by far. Nonetheless, she liked Peggy, with her infectious enthusiasm and friendly manner.

She texted back: *Don't really know the farmers up there tbh. Met that hedge-killer one at work the other day – he bought enough weedkiller to decimate the whole county. Seems pleasant, aside from that.* She added a laughing face emoji and hit SEND. "You judgemental cow," she told herself as the kettle burbled to a boil and clicked itself off. He did seem nice, and what did she know about land management and farming anyway? Hadn't Marcus laughed at her more than once about exactly this.

Back in the summer, when they were still pretending they hadn't got feelings for each other, he'd teased her about her suggestions for managing the forestry at the edge of the river. She tingled with the memory of him brushing pine needles from her hair as they'd ducked through the trees on a Scooby-Doo-style sleuthing adventure, then shuddered as the image of the dead fisherman bobbed into her mind instead. It had been an awful time. But also, it'd had brought her and Marcus closer, so ...

She splashed hot water onto a teabag, stirred it, and let thoughts of Marcus swirl in the steam. *He'll be here soon.* Still smiling, she padded to the sofa, tucked her legs under her, and leaned back with her eyes closed, suddenly longing for that takeaway.

Chapter Nine

Any passing notions Jess had entertained about attending the protest were washed away by the predicted foul weather pounding against her bedroom window when she woke on Saturday morning.

Marcus had stayed overnight, creeping out quietly sometime earlier while it was still dark, but when Jess opened her eyes properly a little after nine, the light bleeding through the crack in the curtains was a dismal grey. She groaned, turned over, and shut her eyes again. No way she'd bother herself to go and see this protest if it was raining. Poor Marcus, having to stand out there in the rain, policing it. *Was he, though? Actually out in it?* She suspected it was beneath his rank, and he'd send out the uniformed Gardai while he spent a comfy morning with his feet up in his office. Not that Jess had any idea what his office looked like. She should ask Kate. Kate had been on the wrong side of the police station inner door about a year ago, when she'd been stopped for drink-driving. Ages ago now. Jess grudgingly opened her eyes, the call of the bathroom stronger than the desire to go back to sleep.

Rather than going back to bed, she made herself a cup of tea and two slices of toast, and curled up on the sofa with the dogs beside her. The weather was bad enough for even Fletcher to feel lazy. She clicked on the TV and idly scrolled channels, settling on none, and switched it off again as soon as she'd finished her toast.

Half an hour later, showered and dressed and the dogs still snoozing on the sofa, Jess stepped into her opposite neighbour's hallway and shook raindrops from her hair.

"Hello, love." Linda greeted Jess with a peck on the cheek, and ushered her to the cosy kitchen at the front of the house. "What brings you over on such a dreary day?" Without waiting for an answer, she filled the kettle, set it to boil, and pulled a cake tin from a stack on the work surface. "Is it too early for elevenses?" She rooted in a cupboard for two pretty china plates, and set a slice of buttery shortbread in front of her guest, her eyes twinkling with mischief. "What's this about you reporting a dead buzzard?"

"Linda! You knew that already. You saw the woman come out on Tuesday, so I know you're trying to wind me up. Who's been talking about me this time?" Jess nibbled the edge of the shortbread. "Mmm. Yum. Never too early for shortbread."

"Gerry told me yesterday; knocked with a parcel and stopped for a chat. Seems the whole village knows you've got it in for poor old Docherty."

Jess smirked. "Young Docherty, actually. I don't know the old ones! Ha!"

"Ah sure, there's plenty of them," Linda acknowledged. "Most of them live up that same lane, or roundabouts. Some down past the school, too. They don't go far from home, the Dochertys. Which ones do you know?"

"None of them, really." Jess took a larger bite of shortbread, her resolve to make it last as long as possible already lost. "I know some of the land up there behind the pub belongs to the Dochertys, and I met Thomas this week, in the garden centre. I'd say I've spoken to him once or twice, but I wouldn't know him, or any of the family."

"Ah well, you've crossed them now, love, calling in the inspectors on them! There's more than one Thomas among them, too. So many children they ran out of names." Linda chuckled at her joke and slid the shortbread tin towards her friend. "You'd best have another piece, to take the sting out of troubling them."

"Inspectors!" Jess laughed. "It was only the Parks and Wildlife woman. I don't think she's an inspector. She's fun. You'd like her. She talks a lot, though." Jess helped herself to a second piece of shortbread from the tin. "A lot. She loved your gingerbread. But who wouldn't? Has no one got anything better to talk about round here than me finding a dead buzzard? I had to report it. Marcus said."

"And how is your lovely Marcus? Take some of this back for him, won't you, love. I know he's a sweet tooth, like you."

The two women passed an hour or so in companionable chatter, not leaving much shortbread for Marcus after all. After a third cup of tea, Jess glanced out the window and frowned. "I thought if I sat here long enough, the rain might stop, but it's blowing a right gale. I don't think the dogs'll get much of a walk today. Thanks again for looking in on them in the week. It's working okay, isn't it? You checking on them? You will say if it's too much."

Without Linda's kindness and help, Snowflake and Fletcher would be left for too long on the days that Jess's new college course clashed with Marcus's day shifts, and Jess wouldn't have known how to make it work.

"I'm so grateful. We both are." She stood and dropped a kiss on Linda's white hair. "I'd better get back to them. And do something useful with my day. Don't get up."

Gusts of furious wind swept Jess sideways as she ran across the street, the rain soaking into her sweater in the few seconds it took to get from Linda's door to her own. Inside, she tugged the wet jumper over her head and dropped it on the bottom stair. "Blimey," she said to Fletcher as he leaped at her chest to welcome her home. "You're not getting any walk in this. Sorry mate."

His chocolatey eyes gazed at her, but he seemed to agree, as he jumped back onto the sofa, turned around twice, and settled to sleep beside his snow-white friend.

Not long after three, Marcus texted to say the protestors had quietly disbanded, beaten by the weather, and he was finishing early, no longer needed.

I need you, Jess thought, with a flip of her stomach.

∞

"Well, O'Malley." Marcus's eyes crinkled in amusement as he studied her face while she sat on the stairs watching him take off his shoes. "You'll be interested in this. You mightn't have bothered your lazy self to come and see the protest—oy!" He expertly sidestepped her swing at him and continued. "But the protest came to you. Well, to Ballyfortnum, at least. As I drove through the village, a little group were huddled outside the pub, smoking."

"How'd you know they were from the protest?"

"Couple of the cars had signs stuck on the windows."

"What side are they on?"

"Some on the driver's side, some on the—Ouch!" He stepped backwards, out of reach of her swinging socked foot. "All right, all right. I knew what you meant. Against the turf cutting. Save our bogs. Protect nature. That kind of thing. Guess they were locals. I didn't recognise them, wrapped in coats and raingear, and with my windscreen running a waterfall. Half a dozen, maybe. Could've been more inside, I suppose." He shrugged. "How's your day been? Did you move off the sofa at all?" He dodged another swipe, and leaned down to pin Jess's arms to her sides, holding her firm and preventing further attack by planting a kiss on her forehead.

"Actually," she said, wriggling free and getting up. "I did. Linda says the whole village is gossiping about me."

Ten minutes later, tea in hand, they sank side-by-side onto the larger of Jess's two sofas. With a contented sigh, she swung her feet up and snuggled her back against him, jiffling to get comfortable before telling him how the news of her buzzard had circulated.

"Do you think I'm a trouble-maker?" she asked, twisting her neck around to try to see his expression.

"I *know* you're a trouble-maker, Miss O'Malley." The laughter in his voice was barely contained, and she nudged into him with her back, showing her objection to his comment while trying not to spill their tea. He said nothing, waiting it out.

"Fair enough," she conceded, after a moment's pause.

"At least it's only a bird and not a person. That makes a nice change."

Chapter Ten

By Sunday lunchtime, the rain and wind had stopped, although the turbulent sky beyond Jess's living room window promised more to come later. A reluctant Marcus agreed to grab the moment of dry weather to walk the dogs together, up the lane by the pub. Being almost opposite Marcus's little cottage, he walked Snowflake here often enough, and knew the land better than Jess.

His reluctance, he told her, was because he knew she only wanted to go that way to snoop around. "It's only a bird, for goodness sake. Wouldn't you rather head for the woods?" He held her gaze, and she almost gave in. His nearly-black eyes, as velvety and endearing as Fletcher's, were hard to resist, and a rush of warmth flooded through her.

"I just want to show you all the hedges that farmer's ripped out." She rubbed her fingertips gently along his arm, and peered up at him with a look hoped was more beseeching than the one he gave her. "I can't believe he's allowed to do it, especially at this time of year."

"I'm off duty. Besides, it's really not a police matter. You'd need to ring the council. Not the Gards, for this sort of issue."

"Just to show you," she said again. "So you can tell me if I'm being dramatic."

Marcus laughed; a deep, warm laugh that crinkled his eyes into those lovely deep lines, and caused flutters in her belly. "You? Dramatic? Shouldn't think so." His voice was deadpan as he pulled her in and kissed her. "I will agree, but only because it's going to rain again soon, and if we walk this close to home, we'll be done sooner and you can cook me a spectacular Sunday dinner when we get back."

"Hmm. We could go to Finbar's?" The hotel restaurant in Ballymaglen had a well-deserved reputation for truly delicious traditional Sunday roasts, along with an assortment of other tempting dishes and a fine array of desserts, without any need to cook or clean up after.

Marcus, having run out of reasons to protest, called the restaurant to make a reservation for that evening, and pulled on the work shoes he'd discarded under Jess's hall table the afternoon before. "We'll have to stop in for me to get my boots. I'll drive. Come on."

***

In the short time since Jess had driven along the pub lane on Friday, the landscape had changed again. Where the hedges on the right-hand side had been replaced with wire, the ground beneath that fence was sodden and swampy from Saturday's torrential rain. Beyond the point where the cottages gave way to the farmland, ankle-deep puddles spread across the lane. The drainage ditches on Billy White's side, between the dandelion-strewn verge and the primrose-laden bank, overflowed and spilled across the grass.

"Wow." Jess stood motionless in the middle of the track, watching the torrent of water flowing along the edges of the road, searching in vain for somewhere to drain to. "Billy White did say that flooding was more of a problem since his neighbour has taken out so many of the trees. I guess the trees suck up a lot of the water, after a storm?"

Marcus, trying to find a dry path through the puddles, shrugged. "That and the roots keeping the soil looser. It's true; it has got worse over the last few years. I hadn't thought about why, though."

Ahead of them, Fletcher showed no such hesitation about getting his feet wet, and ploughed through the puddles as if personally responsible for testing the depth of each one.

Snowflake, more like his master, made for higher ground and drier feet. He made a tentative leap across the overflowing drain and scrabbled up onto the primrose bank, where he trotted along, looking down at his muddy Labrador friend with something between disdain and envy.

Jess, in her rugged Canadian wellies, splashed through the water like a child, kicking up water and jumping from puddle to puddle. "I can't believe it rained this much! It mustn't have stopped all night. It's a mess. Billy White wasn't wrong when he said it flooded, was he?"

Marcus grinned indulgently at Jess for a moment. "Jess, I can see you are having fun, but can we go home now? Look at the state of the dogs!"

She kicked a splash of water in his direction, but only half-heartedly, not really wanting to shower him with a muddy deluge. "Lightweight!" She stuck her tongue out, then caught him up in three large and splashy strides across the water. "Okay. You're right. Let's go get dinner." She slipped her hand into his, and they headed back towards the village, past the scattering of cottages. "Who even lives along here?"

"I don't know all of them. The farmers, but you know that. Billy White and his wife, Mary. A lot of children. Four or five, I think, could be more. Or less. And Dochertys on the other side." Marcus gestured back the way they had just turned from. "Big family. There are two older couples—Thomas and Margaret; Colm and Frances. Not sure Colm and Frances live there anymore, actually—think they've a house down the road by the Geraghtys. They'd be brothers, Thomas and Colm. The farm goes right across to join up with the Geraghtys' land, I think. And their father, another Thomas. The middle one goes by Tom, to avoid confusion. His father's an old fellow now—older than Mrs Harris, even."

Jess laughed. Rumour had it that the vicarage's elderly housekeeper had been in charge of Ballyfortnum's priests for centuries. No one in the village could remember a time when she wasn't there, however many priests had come and gone.

Marcus squeezed Jess's hand. "I'm not sure which of them live where—there's a couple of cottages tucked away back on the land somewhere, and the farmhouse, and a converted stable block too." He shrugged, lifting her hand a fraction as his arm rose and fell. "Then they've an assortment of children, all adults or at college now, I'd guess. You met the younger Thomas the other day, you said?" He threw her a glance, and she nodded.

"Yes, he'd be the one who bought the weedkiller, I guess. He lives there somewhere?"

"Think so."

"Who else?"

"I don't know all their names. Might be an Aoife ... Anne? A Matthew, I think ... I'm really not sure. Some of them have young children, too. The old fellow's a great grandfather and proud of it. There're loads of them."

He broke off and looked at her with a quick laugh. "Why don't you just ask Mrs Dunne?"

She snaked her arm around his waist, pulling him close. "I might. She's a better detective than you, Woo."

He wrapped his arm around her back and squeezed gently. "Or a better gossip."

"Fair. Who lives in these cottages then? Or will I ask Detective Dunne in the shop?"

"Again, I only know one or two. I don't know who's in that one we just passed. This one—" He gestured to the one on their left; the first past the entrance gates to the Docherty farm. "—I don't know either. A youngish couple. Two cocker spaniels. I've seen them out walking once or twice."

Jess hadn't. She'd have remembered cocker spaniels, with their gorgeous silky ears and adorable faces. She'd have to look out for them.

Marcus pointed to the low, wide bungalow on the right of the track. "This one is an older couple. Canadian, I think. Or very north America. She is, anyway. I think he might be from somewhere else. They're renting for a year. She teaches music lessons. Lovely lady. Cindy someone. Striking, with very white hair, but not really old. Sixty, thereabouts? She has two cats. Teddie and Fweddie."

Jess snorted. "Fweddie? What a brilliant name!"

"In the summer, they'd lie out on the driveway, soaking up the sun. She plays the harp, like a real Irishwoman."

Jess snorted again. "I don't know a single Irish person who can play a harp."

"Me either. Donnie Parker. Lives alone. Oldish, maybe late seventies." Marcus pointed to the bungalow opposite the harp lady's. "Bit cantankerous. I didn't tell you that." He squeezed her close again, and inclined his head to the next house on their right. "Elsie Shaughnessy. And family. Children, but grown. University age, I'd guess. Don't know who her husband is, but she does have one. Some of the kids live there, I'd say. A lot of coming and going of young people and loud cars. And Dominic and Lila Finnerty." They drew level with the final bungalow on the lane. "She's a bit of hippy-type, by all accounts."

"I've seen her in the garden. Long flowing hair and long skirts? Seems friendly. Well. Listen to you out-gossiping Mrs Dunne after all, Detective Woo." She leaned in to peck him on the cheek, then disentangled herself from his arm to clip on Fletcher's lead. As she straightened up, she jerked her head in surprise. "Look!" She turned to look more closely at the car in the Finnertys' driveway. The back window displayed a hand-written poster, with large, black, blocky letters: **SAVE IRELAND'S BOGS**. "I guess she was one of the ones you saw outside the pub yesterday?"

"You could be right." Marcus was non-committal and only vaguely interested. "She wasn't the only one, that's for sure. And, having seen that flooding, I'm on her side, I'd say." He bent to attach Snowflake's lead, then hand in hand, he and Jess, one dog each side of them, crossed the quiet main Ballyfortnum street beside the pub.

"I'm not sure it's farming the bogs that's causing the floods," Jess said. "That's more to do with those Dochertys trashing the land. Pulling out the trees and hedges. Compacting the soil."

"You have learned some new land-management terms, O'Malley." His tone was teasing, but Jess's heart thumped with a jolt of pride as she realised that she was indeed learning plenty on her horticulture course. Who'd have thought a year ago she'd have had the first clue about compacted soil?

She called a hello to Mrs Harris, who stepped out of the vicarage doorway as they passed the church. The elderly housekeeper waved cheerily back, and shuffled towards the church in the quick-slow gait of the agile elderly.

The pavement narrowed after passing the church, and Marcus and Snowflake fell into step behind Jess and Fletcher, who insisted on walking sideways from then on to check his friends were still following. In this fashion, they meandered along the pavement for the few hundred yards back to Marcus's cottage, to dry the dogs, get cleaned up, and head out to dinner.

Chapter Eleven

Finbar's restaurant in the Ballymaglen hotel was packed and buzzing with chatter. A harassed-looking waitress guided Jess and Marcus to a corner next to a window overlooking the main street, jammed between a large table with a noisy, multi-generation family and a wood-panelled dividing wall.

Jess slipped out of her coat, hung it over the back of her chair, and eased into the seat facing the room; her back to the wooden wall. Once she'd jiggled in her chair to get comfortable, she gazed around the bustling room in search of familiar faces. Seeing no one she recognised, she turned her attention to the menu, her stomach emitting a low rumble of anticipation.

Under cover of the table, Marcus nudged her foot. "See that couple beside the bar?" he said, keeping his voice low.

Jess swung her head around. "Which couple?"

"There." He nodded towards a silver-haired couple, deep in smiling conversation across a small table-for-two on the other side of the room. "Woman in the pale top; man in a blue shirt. I think they're the couple from

Canada. The music teacher. I think it's them, anyway." He picked up his menu and studied it for a moment, although Jess could predict what he'd choose, and got to her feet in preparation for his next question.

He didn't let her down: "What's the roast today? I don't think she said."

"I'll go look." The Specials board, fixed to the side of the bar, would give her a perfect excuse to check out the couple Marcus had pointed out. Two birds, one stone. She grimaced as the thought of a stoned bird popped into her mind. *Eugh.*

Roast lamb. Boeuf bourguignon. Linguine with marinated vegetables. Seabass. Vegetarian enchiladas. Chicken and mushroom pie. Decisions, decisions. As she squinted at the board, a black-clad waiter stepped from behind the bar and rubbed *seabass* away, leaving a chalky smear in its place.

"Hope you didn't want that," he smiled at Jess. "Not much of the bourguignon left either."

She nodded at him, cast a glance at the older couple, and returned to Marcus to deliver him the news about the seabass. Not that he'd care. They both knew he'd choose the roast. He'd have chosen it whatever meat it was.

"It's lamb. I'll have the pie, I think," Jess said, as she slid back into the seat. "What'll you have?" She tipped her head slightly to the side and assumed an innocent look, biting on the inside of her cheek to stop a smile escaping.

Once the waitress had taken their order and delivered two ruby-hued glasses of house red to the table, Jess leaned back in her seat and sighed in contentment. "It's nice, having someone to eat out with."

"And someone to eat in with, too."

As Marcus caught her eye, warmth surged through Jess. She'd read enough mystery stories to know that this didn't happen in storybooks. In any one of the beloved murder mysteries that lined her landing bookcase or tottered in unstable piles beside her bed, the policeman was an incompetent buffoon. Everyone liked Marcus. He was just so ... nice. Here she was, un-veiler of not one but *two* killers in the past twelve months *and* having dinner with this lovely, kind man who made her heart swell. In mysteries, the person who found the killer was categorically *not* supposed to fall for the detective. Oops. She flicked her eyes towards the non-buffoon and sighed again. "Mmm."

"Mmm what?"

She flashed him a smile and moved her glass aside so the waitress could set down the plate of steaming pie and chunky golden chips. "Well, this, for starters." She gestured at the food. "Yum."

Outside the window, the evening had drawn in, and streetlights cast an orange glow over the darkening street. It was raining again. Rainwater glistened from headlights as a line of traffic waited for red to change to green at the junction by the supermarket. The restaurant lights were dimmed and cosy, and a fire burned in the grate on the long side wall, away from where they sat, throwing a warm, somnolent aura into the room. The loud party on the neighbouring table left. The waitress cleared the detritus and divided the shoved-together smaller tables into individual units once more. An elderly couple sat at one; a family of four took the further one, and the one beside Jess and Marcus remained empty as they finished their main course.

"Can I get you dessert?" The waitress stood expectantly; pen poised over notepad as if she already knew that Jess had mentally selected a gooey order of sticky toffee pudding.

"Sticky toffee, please. With ice cream. And don't think you'll be sharing it if you pretend you don't want anything and don't order your own." She mock-glared at Marcus, who held up his hands in defence.

"Okay, okay. I'll have the brownie. And coffee. Thank you."

As the waitress walked away, still scribbling on her pad, Marcus lifted a hand in greeting.

Jess turned to see the couple he'd mentioned earlier, shrugging into their coats as they made for the door.

Catching Marcus's gesture, the woman swerved from her course and approached their table instead. "Hello," she said, in a soft Canadian lilt. "It's Mr Woo, am I right?"

He nodded in admission as he stood to greet them. "Marcus. We walked past your house this afternoon, with the dogs. Got a bit wet. I was telling Jess you play the harp." His eyes crumpled into their familiar laughter lines and he gestured across the table to Jess. "Jess, this is Cindy. Cindy, Jess. I'm sorry, I don't know your husband's name."

The man stepped forward and proffered his hand. "Walt. Nice to meet you, Jess, Marcus." He shook first Jess's hand, then Marcus's, then glanced through the weather to the orange-lit rain. "Turned nasty again. Our road is flooded. You saw that, if you walked? After our house, fortunately."

"Yes, we turned round. Someone didn't want to get their feet wet." Jess smirked pointedly at Marcus, who nudged her foot with his. "Does it often flood up there? It's not somewhere I usually walk. I live at the other end of the village. Opposite the park."

Walt shrugged. "Happened often enough through the winter, I guess. Neighbours say it's worse lately, but we wouldn't know. We've only been here since August."

His wife nodded. "We retired, you see, and ..." She hesitated, her cheeks pinking a little. "Well, I play the pedal harp—"

"Among other instruments," her husband added, gazing at her admiringly. "She's very musical." He patted her arm.

"So we decided to come and visit Ireland for a year, eh. We're renting that little cottage. It's very pleasant. Although it does rain quite a lot."

The four of them laughed at the understatement as rain lashed against the window.

"Why don't you join us for a few minutes? See if it eases off a bit. We just ordered dessert and coffee." Jess pointed to the empty table behind Marcus. "Pull those chairs over and join us."

Marcus swung around and dragged the nearer chair closer.

Walt stepped around his wife and grabbed the other, placing it for her to sit, in a show of gentlemanly chivalry that made Jess smile.

"Shall I order you something to drink?" she asked, getting to her feet.

Walt waved her down, and headed to the bar, meeting the waitress as she arrived bearing the desserts. Five minutes later, the four sat companionably drinking coffee, while outside, the rain ran in rivulets down the glass.

"I met one of your neighbours earlier in the week," Jess said, between spoonfuls of sticky toffee. "Oh! Two of them, actually. Both the farmers. Billy White and Thomas Docherty?" She raised her eyebrows at Walt and Cindy. "Do you know them? Billy was the one who told me the flooding has got more problematic over the years. He said—" She stopped herself by spooning another bite of the pudding into her mouth. She wasn't going to start spreading gossip about Thomas Docherty.

Cindy peered at her in curiosity but didn't question her abrupt silence. "We've met them both, once or twice," she said. "We like to potter around in the yard. We promised the agent we'd tend the weeds, eh?"

"We've a fair-sized patch back in BC," Walt added. "It seems that any time we are out front, someone is sure to stop and chitchat. It's Mr Docherty who keeps his side of the track clear and tidy, and Mr White who has more affinity with nature. They seem to disagree on best farming practice, that's for sure. We don't often venture in that direction." Walt lifted his cup and took a delicate sip of the hot coffee. "We prefer to take bicycle rides around the roads. That lane is a bit rough for comfort, right honey?" He touched his wife gently on the arm with such affection Jess felt her insides melt.

I hope I have that with someone one day. She rubbed her foot against Marcus's. "I don't really know any of the people who live on your road," she said. "I've only lived in Ballyfortnum a few years myself, and I was caring for my dad for the first while. It's only this last year or so I've begun to get to know people and explore more."

Marcus chuckled his deep throaty laugh. "And look where that's got you," he said, eyes crinkling.

Jess glared at him. "Do you mean meeting you, or outing murderers?" she asked in her sweetest voice, before remembering her manners and clasping a hand over her mouth. "Sorry!" She turned to their new friends. "It's a long story. I don't know if you heard that one of the farmers down my end of the village was killed last summer?" She decided not to mention the other few deaths that had rocked the community over the last year or so, not wanting to worry the couple unnecessarily. "Tell me what brought you to Ireland? Not just the harp, surely?"

By the time the second cups of coffees were drank, and the rain a little less persistent, Cindy had regaled Jess and Marcus with a potted history of their lives to date. Not only was she teaching music—piano and flute as well as harp—but Cindy was also tutoring a few of the local secondary school students in French, including some of their neighbours on the lane. "One of the Shaughnessy kids, two of the young Dochertys. A handful of other teens from around the neighbourhood. Grinds, you call it, eh? One of your funny Irish terms we've learned since we came here. We'd never heard that phrase for extra-curricular study back home."

"It's more about the teachers not doing their jobs in school, and then making a heap of extra cash on the side by giving out-of-school coaching in the very same subject they are supposed to teach properly in school." Jess and her dad had spent many hours complaining about the ridiculousness of this exact thing, starting from way back when she and Eric were struggling with Irish, not having learned it as small children and then expected to pick it up effortlessly when they moved back to Ireland and settled into high school.

"It's one thing getting grinds for the pair of you, for something you haven't had a chance to learn before," George O'Malley would say, "but I'm not forking out for anything you're meant to know from your schoolwork." He'd usually end these tirades with pointed glares at Eric, and a grumbled muttering about someone needing to pull his socks up in maths.

Jess smiled at this memory of her dad, before turning her attention back to the restaurant table and her companions.

"... and Lila's a sweetheart," Cindy was saying. "She plays guitar, so we sometimes have a little soiree in an evening. She's one who's upset about that farmer, now I think of it. She's passionate about the natural world and got in a right state back in the autumn when he felled a patch of woodland."

"That's right." Walt jerked his head up, remembering. "He brought us a load of firewood; said it was arranged with the property owner for the winter. We haven't used it. There was a stack in the shed for us to use this year. That load will be for next year. Farmer Docherty had someone stack it for us. Not our job, he said."

"It was all arranged with the property owners," Cindy agreed. "I mentioned it to Lila and she cussed till her face went blue. It wasn't the wood she objected to, but the fact he'd cut it. Said he's decimating the natural habitat. *Decimating* it. She got mighty steamed up, eh, honey?"

Walt smirked, encompassing Jess and his wife in the half-smile. "She was merry enough on Saturday night when she was singing her way home. Overshot her own home, too. Singing some Irish ballad as she stumbled up the lane. Must've stopped raining, by then, as she looked quite striking in the moonlight when I looked out to see what the noise was about. Beautiful voice, she has, even when drunk …" He tailed off under the weight of his wife's icy glare.

"It's perfectly true—" Cindy winked at Jess, out of sight of her husband. "—but my Walt's not supposed to notice how attractive our neighbour is!" She shook her head, drained the last dregs of her coffee, and stood up. "Walt, honey, we must get back. It was lovely to meet you, Jess. And to chat with you, Marcus. You must call in and say hi next time you are walking by, eh? Goodnight."

Walt held out his wife's coat and she slid her arms into the sleeves. "Goodnight." He shook Jess's hand again and the couple left, Cindy ducking under Walt's arm as he held open the door, then stepping out arm-in-arm into the damp, dark street.

A few minutes later, their bill paid and the last crumbs of pudding cleared from their plates, Marcus pulled Jess to her feet, called goodnight to the barman, and they, too, huddled into their coats and set out into the rainy evening.

Chapter Twelve

Jess set the carton of milk and two bars of chocolate on the shop counter and rummaged in her pockets for the correct change.

Mrs Dunne ignored the money, rested her ample bosom on the counter, and leaned towards Jess with an air of utmost conspiratorial importance. "Thomas Docherty," she informed Jess with far less solemnity than the news warranted, "has passed away."

Jess stood silently for a moment, the chocolate all but forgotten as her brain tried to process whether this news impacted her life. "Which one?" she asked, eventually.

"The young un, of course, else how would old Thomas have told me, eh, love? Serves him feckin' right, didn't he say too, young fecker that he was? Terrible thing to say about anyone, never mind one of your own." Mrs Dunne leaned heavily on the counter and basked in the drama of being the one to break the news.

The death of the oldest Thomas Docherty, who Jess had so recently learned was over ninety and not exactly in the prime of his health, would have been of little surprise. The death of his grandson, the youngest Thomas, who Jess had just met a few days ago, sent a shockwave through her body. She clutched at the counter as her legs buckled.

"Huh? He can't be. I only spoke to him the other day!"

Mrs Dunne shifted her weight and patted Jess's hand. "Sure, what difference does that make, now? You'd not think it of him, but old Thomas's mind's still sharp as a thumbtack. He was delighted to have outlived his grandson, God rest his soul." A little belatedly, she crossed herself and plastered a sorrowful look across her face. It didn't last. "Mind, he didn't say much more than that, but stands to reason he didn't pass from old age, that's sure enough. Only a wee bit older than you, I'd say. Thirty-seven? Thirty-eight. Not forty yet, least there'd have been a do." She gazed into the middle-distance as if searching through an invisible calendar of Ballyfortnum's past few years of social engagements. "And there hasn't been a do."

"When? When did it happen?"

Mrs Dunne snapped her attention back to the news in hand. "Found early this morning, so he was. That's about all Old Thomas said about it, to tell the truth; picked up his cigarettes and paper, same as always, and out he went. Gardai will be out right enough, shouldn't wonder. Your Marcus will know what's what now, eh love?"

Jess didn't quite follow Mrs Dunne's incongruities, nor her obvious enjoyment in being the bearer of such tragic gossip, but she was right about one thing: Marcus would know. She scooped up the milk and chocolate and left the shop, without another word to Mrs Dunne.

Outside the shop, Kate was rocking a baby buggy back and forth, an impatient Fletcher straining on the lead she held in the hand that was not rocking the pushchair, and Snowflake sitting demurely at her feet.

Fletch jumped up at Jess as if he'd been waiting all his life for her return, not just the five minutes or so since she'd gone in for milk and come out with trembling legs and the feeling someone had slapped her in the face.

"What kept you? You've been ages!" Kate let go of Fletcher's lead, no longer able to contain his bouncing and keep the pushchair on an even keel.

Jess trapped the lead under her foot before Fletch could dart into the road. "Thomas Docherty died. Mrs Dunne was telling me about it."

"Thomas Docherty? Which one?" Kate echoed Jess's own question as she swung the pushchair around to face the way back towards Orchard Close.

"Younger. I only saw him last week." Jess heard the tremor in her voice, and leaned against the shop wall to catch her breath. "How can he be dead? She said the Gards are on the way. Did someone kill him, do you think?"

Kate turned from the sleeping baby and cast an incredulous look at her friend; plucked eyebrows raised into her dark-blonde highlights. "Oh Jess, not another one! Are you sure you're safe living here? You should really think about moving away to a safer neighbourhood, like Howardstown!" Kate named one of the roughest, most notorious areas of Dublin, and Jess laughed weakly.

"Yeah, this doesn't seem the safest place in Ireland, that's for sure." She pushed herself away from the wall's support and rested her fingers on the handle of the pushchair. "Come on, let's get back. It was probably just a farming accident. That's bad enough, of course … I'll call Marcus while we walk. Let's get out of the village first. The dogs will walk more sensibly once we're past Marcus's house."

Kate glanced down at Snowflake, walking neatly alongside the pram in which her seven-month-old daughter slept contentedly. "You mean Fletcher. Not *the dogs*. You can't accuse this little guy of anything."

The initial shock of Mrs Dunne's news having subsided, Jess and Kate strolled through the village centre, enjoying the sunshine and saying little. After the weekend's deluge and Monday's overcast chill, today had brought blue skies and puffy storybook clouds. Only the battered spring flowers in the village gardens gave any hint of the weekend's storm. Even Henry and Elizabeth's garden had taken a beating, and looked less well-tended than usual. As Jess and Kate drew level with the gates, Stanley and Daisy careered down the drive towards them, barking madly.

Alerted by the noise, Henry straightened from a kneeling pad halfway up the drive. "Jess, Kate. How're you?" He tipped an imaginary hat to them both. "Hello Fletcher, who's a mighty handsome dog, then? And you too, Snowflake. How are you girls?" He glanced at Kate's pram. "And the little one? I expect Elizabeth would love to see you. I'll give her a call. Come on in."

Jess and Kate exchanged an unspoken question—*Shall we?*—and nodded to one another in silent agreement—*Okay then, but not for long.* Jess unlatched the gate as Henry, already nearing the house, called to his wife through the open front door.

"Elizabeth, visitors!" He turned back to Jess and Kate. "I'll be getting on then." He tipped the imaginary cap once more, and groaned as he sank to his knees in front of the rain-beaten spring bulbs and took up the discarded trowel.

Elizabeth appeared in the doorway, all smiles and warmth.

Fletcher, not a fan of Daisy, tangled his lead around the wheels of the pram and dragged it sideways in his efforts to avoid her growls and snarls.

Jess shooed the whippet-mix away with a hiss, and Henry dragged himself up once more.

"I'll shut her in," he sighed, with the air of one who had been infinitely more reluctant than his wife to welcome their ex-neighbour's bad-tempered dog to their household, after the neighbour left the village last spring. "Come here, you brat." His voice was soft, and dissolved any hint of malice from the words. Henry was a pussy-cat, who hadn't a malicious bone in his body, but as he often told Jess, he really *would* prefer a quiet life now he was retired. He grabbed Daisy's collar and scooped her into his arms. "You too, Stanley," he told the King Charles, who was also running circles around Jess, Kate, and the pushchair, but in friendly excitement at having his friends to play.

"If you can shut Daisy somewhere, I'll let Fletch and Snow off," Jess suggested. "The boys all get along fine."

"I know, I know." Henry's eyes twinkled. "It's the girls that cause the trouble. Isn't that right." He cast another smile towards the now-awake baby, tucked Daisy under his arm, and set off up the drive.

The dogs dealt with, Jess strode to the door and greeted Elizabeth with a peck on her cheek. She'd become increasingly fond of Elizabeth since Elizabeth had almost died at the hands of a neighbour whose jealousy of Kate's slimming group members had driven her to murder. The imposed break Kate had taken from the group when her daughter was born had allowed the group to recover from the shock that one of their own had turned on them, and the group had reconvened in January full of fresh intentions for a new year and a clean slate. Kate didn't like to talk about it, not least as the father of her daughter had been one of those caught up in the tragic events. Poor little Della would never know her biological father, although Kate's husband Declan was doing a grand job of being Della's dad.

Jess grinned as she remembered Kate's initial mad notions of naming the baby Davida, after her real father, and how she, Declan, Linda, and many others besides had tried to conceal their horror at the idea while calmly suggesting she rethink. There was only so much Declan could be expected to forgive after Kate's short-lived dalliance with one of her clients, and a constant reminder in the baby's name would seem a step too far for even the most reasonable of men, never mind for a laddish wide-boy like Declan.

Elizabeth, already cooing over Della in babbling baby-talk, urged them to come in for a cup of tea. "The dogs can stay out here with Henry. He'll not mind." The sparkle in Elizabeth's eyes told Jess and Kate that Elizabeth thought her husband might in fact mind, but he wouldn't complain.

"If you bring me a cuppa," Henry mumbled from the flower border. "Go on in. We'll be grand enough out here."

Kate released Della from the buggy, scooped her into her arms, and followed Elizabeth and Jess inside.

Chapter Thirteen

In the bright sunny kitchen overlooking the distant mountains and Henry's beautifully-tended garden, Elizabeth fussed over the baby, cooing and gurgling as if she, too, were only seven months old.

Jess picked up the kettle and filled it. "Go on, I know you're dying for a cuddle. I'll make the tea." She smiled at Kate and Elizabeth indulgently. "I don't mind."

Some minutes later, as the three women sat around the kitchen table, cups of tea half-drank and a packet of low-fat biscuits open between them, Jess suddenly remembered the news Mrs Dunne had shared only half an hour earlier.

Fortunately Della was now snuffling contentedly at Kate's breast, so when Elizabeth paled at the news and her hands trembled, it was only a half-eaten biscuit that fell from her hands and not the baby.

Jess was instantly contrite, not having predicted how news of another potentially suspicious death in the village might cause Elizabeth such a fright, after her own terrible experience the year before. "I expect it was a farm accident," she hastily clarified. "I was going to call Marcus, and see if he knows what happened, but then we saw Henry, and well …" She gestured around the cheerful kitchen. "Here we are."

Elizabeth picked up the broken biscuit and dropped it onto a plate beside the sink. Her composure recovered, she topped up the teapot for a fresh brew and returned to the table. "I wouldn't be so confident it's an accident," she said, thoughtfully. "He's ruffled a few feathers lately." She chuckled softly and turned her pale blue eyes to Jess. "No pun intended. Actually, I hear you started it. You reported a dead buzzard, I heard?"

Now it was Jess's turn to falter. She lowered the biscuit she was about to bite into, and studied her friend. "Yes, I did … but … well … Firstly, I didn't know who might have hurt it anyway, and secondly …" She tailed off, not sure exactly what she was defending herself against. "What do you mean, I started it?"

Della hiccupped quietly.

Kate lifted her upright against her shoulder, gently rubbing her back with a soft circular motion until the baby let out a loud burp. "Good girl." She switched her attention from Della to Jess, then Elizabeth, then back to Jess. "Yes, what's Jess done this time?"

"Oy!" Jess glared at her friend. "I haven't done anything, and what do you mean, 'this time'?"

Kate nuzzled her face into her daughter's wispy strawberry-blonde curls in a futile attempt to hide her smirk.

Elizabeth patted Jess's hand from across the table. "Nothing, dear. It's only that … well … Mrs Dunne said Parks and Wildlife had been out to interrogate the local farmers, and then Gerry told Henry that on Saturday evening there was a bit of trouble up that way too—"

"Trouble?" Jess interrupted. "What kind of trouble? I didn't hear anything about any kind of trouble."

Elizabeth ducked her head and picked at a crumb on the table. "You know I don't like to gossip, but I thought this was common knowledge. It's not a secret, that's for sure."

Jess nodded. "You're not a gossip, Elizabeth. We know that." It was true. Elizabeth only had kind words for everyone. A nurse before she'd retired, Jess could easily imagine Elizabeth's patients enjoying her gentle bedside manner and the best of care in every sense of the word. "But Marcus didn't say anything, and we saw another couple who live up that way, on Sunday, in Finbar's, and we got chatting to them, and they didn't mention anything either. What happened?"

"Yes, go on." Kate jiggled Della on her knee. "What happened?"

Eizabeth sighed, and straightened on her chair. "Let me just pour the tea first, and then if that gorgeous poppet is done feeding, pass her back to me so you can enjoy a cup of tea without worrying about her."

Jess took the teapot from Elizabeth. "I'll do the tea."

Kate handed over the baby, and held out her cup for Jess to fill. "So," she asked Elizabeth, "what did we miss that Mrs Dunne didn't feel it necessary to tell Jess about?"

Jess laughed. "I expect she forgot, with the new, better news."

"You'd have heard there was a protest about the farmed bogs? In town on Saturday?"

The two younger women nodded.

"Marcus said a few of them were gathered outside the pub afterwards, on Saturday afternoon?" Jess said.

"A few of the locals were there all right," Elizabeth agreed. "Seems that some of them had got wind of the Dochertys draining the bog for grazing, somehow. It's been said your Parks and Wildlife one was giving out about that, too." Elizabeth peered shrewdly at Jess from over Della's head. The baby let out a gurgle of displeasure at Elizabeth's shift of attention, and grabbed at the glasses that hung on a thin chain around Elizabeth's neck. "You can't have those, no you can't." She removed the glasses and set them on the table, waggling her fingers at Della. "And somehow, that got back to the group, and they went trampling up there to see what's been going on. When they saw just how much of the woodland had been cleared, and how much of the bog had been fenced in for grazing, and that the hedges were gone too, they took their placards and their annoyance up to the Dochertys' yard and made a bit of noise and bother."

Jess closed her mouth, realising she'd had it hanging open. How come Marcus hadn't heard this? Why hadn't Cindy or Walt mentioned it? "Were they violent?"

Elizabeth babbled at the baby for a moment, then in that baby-talk voice people use when they are speaking to infants, she replied to Jess's question, still talking to Della. "Not a bit of it, were they, no they weren't. Some of the kids came out, and they'd all have been in school together, or played together when they were smaller, yes they did, yes they did, and then they set off back down the pub with the Docherty kids in tow and that was that, yes it was, yes it was." She bounced Della on her lap, smiling as the little girl gazed adoringly up at her, before turning her attention to Jess. "From all accounts, it turned into quite a gathering. The kids are all home for the holidays. A couple of the White children; one of the Shaughnessys, the whole lot of them, all having fun and getting along like they always did. Not a bother on them, once they were back in the pub, a bit of excess drink aside. They're good kids, most of them."

"Hmm," Jess drained the last of her tea. "Doesn't sound like it was anything to worry about, so."

"Not really," Elizabeth agreed. "Only that you might wonder how they felt the next day, once their heads were clear. Might one of them have remembered they were supposed to be all for protecting the bogs, and gone back up? It doesn't seem likely. They're only kids. Mind, some of them would be your ages by now, come to think of it. Not really kids anymore. In their thirties, most of them, I suppose. Where does the time go, eh Della?" She shook her head sadly as she jiggled the baby. "But even so ..."

"You never know," Kate finished for her. "You just never know what people'll do to each other." Her face clouded over and she lifted Della from Elizabeth's lap. She held her daughter close and buried a sigh into the baby's hair, and Jess knew she was thinking about Dave; Della's father who'd been run off the road and would never know his daughter.

"Let's hope not. Let's hope it was just an accident." Jess gathered the tea things and tidied them onto the worktop.

Kate wrapped Della into her coat and pulled a fleecy beanie hat over her soft curls. She got to her feet, dropped a kiss on Elizabeth's cheek, and thanked her for the tea. "Good to see you. Come back to the group soon, yes?"

On the doorstep, she bundled Della into the pushchair and pulled a blanket up around her chin, while Jess bade her farewells to Elizabeth and called to the dogs.

"She hasn't come to Get Slim since ..." Kate told Jess as they turned out of Elizabeth and Henry's drive and headed homeward.

She didn't need to finish the sentence for Jess to know Kate meant Elizabeth hadn't attended the Get Slim meetings in the whole year that had passed since the slimming group murders.

"Poor Elizabeth, she's so lovely." Jess wrapped Fletcher's lead tighter around her wrist to pull him back onto the pavement and out of the path of an oncoming car. "Let's get back for some lunch, huh? That little stroll to the shop turned into quite a day trip! I'll call Marcus while we walk; see what he knows."

With Fletcher reined in close, and Snowflake trotting sensibly along beside Della's buggy, Jess paused to ease her phone from her pocket and thumb the buttons to bring up Marcus's number.

"Dammit. Voicemail."

Kate shrugged without turning around, and Jess slipped the phone back into her pocket. With two quick strides, she caught up with her friend and the two walked side by side until the pavement ran out and the road narrowed as the village gave way to the fields.

Chapter Fourteen

By the time Kate left, after a leisurely lunch and a trip over the road to see Linda, which turned into another hour of tea and cake, Marcus had still not retuned Jess's calls. She'd tried to call him again a few times as she and Kate had walked home from Elizabeth's house, but each attempt only connected to his recorded voicemail message.

Eventually, Kate had whisked the phone from Jess's hand and shoved it in the pushchair behind Della. "Leave him alone! He'll call when he can. How about introducing your goddaughter to a few cows, since she's awake?" At that, Kate had tugged the buggy into a gateway, and hunkered down next to her daughter, pointing out the livestock. "Cow. Cow. Mooooo. That one looks like Auntie Jess, look."

"Oy! Don't teach her that!" Jess smacked Kate gently with the end of Fletcher's lead. "Look, Della. Mummy." She bent over the pushchair and took the little girl's hand, pointing it to a particularly long-lashed cow.

Della, delighted by the approach of the herd of curious cows, cooed and giggled, either in appreciative amusement of the cows or in happy agreement of her mother's and Jess's snarky bantering.

Now, an hour or so after Kate had left, Jess was making the most of the still-dry weather to potter around her garden for half an hour before she'd need to stop and make dinner. She'd cook for Marcus tonight; bribe him into spilling whatever gossip he might have from the day. Had he been in Ballyfortnum, investigating what had happened to Thomas, or snowed under with something else? He wasn't rostered to work tomorrow, so hopefully he'd stay the night, too. She tugged a tangle of new buttercups from the border and tossed them into a rapidly-filling bucket of weeds. Spring *must* be on the way, if the weeds were growing this much already.

A beady-eyed robin hopped onto the rim of the bucket and peered hopefully inside.

"I'll be done in a minute," Jess told it. "Then you can peck away at the soil and tidy up after me."

The bird cocked its head to one side, and flitted down to perch on a woody stem of rosemary, just inches from Jess's arm. She sat back on her heels and sighed; the low sun still just about warm on her face. Was this the end of the dark days of winter? She really hoped so.

※

A few hours later, Fletcher leaped to his feet, flung himself from the sofa, and scrabbled to the door, barking as if his life depended on it.

Snowflake followed, his white tail wagging against the hall table like an over-enthusiastic feather duster.

"All right, all right, let me get in." Marcus shut the door behind him and patted Fletcher's head while simultaneously pushing him back down to the floor so he could greet his own dog, who patiently waited his turn while trying to keep out of the way of Fletcher's flailing feet.

Jess leaned against the living room door frame, biting her cheeks to stop from laughing as Marcus tried to negotiate removing his shoes without being licked to death. "Clearly they have missed you far more than I have," she said dryly. "I could call them off …"

"And spoil your fun?" Marcus, still bent over his shoes with Fletcher almost on top of him, smiled up at her, and a thousand butterflies fluttered in her chest.

"All right, all right. Fletcher! Come here!"

Snowflake trotted over to Jess and sat at her feet.

The Labrador ignored her completely.

Jess shrugged. "I tried. What can I say? I blame his owner. He's obviously badly trained. Fletcher!" She sharpened her voice and aimed to emulate the no-nonsense tone Marcus used to get her dog to behave, but backed up her attempts to discipline her dog with stepping forward and grabbing his collar. "Fletcher, come here!" She shoved him into the living room, pulled the door smartly closed, and pulled Marcus into a hug. "My turn."

A moment later, she pulled back, her arms still around him, so she could meet his eyes. "What happened to Thomas Docherty?"

"Hello Jess. How was your day? Yes, thank you, mine was hard, and I'd love a cup of tea. Mmm, something smells good? Yes, thank you, I'd love to stay and eat. How's Snowflake been today? How was Kate?" The wrinkled laughter lines deepened with the barrage of questions and Jess wriggled out of the hug and led him through to the living room.

"Actually, I already made tea. The dogs always know when you are nearly here; they were both up on the back of the sofa watching for you five minutes before you pulled up. I put the kettle on as soon as they pressed their noses to the window. And I already know you had a busy day, since you haven't answered your phone all day long and the Gards were up the pub lane earlier, which is why I have made you a truly fabulous lasagne. And garlic bread. And you know full well how Snowflake has been because you, at least, have a perfectly well-trained dog who never puts a paw out of place." She pushed him onto the sofa and grinned at him. "Is that it? Oh, no, and Kate. Yes, Kate is fine, thank you. Della is growing so fast. She's a little cutie, as far as babies go. Now, that's it, all covered. So. What happened to Thomas Docherty?"

She dropped a kiss on his forehead, padded to the kitchen, picked up the two mugs of tea, set them on the low side table by the sofa, shoved the two dogs out of the way and snuggled against Marcus before either of the dogs could claim the space. "What happened?" she said again.

Marcus picked up his tea and pretended to savour it.

"Marcus! Do you *want* lasagne? Or do you want to go home to your empty cottage and cook for yourself?"

He took a slurp of the tea, draped his free arm around Jess, pulled her close until she leaned her head on him, and sighed. "He's dead."

Jess squirmed away from him, snatched up a cushion, and brandished it threateningly. "Looks like the lasagne is all ours, Fletch." She nudged the Labrador with her foot and he rolled over obligingly for a belly rub.

"All right. Put down the cushion and share the lasagne." Marcus used the voice Jess thought of as his firm policeman voice; the one he must use when talking people down from tall buildings and away from unexploded bombs. Well, the one he would use if the Irish midlands had any tall buildings or unexploded bombs, anyway.

"Actually," Marcus said, his voice serious now, "you almost got a visit yourself. Only that I said I'd speak to you, and also that I was with you."

"Huh?"

"Your name came up."

"Huh?"

"Jess, Thomas Docherty was murdered. He was found riddled with shotgun pellets and rat poison. Does that sound familiar to you?"

The room tilted and a rush of noise whooshed in Jess's ears. Heat rushed to her head. The room, still tilting and whooshing, blurred, and everything began to sway. Marcus was still talking, but his voice seemed to come from somewhere far, far underwater, lost in the white noise in her head. The mug was removed from her hand and the arm around her shoulders was all that held her up.

"Breathe, Jess. Breathe. Come on. Put your head down." Marcus twisted her body until she lay with her head on his lap. He stroked her hair until the room stilled, then picked up his tea and drained the mug. "Okay now?"

She opened her eyes and stared up at his worried face.

His thumb caressed her forehead, smoothing back her hair.

"Pellets? And poison? Like the buzzard?"

He nodded, still stroking her face. "Just like the buzzard. But you, luckily, have a perfect alibi. I was here with you at the time of death. It happened in the night sometime. And I was with you all night." He smiled down at her, his eyes filled with concern. "And as I left this morning, you were running across the road to Linda's, so you—"

Jess jerked her head, knocking his hand away.

"It's okay, we called her to confirm it. We had to. You were high on the list. Shots were heard 'in the night'." Marcus made speech marks with his fingers, momentarily lifting his hand before resuming its soft smoothing of her hair. "But no one seems to know *when* in the night. And at this time of year, there's still a lot of night. Until the coroner determines a more exact time of death, we need to account for *all* the hours of darkness. I knew you'd gone over to Linda's when I left here this morning, but we still had to confirm how long you'd been with her. John called her, just to double check."

"Blimey. Good thing you stayed last night. And that Linda's lights were on when you left. I saw she was up and about, and wanted to check if me and Kate could pop in. We did, this afternoon. She didn't mention anyone had called her. Mind you, she was too busy adoring Della and plying Kate with cake. We didn't even tell her Thomas was dead, come to think of it ... Guess we got distracted by Della."

"John didn't either, I don't think. Tell her. He wouldn't have needed to. He just said who he was, and that he needed to confirm that you had seen her that morning. He'd have asked her not to say anything to you." He put his hand back on her hair, stroking her like a cat. "So you were with Linda from about eight ... I left around eightish. And shots were reported sometime during the hours of darkness, but no-one could quite determine what exactly they meant by *in the night*. We suspect it was likely to be between eleven last night and six this morning, after the family was settled for the night and before this morning's sunrise, but that's speculation at this point. So we need alibis from seven last night to eight-thirty this morning, erring on the side of caution. It was getting light before that, of course, but anyone still sleeping with curtains closed may have assumed it was still dark outside, if they didn't look at the time. And none of them did." He tapped her nose gently with his fingertip. "And you, my lucky little thing, are unarguably accounted for, for almost all of that time."

"Almost?"

"Linda doesn't know exactly how long you were with her, but it doesn't really matter, as it was already almost light when I left, and even if you were only at Linda's for five minutes, which you weren't, because she says you had a cup of tea with her in your pajamas—" He smirked down at her, and she jabbed his leg with her finger. "—it still would have been fully light by the time you could have got to the farm, and that really doesn't tie in with the witness reports about the shots, and there were several people around at the farm by eight, too. But I could assure my colleagues that you were snoring under the duvet with Fletcher on your feet from about midnight until my alarm went off, and that I was with you all evening."

Jess frowned up at him. "I don't know whether to be more offended that you think I snore, or that you told your mates I do."

He bent his head over hers and kissed her pouting mouth. "Jessica O'Malley. You were this close to being a murder suspect at eleven o'clock this morning." He held his thumb and forefinger millimetres apart to show exactly how close she'd been to interrogation. "So if I can tell someone you were snoring at that time, you should take it. It wasn't great for me, either, you know, having your name on the top of my suspect list." His brow wrinkled and a flash of worry darkened his already nearly-black eyes.

"Mmm, guess so. Must have been a bit awkward." She sat up and swung her legs to the floor. "I need to put the garlic bread in, or you won't be getting any. And some veg?"

He nodded.

"But you haven't told me *why* my name came up? I mean, it's sort of obvious ... I found the bird, and I suggested that maybe he'd killed it, and that whoever did it deserved to be shot—" She broke off with a shudder. "I didn't mean it literally, though. But anyway. How did your lot know I'd thought that?" She froze, midway to the kitchen. "Did you tell them?" Her mouth hung open at the thought. Surely not.

Chapter Fifteen

Alone in the kitchen, Jess freed a stick of garlic bread from a packet, placed it on a baking sheet, and slid it into the oven beside the browning lasagne. A waft of melting-cheese-scented steam clouded her face, and for a moment she basked in the heat of the oven.

Thomas Docherty had suffered the exact same fate as her buzzard.
That couldn't be a coincidence.
Dammit.

The heat of the oven prickled her eyes. How *could* Marcus have told his colleagues about that and put her in the frame? Why would he do such a thing. She closed the oven door and straightened, then leaned over the worktop with her head in her hands. He *knew* she wouldn't hurt anyone, so why would he even suggest her name? She balled her fists and rubbed at her eyes as Marcus came up behind her, slipped his arms around her waist, and gently turned her to face him.

"I didn't, Jess. I didn't say a thing. Why would I? I know you wouldn't hurt a fly."

She peered at him from under a loose strand of hair. "I hate flies. I would kill them if I could catch the buggers." She wiped her eyes on her sleeve and offered a feeble half-laugh. "If not you, then who?"

Marcus sighed and nudged her gently towards the table. "Sit. I can see I'd better stay again tonight, just in case you need another alibi for murder, so—" He took a hasty step backwards as she shot him a daggered glare. "Calm down, I was only going to say I'll open a bottle of wine!"

Jess bit hard on the inside of her lip to stop a smile escaping. "Damn you, Marcus Woo. Yes, I suppose you should stay ... If you must." Now the laugh did break free and she got up to extract a pair of wine glasses from one of the wall cupboards. With her college course on a break for the Easter holidays for the next two weeks, and Marcus between shifts, neither of them had to get up early, so if he stayed, she'd get a lie-in. She'd make him let the dogs out and bring her a cup of tea to enjoy in bed. Win win.

"Your name came up from one of the Dochertys. More than one of them, in fact. They'd heard it was you who sent Parks and Wildlife round. When asked who they'd heard it from, they didn't seem quite sure. It could have been the NPWS officer who let it slip?"

"Or anyone," Jess said, as the timer bleeped to announce dinner would be cooked. "Mrs Dunne knew." She got up to retrieve the lasagne from the oven; the aroma of herbs, garlic, and melted cheese filling the kitchen as she eased open the oven door.

"Good point." Marcus grinned at her and inhaled deeply. "Mmm. Smells so good. Want a hand?"

"Just do the wine? It's a veggie one, hope that's okay?" She waved away his offer, and spooned a generous helping onto each plate.

"Veggie wine. My favourite."

"Idiot." She set the laden plate in front of him, and the dish of portioned-up garlic baguette between them. "The lasagne. Veggie. Help yourself." She gestured to the bread. "Did they interview Peggy then? The Parks woman?"

Marcus took a mouthful of garlic bread, catching the buttery drips with his finger before he answered. "Yes. And no. Someone got her on the phone, in the end. Hard woman to track down. They've asked her to call in to the station this evening."

Jess was quiet for a moment, thinking of the vivacious woman who'd sat on the very chair on which Marcus now sat, just a week ago. And the long friendly chat they'd had on the phone on Friday morning when Peggy had told Jess about the vet's report. And the long, chatty messages on Friday afternoon after Jess's momentary annoyance that Peggy'd gossiped to Mrs Dunne. She liked the woman; thought they could become friends ... But ... "Marcus, is she a suspect?"

"Should she be?"

"She was really angry about the buzzard and the mess he's made of the land."

"So were you."

"Yes. I was. I am. But ... well, we both know I didn't kill him over it. But ..." She tailed off, watching Marcus. "I like her. But she did say how fed up she was, and that something should be done."

"So did you."

"But I didn't kill him."

"So probably neither did she? But I suppose we need to check her out more thoroughly. I'll call in the morning and see if they managed to interview her this evening in the end or not. Take it from there."

Jess quietly chewed another mouthful of lasagne, reluctant to consider that her new friend could be a killer. Even if Thomas had deserved it. She gave herself a mental jolt. *No one deserves that, Jess. No one.* "She'd have known exactly how the buzzard died. The pellets; the poison."

"But thanks to you and her and Mrs Dunne, she was far from the only one, right?"

Jess frowned, wanting to be angry at the accusation but knowing it was true. She had mouthed off to Peggy. And to Linda, and Kate, and Marcus. And Peggy had told people too, and once Mrs Dunne knew, well, there'd be no stopping the spread of the news. He was right. "Yes. *Everyone* knew." She sighed, and searched his deep, dark eyes for some kind of answer to an unasked question.

He broke off another chunk of garlic bread. "So the real question is, who is *everyone*?"

"Exactly. And which of those everyones would have the means and the motive?"

"And that, Jessica O'Malley, is what the police will be finding out. Now, what's for dessert?"

"Dessert? You think I've nothing better to do than cook for you? What is this, the nineteen-fifties?"

"No, but I know you saw Linda, remember."

Jess laughed. "Oh, you detective, you. Look in that tin." She nodded towards the end of the table, where a biscuit tin sat, displaying a cheerful Christmassy snow scene. She reached for the tin and slid it across the table towards him, then swivelled in her seat to extract two side plates from a cupboard, all without getting up.

"Chocolate cake!" He was up and rooting for a knife before she'd even set the plates down. "Big slice or small slice?" Without waiting for the answer, he cut two enormous chunks, topped up their glasses, and sat back with a contented smile. "The way to a man's heart, Jess, the way to a heart." He took a large bite, sighed, and added, "I know we have something here, and I like you very, very much, but would you mind terribly if I left you for Linda?"

※

Curled up on the sofa, full, half-asleep, and a second bottle of wine half-empty, Jess dozed happily, enjoying the peace and the comfort of having Marcus there with her. The dogs sprawled across the other sofa, and Marcus was half-watching a rugby match.

With an almighty jolt, Jess sat up, sloshing Marcus's wine and bashing her head on his chin. "Oops, sorry! I just had a thought. Billy White. He said he'd shoot him."

Marcus, rubbing his chin and dabbing at the wine, hit the remote control and paused the match. Johnny Sexton's handsome face froze on the screen, marred only by his gum guard distorting his rugged good looks.

Jess didn't know much about rugby, and couldn't follow the rules, but she knew who Johnny Sexton was, all right. She pulled her focus from the rugby player and looked at Marcus. "Remember how I told you about how mad he was about the flooding? Billy, I mean, not Johnny Sexton."

Marcus flashed her a wry grin but said nothing and Jess could sense him weighing up whether to ask her to expand or to tell her to leave it to the police. Eventually, his professionalism won over, and he went with the latter: "We'll be talking to all the neighbours. But you, Miss O'Malley, are not to get involved. Not again."

She said nothing.

"Really Jess. No. Do. Not. Get. Involved." He stared at her for a long moment.

"But—"

"No." He cupped her face in his hands and kissed her, effectively silencing her protests, then topped up her glass and unfroze the rugby. "Now let me watch the rest of this?"

With a sigh, Jess scooped her open book from the table and tried to remember what Miss Marple had discovered in the last chapter she'd read. Marcus was right. She didn't even know Thomas Docherty. No need at all for her to get involved. *Leave it to the police, Jess. Leave it to Marcus.*

Chapter Sixteen

By the time Jess dragged herself out of bed on Wednesday morning, Marcus had walked the dogs around the park, made her two cups of tea and breakfast in bed, taken a delivery of hot cross buns from Linda, and been called in to work.

"Must you?" Jess complained. "Surely they can cope without you for one day?"

"We've a murder investigation to deal with. I'll be as quick as I can," he promised. "Do you want me to pick up anything in town once I'm done? Easter eggs or anything? Or are you all set?"

"Maybe I'll run in myself, after lunch. I got the girls' eggs on the way home on Monday. Think I've most of the meals planned now. I guess I'll do some baking."

Eric, Belinda, their two daughters, and Alice were all coming for the Easter weekend, and Jess had plenty to get on with. Once she'd got over the disappointment of losing her expected lazy day with Marcus, she'd be grateful for the time she'd gained to get organised. She waved Marcus off, cleaned up the breakfast things, made another cup of tea, then sat at the kitchen table to make a list:

Make beds.
Make cake.
Make shopping list.
Plan egg hunt.
Shop for food.

If she could get most of that done today, she wouldn't need to juggle working at the garden centre over the next two afternoons with getting ready for her family, and she would be calm and organised and ready to relax by the time she met Alice's train on Friday evening.

Alice, it seemed, had other ideas. As Jess wrestled with putting fresh bedding on the double bed in the spare room, Alice texted to say she had Friday off and could she come tomorrow night instead?

Of course, Jess replied. *I have to work Fri afternoon, but only for a few hours. See you tomorrow, tell me train times xxx*

It would be good to have them all here, but an extra night with her sister without their nieces demanding non-stop attention would be nice too. She pulled a set of single bedding from the airing cupboard and wrangled it onto the narrow bed in the box room, for Clara and Bryony to share. *Or Alice. Hmm.* Alice had slept on the sofa last time they'd all come to stay, but she might not be so happy to do that if Marcus was staying too … But then the girls would have to bunk in with Eric and Bel … She'd better tell Eric to bring sleeping bags and their camping mattresses just in case.

By early afternoon, a rich fruit cake was cooling on the counter, and the shopping list was tucked in her wallet so she couldn't forget to bring it to the shops. Now all she had left to check off was planning the egg hunt and going shopping.

She texted Marcus: *How's it looking? You be done anytime soon?*

If he was on his way, they'd reclaim some of their day and he could help her with the egg hunt. If he was going to be caught up at the Garda station for a while yet, she'd shop today and do the egg hunt with Alice on Friday morning.

His reply was swift and unfavourable: *Couple hours yet, sorry x*

She pushed the still-warm cake far back on the worktop out of reach of the dogs, threw a clean tea towel over it to lessen temptation, pushed her feet into her trainers and grabbed the car keys and her bag.

She called the dogs in from the garden, ignored their hopeful faces, and squeezed out of the front door without letting them escape. "Be good, you two. I'll bring you a bone." *Maybe.*

○○○

The supermarket was busy and the shelves poorly stocked. With it being the Easter holidays, excited children sprawled into every aisle, and there were trolleys abandoned at haphazard angles in front of every shelf. Good thing she'd got the Easter eggs already, as all that were left were a few small Double Decker ones that no one liked anyway, and a crumpled pink-foiled Thorntons one that had probably been dropped.

She whizzed around the store as fast as the chaos allowed, having decided to go home via the large greengrocer on the outer ring road for the fruit and veg instead of picking through the bruised remnants left in the supermarket.

An hour later, she stood facing a rainbow of piled produce at Fresh For You, weighing up a pair of aubergines, one in each hand, trying to decide if one was enough to add to a dish of roasted vegetables or if two would be better.

From the other side of the laden shelves, two women were chatting in increasingly rising voices, which Jess allowed to wash over her until a familiar name caught her attention:

"Those poor Dochertys ..."

"... trouble he's brought on them ..."

"... his poor mother ..."

Jess laid the aubergines gently in her basket on top of a cushion of feathery carrot leaves, and sharpened her ears.

"Always did think a lot of himself, so he did, and look where it's got him—"

"Dead in his grave before he's even forty, God rest him, but I'd say there's many not sorry he's gone—"

"That's a shocking thing to say about anyone ... true as it may be ..."

Jess edged sideways along the shelving unit. As the display of aubergines gave way to peppers, tomatoes, onions, then segued into an array of several different pots of growing herbs, the shelving lowered, and lowered again. She selected an aromatic grey-leaved pot of sage, then discarded it: *you've sage in the garden, you daft cow*. Beside the herbs, mushrooms in every shade of brown lay like beach pebbles across a waist-high table; some in large cardboard trays, some in small cardboard punnets, and some in blue plastic containers covered in shrink-wrap.

Here, Jess could see over the divider and get a glimpse of the two gossiping women. She needed mushrooms, anyway, and it would be perfectly natural if she were to glance up and acknowledge fellow shoppers while making her selection. Polite, really. Perfectly acceptable and not at all nosy. Rooting through the mushrooms—oyster, shitake, big flat ones, small round buttons; she'd get a mix for stroganoff tomorrow—she stretched across the table to reach for a pack on the far side from where she stood, just as one of the women reached for the same pack.

"Oh, sorry." Jess withdrew her hand. "You go ahead." She smiled as she looked up at the woman. "Sorry to be nosy, but I couldn't help overhearing … Is it Thomas Docherty you were talking about?"

The woman squirmed and glanced at her friend.

"Oh don't worry—I don't know him, not really. I live in the same village. I couldn't help hearing you say he wasn't well-liked? I got that impression too." She cringed inwardly, uncomfortable at talking ill of someone who'd just been brutally killed. "I met him last week, actually. He seemed nice enough." *Aside from massacring an entire environment and buying up enough weedkiller to clear a forest.* She gave herself a mental nudge. *Jess! Be nice. A man is dead!*

The woman laughed nervously and flicked a sidelong look at her friend. "Rumour has it he's running that farm into the ground, is all. My husband contracts for him sometimes—does the silage, you know?"

Jess didn't, but she nodded, smiled, and scooped up two packs of mushrooms—one large tray of the flat ones, and a smaller carton of buttons. She set them in the basket and added a packet of the mixed varieties. "Running it into the ground? How do you mean?"

The other woman piped up. "These big dairy farms; so intensive. All overmilking and no animal welfare. This country is going to the dogs and the farmers are to blame for a lot of it." Her eyes flashed with anger, and she looked suddenly familiar.

Jess squinted at her, searching her face. "Have we met before? I think I know you from somewhere?"

The woman shrugged. "I live in the village too. Lila." She held out her hand over the mushrooms. "Lila Finnerty. I live behind the pub. I don't remember meeting you." She shrugged again, apologetic.

Jess's mouth fell open. "Small world," she said. "I met one of your other neighbours on Sunday, too. Cindy? The Canadian woman."

Lila smiled. "Oh, yes, she's lovely. Musical. We play together, sometimes."

"Did you know Thomas?" Jess asked, setting her basket on the edge of the table to support the weight of the vegetables while she stopped to natter.

"Yes and no." Lila nodded then shook her head. "In passing, of course; he was up and down past our house often enough; they all are. There's a lot of them." She *hmph*ed in a short almost-laugh. "Typical Irish farming family: lots of them and all stayed close to home. I'm friends with Anne—his youngest sister. We were in school together. I'd drink with any mix of them now and then. Siobhan was in our year too."

"Siobhan?"

"One of the cousins. We were always friendly enough; still pass the time of day, hang out together. Her da is a brother of Thomas's da."

"You said ..." Jess faltered. Was she being very rude? And a total gossip, at that. "You said ... you implied ... the family hadn't had a lot of time for him?"

"Some weren't too keen on what he was doing to the farm. Preferred the older ways; the more gentle approach. You'd have heard he's felled a lot of—oh!" She clapped a hand to her mouth. "It was you!"

Jess's stomach flipped. She knew what Lila was about to say. She nodded. "Yes," she said quietly, just as Lila spoke again.

"You found that buzzard and reported it." Lila lifted her chin, looked directly at Jess; held her gaze unwaveringly with her hazel-flecked green eyes, held out her hand again, and said, "Frickin' well done. Nice to meet you, Jess."

The other woman looked from Lila to Jess, a look of understanding crossing her face. "Oh. Well done. Were you at the protest on Saturday? There was a fine turnout. It's criminal what's happening to our heritage. So sad to see the bogs being lost. All that destroyed habitat ..." She tailed off, her face clouded in sadness, and Jess imagined tragic, barren images of Ireland's decimated boglands spooling through her mind.

As Jess imagined the other woman's thoughts, the images of barren peatbogs morphed into pictures of sterile strips of grassland:

Neat, even squares of grass, boundaried by single strands of wire.

Butchered tree stumps, their sawn tops pale against the dark earth where the hedges once flourished.

A shed crammed full of lowing cattle.

The buzz of insects replaced by the thrum of silence.

A dead buzzard, glassy-eyed and still on a dusty lane. She sighed. "He has certainly messed up that lane, hasn't he? I walked down there a few times last summer, and it was buzzing with insects. Buzzing. I'd usually see buzzards, too. Flying, I mean, not dead. Wakes of them, someone told me they were. A group of buzzards is called a wake, did you know that? I just heard it a few months back. Fitting, now they're all dying." She turned up one side of her mouth in a wry smile. "A wake. All laid out in a row, dead. That's how I imagine them now. Not soaring through the sky. It's such a shame." Her face warmed in sudden embarrassment. "Sorry, I do run on."

"No, you're right. Something needs to be done." The woman whose name Jess still didn't know nodded her agreement. "Well," she snorted, "seems something *has* been done. I'm not saying it was *right* to kill someone, but if that someone's responsible for murdering a whole lot of wildlife, well maybe there's some karma in that. Just saying." She huffed, smirked, and selected a tray of organic mushrooms to add to her shopping basket. "Maybe whoever takes over the farm will put it to rights."

Chapter Seventeen

Ignoring her promise to Marcus, and to herself, Jess had her notebook propped open on the worktop beside the half-decorated Easter cake. She was keeping it simple; a circle of marzipan and ready-roll icing on top, with a circle of marzipan eggs around the top and around the base, reminiscent of a simnel cake. Ultimately, no one would care what it looked like as long as it tasted good and included a good lot of the requisite marzipan she and Eric loved.

On the open notepad, as well as a light dusting of icing sugar, was a list of potential suspects, each of whom may have wished Thomas Docherty dead.

~~1 Me!~~

She'd crossed that out as soon as she'd written it, but after Marcus's revelation that her name had come up as a suspect, she'd added it anyway, just for the fun of it. And so she could very emphatically cross it out.

2. Billy White

3. Ella's man's dad (not really him, but anyone like him who wanted to see the bogs left for harvesting, not turned over to grazing or left to nature)

4. The protestor types – the ones <u>against</u> farming and <u>for</u> nature

5. Who was in the pub Saturday night? local? any that match number 4?

6. Lila Finnerty, then. Should've asked her when I saw her!

7. Other neighbours affected by the mess he's making of their lane – who else is annoyed by the floody road? Could call on Cindy???? Ask her?

8. Family. Lila said they hated him!!

It was a long list.

She chewed the end of her pencil, studied the names for a moment, and added SUSPECTS in neat capitals above the list. She blew the icing sugar from the paper and turned the page with her pencil, mindful that her hands were marzipan-sticky. On the top of the next page, she wrote **WHY?**, then added MOTIVE beneath it in slightly smaller letters.

She chewed at the pencil again, then swapped it for a little ball of marzipan; almondy, grainy, sticky, and infinitely more satisfying than the woody pencil-end. Yum. She broke another piece from the gooey golden wodge, popped in her mouth, washed her hands, and set about finishing decorating the cake before she accidentally ate all the decoration. As she rolled the yellow paste into neat egg shapes, she rolled potential motives through her mind.

It all *seemed* to come back to Thomas Docherty's desire to have a neat, orderly farm, without trees, hedges, or any obvious regard for animal welfare, and with every inch of the farmland given over to grass. The dead buzzard; the flooding; the destruction of the bog and the woodland; the discontent among his neighbours and family ... It all came back to the way he managed—or mismanaged—his land. She lifted the finished cake and eased it into a tin, pushed the lid firmly on, and slid the tin to the back of the worktop. Another job done. Time for tea, then. She put just enough water in the kettle for one mug, set it to boil, and extracted the last piece of Linda's gingerbread from another tin, where it had nestled beside a hunk of the delicious chocolate cake she and Marcus had enjoyed last night. She'd done well to make the gingerbread last, she thought with a swell of pride far greater than the achievement warranted. *I deserve it just for that. A reward for not having eaten it sooner!* Chuckling to herself, she took a large bite and remembered someone else she needed to add to the list.

Setting the gingerbread on a plate, she turned the page of her notebook back to her list of names, and added number nine: *Peggy*. She stared at the names for a moment, searching for something she couldn't see, turned on the radio, made herself a cup of tea, and sat down, notebook in front of her, to finish the gingerbread before unpacking the rest of the shopping and thinking about what to make for dinner.

Humming along to the radio as it played out the last of the songs before the news, Jess chopped onions and cubed a hunk of butternut squash, to turn some of the day's groceries into a risotto for tonight. She diced half a red pepper, then rummaged in the cupboard for a packet of pine nuts and the arborio rice, letting the days' news wash over her.

As was usually the case, there was nothing that caught her ear. Thomas's murder was already old news, at least until there were any developments in the investigation, and wasn't mentioned. The news segued into the weather forecast—blustery, until Friday, but a promise of a calm Easter weekend—and on into the day's obituaries. They'd read Thomas Docherty's out yesterday, but would repeat it several times a day until the funeral was over, so it was no surprise to hear it again now. The funeral, the voice intoned solemnly, would take place at the church of Our Lady, Ballyfortnum, before the regular Good Friday service. Even the funeral announcement didn't give the church its full, long title of *The Catholic Church of Our Lady, Mary, Blessed Virgin and Sacred Mother of Jesus Christ,* Jess noted with a grin. Who'd blame them? Most of the locals referred to the church as nothing but 'Mary's', although whether in laziness, affection, or disrespect was an argument none voiced aloud. The announcer droned on, and by the time another five deaths had been read out in the bored monotone, there were barely forty-five minutes left for '80s hour. Again.

The peppy sound of Rick Astley hot on the heels of the obituaries brought an image of Father James into Jess's mind. She'd not seen him for ages. Not even zipping around the village on his bike in his too-tight Lycra. Maybe because she'd not walked into the village so often lately? What with going up to the river, or driving to the pub to walk up the lane where she'd found the buzzard, and adapting her times to suit her new hours at work and at college, maybe it was inevitable their paths would cross less often. She'd call in to see him soon. Tomorrow morning, perhaps.

Father James wasn't like most Irish priests: he was young, about Jess's own age, with fading red hair and a freckled face, not dissimilar to Eric's stereotypical Irish appearance. He'd been so kind to her over the years, and even more so since her dad had died. Besides, he shared Jess's love for scones and there were always some on offer in the warm, cosy vicarage kitchen.

"We'll go see him tomorrow, eh, Fletch?" She nudged Fletcher with her socked toe, and he rolled over onto his back. Obliging, she rubbed his belly as he squirmed in approval. "Shall we go for a quick walk, before dinner? Shall we?"

Fletcher thumped his tail on the kitchen floor in agreement.

"I'll call Marcus, see if we have time."

⁂

As Jess and the two dogs meandered up the dead-end farm track to the east of Orchard Close, she mulled over her list in her mind. The list of people who seemed to dislike Thomas Docherty was a long one, and given the level of disapproval the man seemed to have, it stood to reason there may even be more names to add. Still, at least she'd crossed one person off for certain, even if it was only herself! Her sudden burst of laughter startled a sparrow from the hedgerow and she laughed again as it made her jump backwards in surprise.

A few yards on, she stopped to pick up a stick to toss for Fletcher, and flung it through a gap in the hedge, into the empty field.

He ignored it, and continued up the muddy track, nose to the ground in pursuit of something far more odorous than a dry stick.

Snowflake flashed her a baleful doggy look, and trotted after his friend.

"Ah well. Don't say I didn't try to play with you, you brat," she muttered after her ungrateful Labrador, smiling as she watched the pair of them enjoying the freedom of the off-lead walk. She swung the leads in circles, one each side of her, and let her mind drift back to Thomas Docherty.

With so many suspects on her list, she needed a way to narrow them down.

Okay... everyone has motive, but who has means? Not having brought her notebook out on the walk, she tried to conjure an image of the page. Who was first? *Billy White. Well, he has a gun—I saw him up at the Gun Club the other day.* She supposed that meant he had a gun, anyway. She hadn't *actually* seen him with a gun. He'd know about poison too. Farmers did, didn't they?

So would Peggy. She really didn't want to consider Peggy could be capable of killing anyone, but she had to admit the woman was passionate and fiery. And she knew exactly what the buzzard's injuries were, so she'd be perfectly able to replicate them. She'd probably know all about poisons, too, wouldn't she? But where would she get a gun? Jess couldn't imagine that Parks and Wildlife officers would have any need or wish to use guns. She kicked a stone across the track, and it clunked satisfyingly against a fence post embedded in the hedge. Who knew what anyone did in their free time? Maybe Peggy was from a farming family and *did* know how to shoot. She shook her head emphatically. Peggy really didn't seem the type to shoot someone. She really didn't.

What about those protestors, then? But they wouldn't know anything about what Thomas was doing to that stretch of bog ... How would they? It was way up at the end of a little-used lane; not farmed commercially or tended by *Bord na Móna* ... was it? She didn't think so, but she should ask someone. Who? But she *had* seen evidence that locals still harvested rows of cut turf for their own domestic use. Hadn't she guessed that was why there'd been that empty coal sack caught in the hedge? The one she'd used as the bird's death shroud. So many rural Irish homeowners still used turf for their fires, despite the laws against it. What was it Marcus had called the rights for locals to claim a strip of the bog for their own? Tubby rights? Something like that ... Tubridy rights! That was it. No, he was the man off the telly ... Turbary. Turbary rights.

She'd Googled it some more, after Marcus had talked about it. People could claim a stretch of land, linked somehow to their house and the old estate boundaries. Local farmers would come in with the heavy machinery and cut it, laying it out in bricks. She'd imagined the machine working a little like a pasta extruder. It used to all be done by hand—by men wielding murderous-looking tools like a cross between a scythe and a cookie cutter—but things had moved on since then. The same farmers with the machinery could stack and dry the cut turf, but for a price, so most of the locals would still do their own stacking. Footing, it was called. They'd pile up the bricks like a Jenga tower, so the wind and the sun could dry the peat into rock-hard bricks. Once dry, they'd bag them up, or load them in loose piles onto trailers, begged or borrowed if not owned. Most of the old local families had a trailer and a little tractor kept just for this purpose. Come high summer, the lanes would be full of old-fashioned tractors in every colour, chugging along at the speed of a drunken snail, hauling an overflowing load of the black turf bricks. Usually with a couple of children or teenagers balanced precariously on top of the heap, enjoying the ride. Fallen bricks would dot the roads for several weeks in summer, either to be retrieved by thrifty passersby to add to their own fuel stores, or crushed back into crumbly earth by the passing traffic.

Having only lived in the countryside for the last few years, Jess still took pleasure in this glimpse of rural Irish heritage, unfolding like a play every July and August. It hadn't happened in Dublin, where the houses no longer relied on open fires or solid fuel ranges to heat their homes. It was a bit archaic, out here in the boglands, she thought to herself, as she neared the end of the track. Was fighting over the bogs where the expression *Turf Wars* had come from? Is that what had killed Thomas Docherty; a good old-fashioned turf war? She spun around on the ball of her foot and started back towards home.

Chapter Eighteen

The second thing Jess did when she got home was send Eric a text. The first, of course, had been to put the kettle on.

It's a good thing you're coming at the weekend. I've another fine mystery for the Lollipop Club!

Before giving him time to answer, she sent another: *Good thing Alice finally joined us! This one's a tricky one!*

And another: *Should we let Marcus in? Tell him the password?*

Not that they actually had a password anymore; not for about the last twenty-five years or so, when Jess and Eric had filled their childhood with solving mysteries, emulating their then-heroes from the old Enid Blyton mystery books—The Secret Seven; the Five Find-Outers, and suchlike. Alice, older, aloof, and already struggling with an eating disorder, had rarely engaged with her two younger siblings back then. It was only in the last few years that her health had improved to the point where they had all dared to say out loud that maybe she was really better at last. Alice, who had hidden herself away, hated the countryside, or family get-togethers, or anyone inquiring endlessly about what she had or hadn't eaten that day, had finally, *finally*, become the older sister Jess had yearned for throughout her childhood and on into her twenties. By the time Jess turned thirty, Alice's absence from her life no longer caused any surprise. Even while Jess had nursed their father through his terminal illness, and dealt with the aftermath of his death, falling into a darkness of her own, Alice had remained absent.

About a year ago, something had changed.

Around the time that Linda's beloved husband Bert had died, Jess, determined not to slip back into depression after losing another loved one, had instead doggedly uncovered the killer of the Get Slim members, setting her sights firmly on both justice and the prevention of more deaths. Alice had stayed away for Bert's funeral, but had met with Jess soon after, for lunch in Dublin. That had been the first time Jess could ever remember Alice suggesting lunch. And eating it.

From that point onwards, Alice had steadily proved her years of counselling and care had finally come good. She had come to stay with Jess in Ballyfortnum several times, and Jess and Alice had embarked on a new, exciting, heart-warming sisterly relationship, at last.

Last August, Alice had even helped Jess expose another killer in the village, and become a fully-fledged member of The Lollipop Club two-and-a-half decades after Jess had first drawn a wobbly, childish picture of a magnifying glass as a logo for her and Eric's detective club.

A magnifying glass Alice had said looked like a lollipop.

The original name of Jess's and Eric's detective club was long forgotten, and the other original members—Watson, the family's dog at the time, and an assortment of Jess's stuffed animals—long gone. But two separate spates of murder in Ballyfortnum last year had seen a semi-joking, semi-serious revival of Jess's sleuthing and with it, their Lollipop Club, and this time, Alice was definitely *in*.

The bleeping of her phone jolted Jess out of her childhood reverie, and the slightly sepia-tinted memory of her and Eric stalking a young couple along a hedge-lined street to see which car they got into vanished from her mind as Eric's name lit up her phone screen. She opened the message.

No way! No policeman allowed! Would the Fine-doubters have let Goon in? No they would not. But, tell you what, little sis, as he is useful AND we like him, he is allowed to visit so we can exploit him for information. How does that sound? I'll bring lollipops. I mean magnifying glasses. I mean bribes. And two fine clue-hunters in the forms of B and C. CU Fri xx

Jess laughed at the screen, imagining her nieces creeping about, hunting for footprints—Bryony would never be subtle enough to make a sleuth. She'd give them clues to hunt for, all right, but the clues would lead only to chocolate eggs, not murderers.

Maybe there was a way her family—the girls included—*could* help her narrow the list of suspects … but what?

She made herself a cup of tea, threw open the French doors to let some air blow through the house, and pulled up her favourite playlist on her phone, then set about cooking the risotto she'd prepared earlier.

As the stock simmered and wafts of rosemary and sage filled the kitchen, she thumbed through her notebook with one hand, all the while stirring the risotto pan with the other. Stopping on the page with the list of suspects, she squinted at the scrawl of words, hoping something would jump out.

Ella's man's dad. Hmm. She'd ask Ella more about Finn's dad and his colleagues, but it seemed too tenuous a link to Thomas Docherty. First, the peat processing plant was a good few miles from Ballymaglen, and second, it was a very different problem to Thomas's methodical amassing of more grazing land from scrubland, woodland, and bogland. She pencilled a faint line through *Ella's man's dad*, but underlined the bracketed note she'd scribbled beside him—*anyone like him who wanted to see the bogs left for harvesting*—and added a note beside it: *Who like him lives near B'fortnum?*

"And how would I find out?" she asked the steam rising from the pan. She turned down the heat, added another splash of stock, and turned back to her list of suspects.

Lila. Lila who Cindy had said was on the road late Saturday night, drunk and merry. What was Lila doing past all the houses? Only the two farms lay beyond Cindy's house, didn't they? She counted out the cottages in her mind, tapping her pencil against the worktop as she tried to remember who lived where. Lila and her husband, tap. Shaughnessy someone, tap. Cindy and Walt, tap. Billy White, tap. No, wait! There was the one with the rusty car in between. Who lived there? She added a note to the page: *Who lives in rusty car house by White farm?*

On the opposite side of the lane, she walked mentally back down the track: Dochertys. Tap. Cocker spaniels. Tap. Old man. "What's his name?" she muttered to the unresponsive page. Tap tap tap. She wrote *cocker spaniels* and *old man* below the line about the rusty car, and added three big question marks.

Why did Lila go *past* her own house on a rainy Saturday night? Was she just too drunk to notice her own house? Not likely. Who gets *that* drunk?

Who else lives on the Dochertys' farm then? That must be worth checking out. Marcus had said they were a big family. Farm labourers, too, probably. Would any of them dislike Thomas enough to kill him?

Jess turned off the heat under the pan and covered it with a lid to absorb the rest of the liquid. She'd give Marcus another ten minutes, then eat without him if he wasn't back. She leaned her bum against the counter and sucked grains of sticky risotto from the wooden spoon. The problem was, it wasn't enough to dislike the man enough to kill him; it was combining that with the *means* to kill him. And, most crucially, combining that with the knowledge of how the bird had been killed. That couldn't be coincidence, surely. The method had been too similar; too contrived; too much of a statement. "Look!" it screamed. "He did this to a defenceless bird and he must be punished for it." The bird, somehow, was the clue.

She dropped the spoon into the sink, scooped up her phone, and texted Peggy: *Hi, it's Jess. Weird question, but who did you tell about the bird's EXACT injuries?*

While waiting for an answer, Jess began a new list:

WHO KNEW ABOUT BUZZARD INJURIES?

Me.

Marcus.

She'd told him what Peggy had said, she was sure. *Hmmph! If I was a suspect, he should be too!* She smiled at the thought of informing Marcus he was on her list, and drew a line through both their names. Not us. Anyway, we are each other's alibis. A warm flutter rose in her chest and suddenly she longed for him to be home. *Home.* Was Marcus beginning to spend so much time at Number 7, Orchard Close, that she could think of it as his home too? She shook away the thought and jotted a note to remind herself to talk to Eric and Alice again about what they wanted to do with the house that legally belonged to the three of them. She tore out the page and pinned it to the fridge door with a garish magnet Kate had brought her back from a holiday in Crete a couple of years ago.

Oh! Kate. She'd told Kate.

But only as they'd walked to the shop the same day he'd been killed. Phew. Not Kate. As if she'd have time to go out and kill anyone while raising a seven-month-old baby anyway. She giggled at the thought of Kate tucking the baby under one arm and firing off a round of pellets with her other, gangster-style, and with not a hair out of place or a smear in her makeup.

So, who aside from her and Marcus, then? She added Peggy's name to the list, and under that wrote *NPWS vet*, although that seemed as far-fetched as the idea of Ella's boyfriend's dad trekking over from a village ten miles away to shoot someone he didn't know about land he didn't care about.

So who else had Peggy told? Mrs Dunne, perhaps, but anyone else?

Fletcher and Snowflake bounded in from the garden and leaped onto the sofa to gaze out of the bay window facing the road, tails wagging a chilly draught across the living room.

Jess shut the French door and turned up the heat under the pan. She took a wedge of Parmesan from the fridge and was grating it into a small bowl when she heard a car pull up outside the house.

Fletcher barked, jumped from the sofa, and charged to the door, Snowflake scrabbling to keep up, to welcome Marcus home.

Chapter Nineteen

Jess left it to the dogs to greet Marcus and usher him in. Peggy's reply had just pinged in, so she'd abandoned grating the Parmesan, and wanted to jot the information into her notebook before Marcus saw what she was up to. To the background noise of his slow progress while he navigated the two happy dogs, she scribbled *Peggy → nosy shopkeeper, colleagues—NPWS, others at Dochertys' farm.*

Thomas hadn't been there himself, Peggy's text had said. She'd seen a handful of other people, but didn't know who they all were. Peggy's text was long and rambling and punctuated with the usual overkill of questions and exclamations. Aside from whoever she'd spoken to at the farm, she said she'd 'probably' given the gory details to Mrs Dunne, but couldn't be sure exactly what she'd said. She'd definitely gone into the full descriptive detail at the farm—*wanted them to know exactly what they'd done! Showed them photos, too!*—but didn't know who she'd talked to, exactly. And of course her colleagues would know, including the vet and anyone else who'd heard her moaning about it in the office, and anyone who *hadn't* heard her moaning in the office but had read the report afterwards.

A second text pinged in as Jess was frantically scribbling; ears pricked for Marcus closing in on her as he made his way through the living room. Peggy again: *Oh, and there was someone in the shop too, dunno who. A man. I think.*

Jess added *man in shop – who?* then closed her notebook and bundled it into the overflowing junk drawer, which jammed as she tried to shut it. She opened it, jiffled the contents around, shut it again, and turned to greet Marcus with a hug.

"Good day?" she asked, hoping she didn't look guilty or suspicious. "I made risotto."

He wrapped her in his arms and sniffed appreciatively. "Mmm. Smells lovely."

If there was one thing she knew about Marcus, it was that she could distract him with food. At least temporarily. She nudged the drawer with her bottom, making sure it really was closed, and sighed. "I missed you, a bit." She smiled, losing herself for a minute in his deep brown eyes. "Hungry?" Not waiting for the answer to what they both knew was a rhetorical questions, she rooted for dishes and cutlery, and gestured to him to sit. "I know you're only just in, but it's ready and I'm hungry too. Tell me how you got on while we eat? Have you solved the case? Caught the killer?"

He prodded her back gently. "You know I can't discuss police business. Sorry I was out all day on our day off though."

Jess set the steaming bowls of risotto on the table and sat opposite Marcus. "Okay, so you can't *tell* me but blink once for yes, two for no. Were you out all day because you were working on Thomas Docherty?"

He stared into her eyes, and slowly, deliberately, blinked. One. Two. Three.

Jess giggled and stuck out her tongue. "All right. Don't tell. I guess if you don't want to talk about work, you don't want to hear my news or thoughts either." She shrugged nonchalantly, and turned her attention to the risotto, carefully ignoring Marcus and trying not to laugh. In her head, she counted. One. Two. Three. Four. Five. Six.

"Actual, relevant news? Or just gossip?"

She smiled. "Six seconds, Woo. Six seconds before you needed to know." She forked a heap of rice into her mouth and chewed slowly, making him wait. And then she changed the subject, having learned he'd be far more likely to let things slip once he thought she'd stopped asking. "Want to help me make the egg hunt for Bryony and Clara? Are you any good at *making* clues? Or is that too much like multi-tasking?"

He stretched a socked foot out under the table and nudged her leg. "We can't all be as multi-talented as you, O'Malley. I assume you've not only worked out exactly how Docherty died, but also planned the entire egg hunt in your mind already?"

"Thought the Gards didn't do assuming, huh?"

He pretended to glare, and ate the rest of his meal in quiet thought. When his eyes darkened and he began pushing the last few mouthfuls around his plate, Jess made another assumption and rubbed her foot against his.

"Thinking of Lily?" she asked softly. Lily was Marcus's daughter. She was the same age as Jess's younger niece, Clara, and Jess knew that time spent with her brother's daughters was bittersweet for Marcus. Since his wife had taken off to America two years ago, Marcus barely saw his little girl, and their attempts at video calls left much to be desired. He had last seen Lily at Christmastime, when he'd flown over to the States for a week to visit.

"She's all but forgotten me," he said now; a refrain Jess had stopped trying to contradict or reassure against because, sadly, it seemed to be true. Lily had left Ireland with her mother at just four years old, and hadn't the attention span for chatting on the phone or a video call, and only became really animated when Marcus brought Snowflake to the camera for the child to talk to.

Jess's heart ached at the sadness on his face, his deep frown lines marking the uncountable hours without his child. She shoved back her chair and went to him, taking him in her arms and pulling his head to her chest. "Oh Marcus. I wish I could help. I'm sorry."

"You do." His voice was thick and muffled. He touched his fingers to her cheek. "You do. At least I have someone to share my time off with again. That's nice."

"Nice? Is that the best you can do? Nice?" She forced a teasing tone, hoping to cheer him up with banalities.

He smiled weakly. "Quite nice?"

She batted his head with her chin. "Oy. Have you considered a family grudge against Thomas Docherty?" Talking about work would be easier than thinking about Lily, even if it meant he'd talk only about *not* talking about it.

"Jess ..."

"Because I met Lila Finnerty in the greengrocer's this afternoon. And when I say met, I mean I heard her before I saw her, and she was talking about him ..."

Marcus pulled back from Jess's embrace and gestured her to sit again. "Okay, okay. I'm listening. Go on. You know you're dying to tell me your gossip."

Jess relayed the conversation she'd had in the shop, and how Lila had implied that most of the Dochertys vehemently disagreed with Thomas's heavy-handed, sterile approach to farming, and how as he'd made the farm increasingly commercial, the family had collectively seethed at the impact on their home and land.

"All of them?" Marcus raised his eyebrows.

"Actually, mad as it sounds, she seemed to think yes. *All* of them. You'd have thought he'd need at least some of them onside, to have made the decisions he made. I mean, it's not just his farm, is it? There's his dad, and uncles and brothers and cousins … And his sisters too, obviously. There are plenty of women farming around here; it's not just a man's world, not these days. Why don't any of *them* have a say? Is—was he that belligerent? Was he a bit of a bully, I wonder? Or just strong-minded and persuasive?"

"Arrogant?"

"Convinced his way was the best way?"

"Did it anyway, even if his family objected?"

"His way or the highway?"

"Something to look into. You win, O'Malley. You've given me something to check out." He got up and gathered the dirty plates. "Thank you for dinner. Go on and relax while I clear up and make you a cup of tea." He nodded towards the living room, and Jess did as he suggested.

Fletcher wriggled out from under the table and followed. He jumped onto the sofa, turned around twice, scrabbled at the cushion, and curled onto Jess's feet with his head in her lap.

Snowflake, loyal to his master, stayed in the kitchen and hoped for dropped leftovers, even if they were only vegetables and not delicious chunks of meat.

The clanking of dishes and splashing of water from the kitchen washed over Jess as she sat back and closed her eyes, trying to untangle the mass of words and ideas she'd committed to her notebook. How could she find out more about the Docherty family? She lifted her bum an inch off the sofa to pull her phone from the back pocket of her jeans, but it wasn't there. Dammit. If she went to the kitchen to get it, Marcus would wonder what she was up to. If she thought really, really hard about what she wanted to ask Kate, would Kate get a psychic message? *Don't be stupid, Jess!* She rubbed Fletcher's head and turned on the TV, resigned to not asking Kate if any of the Dochertys had attended her Get Slim group until later.

In the kitchen, the kettle boiled. Water splashed into mugs. The fridge door opened and closed again with a soft thunk. The metal clink of a teaspoon on china. The bleep of an incoming message.

A moment later, Marcus handed Jess a mug of tea and her phone. "Your phone made noise. Here."

Perhaps the psychic thing had worked after all. She took both from him and pressed the button to bring her screen to life. Not Kate. Alice. But at least she had her phone, and could text Kate without Marcus knowing she was sleuthing. She squinted at the screen, first reading Alice's message confirming her train time for tomorrow, and firing off a quick reply, then composing a text to Kate to ask if she knew any of the Dochertys.

"Alice's train gets in at seven," she told Marcus. "I guess I'll hang around after work rather than come home first, and see you on Friday?" Marcus was scheduled for a night shift on Thursday, so he'd be able to mind the dogs well enough without them needing Linda to help out. "It'll be good to see Alice. She's looking forward to seeing you again, too."

Kate's reply pinged in. *Think maybe. Not sure how they're related. Will check, but prob can't tell you much. Confidential info!*

Jess smirked at the screen, hearing Kate's voice in her head. Kate was forever telling Jess the Get Slim client information was confidential, and then immediately spilling the beans. She'd relaxed about it a lot more since Della's arrival. She didn't take herself nearly so seriously now she had to juggle a baby's needs into her own high-maintenance lifestyle. She'd even called around without makeup on once or twice in the past seven months, heaven forbid! Jess chuckled, typed *oh go on, it's a murder investigation!* and set her phone face-down on the arm of the sofa.

Marcus coaxed Fletcher to shift along to the other end of the sofa and took his place beside Jess.

"Oy, he was keeping my feet warm."

Marcus obligingly tucked her feet under his thigh, and she squirmed to get comfortable again, retrieving her legs so she could twist around the other way and rest her head against his chest.

"Shall we plan this egg hunt, then?" he asked. "Will it be here in the garden? Or somewhere more adventurous?"

Last year, Jess had set a simple trail of clues around the garden, but maybe Marcus had a point. Why not go somewhere with more space? Like the woods or the river path ... or the bog, perhaps. The woods, although an obvious choice, would be busy with families out walking over the Easter weekend. The river path was maybe too risky with the fast-flowing currents of the Tunny just a misstep down a grassy bank. Clara could be trusted to stay close, but bouncy Bryony? Jess shuddered as the bloated, floating image of the fisherman she'd found in the Tunny in August bobbed in her mind. Not the river. "We could take them to the bog? I haven't really shown them the bog. Even Eric hasn't really been out on that section of it; only the bit near the river."

Marcus jostled her gently with a wriggle of his shoulder. "Jess O'Malley, you are the most unsubtle detective I have ever met. You may as well have *ulterior motive* tattooed on your forehead. Besides, isn't it too wet up there still, after that rain?"

She supposed he was probably right.

Chapter Twenty

Jess took a deter along the lane beside the pub on her way to work on Thursday afternoon, to check Marcus's prediction about the state of the bog. He was right. Although the water on the lane had drained away, the open bogland was wet and sticky. It would be far too squishy to bring the girls. In winter, or after particularly heavy rain like they'd had over the weekend, this peaty earth acted like quicksand, and besides the obvious dangers, they would all get absolutely filthy. An Easter egg hunt across the bog was a non-starter.

She drove back down the lane, scanning the open fields in front of the Dochertys' farm with undisguised curiosity. The air was still and silent, and there were no signs of activity. The fields, as usual, were empty of cattle, although on Billy White's side of the track, sheep dotted the field like apple blossom fallen in the wind, small and distant at the far end of the land. The rain had muddied Billy White's fields, and the vibrant green of new spring grass was nowhere to be seen. A platoon of camouflaged soldiers could have hidden easily in the patchy brown-green mix of bare earth, wet mud, and yellow-green winter grass. On the verges in front of Billy's muddy field, the dandelions and primroses shone brightly against their dulled backdrop; the only signs that spring was supposed to be here.

On the Dochertys' side, the grass was greener, unsullied by the trampling hooves of livestock. Jess smiled wryly at the thought. *The grass may be greener on the other side, but his life didn't turn out so good.*

Was Billy White jealous? Was he upset that the grass was greener on his neighbour's farm? She didn't think so. Rage over the impact Thomas's green grass had on Billy's land, maybe, but certainly not jealousy. Billy had made it quite clear he didn't want Thomas's way of farming. *So not jealousy, but enough anger to kill him? Hmm.*

Opposite the Dochertys' drive, the house with the old car stood still and quiet. The man she'd seen before was nowhere in sight.

As Jess approached the next cottage—the one beside the Dochertys' driveway—two dogs ran to the gate, barking loudly: one golden, one black. The two cocker spaniels Marcus had mentioned. If only she was walking, she could've stopped to greet them, but in her car, to stop and talk to a pair of dogs would only make her look deranged. She slowed, and tried to see if anyone lurked behind the net-curtains, but although the volume of the dogs' barking escalated, no one appeared.

At the next bungalow, an elderly man emerged from a corrugated tin shed in the garden, clutching an armful of peat bricks for his fire. Jess raised an arm in greeting and he acknowledged her with a dip of his head.

The next bungalow was the one at which Marcus had said the Canadian couple lived. A large tabby cat sat on the window sill, licking its paws and watching nonchalantly as she passed by. A car in the driveway and smoke from the chimney implied someone was home. Jess glanced at the clock on her dashboard, which told her she didn't have time to call in.

At the next two houses, all was quiet. She reached the junction, turned left, and drove on towards her afternoon in the garden centre and her evening with Alice.

※

A little after four, Alice texted to say she'd caught an earlier train and would be at the station in about half an hour, but the garden centre still thrummed with a rush of Easter-weekend gardeners and gift-buyers.

There was no way Jess was sneaking out early, not today.

Come and find me at work? Jess texted. *Ballymaglen garden centre. 10 min walk from station – turn left out of station, walk to town, can't miss it.* She refilled the gaps on the plant tables, stuck her head into the portacabin office to check on Shay and see which of them might have a minute to make tea, and beetled back into the busy shop to serve an ever-increasing line of customers, most of them bearing flowering plants of some kind or another.

Ella flashed a welcome half-smile—*thank goodness you're back, help me!*—and directed half the waiting customers to the second till, while Jack lugged various items up and down the aisles or out to customers' cars.

By the time Alice arrived, Jess had forgotten she was due. "Sorry!" she mouthed to her sister over the head of an elderly woman who fumbled in a battered leather purse for change. "With you in a bit." It was probably a lie, as there seemed no end in sight to the busy day.

"Alice!"

Jess and Alice swung in unison towards Shay's voice. He'd only met Alice once, last summer, when Jess had thought she and Shay might become a couple and he'd come for dinner to meet her family. The exact same weekend that she'd finally realised—and admitted to Alice—how strong her feelings for Marcus were. Shay had been remarkably gracious about it, and it hadn't taken long for their friendship to recover; something for which Jess was eternally thankful, as she loved her days at the garden centre and relished the help Shay had given her in securing her place on the horticulture course in Kildare. She flashed him a grateful smile as he set tea down beside the till, one for her and one for Jack, and a can of cold coke for Ella, who detested tea with a passion Jess couldn't understand.

Alice beamed at him, clearly delighted to be remembered.

"How're you?" They greeted each other in unison, still grinning as they matched each other's words.

Shay glanced around the shop, took in the madness, and gestured Alice to follow him to the yard. "Keep me company in the office if you like? Until it eases off in here. We close at five-thirty." He checked his watch. "Not long now, thank goodness," he added *sotto voce*, throwing a furtive glance at the queue by the tills. "C'mon."

With a not-very-apologetic look at her little sister, Alice followed him out.

Ella smirked at Jess, her carefully-plucked eyebrows raised in an exaggerated suggestion.

"She's my sister," Jess explained. "They met before."

Ella nodded. "Yeah, right." She ducked her head over the till, still smiling to herself.

"Ella," Jess said, suddenly bored of the repetitive small talk they'd been exchanging with customers since she'd arrived for work at one o'clock, "how's Finn's dad? Any news on his work?"

Ella looked up; her brow wrinkled in puzzlement. "Huh? Why? Oh, yeah!" Understanding lightened her face as she recalled the conversation from the week before. "Nah, he didn't go to the protest, weather being so shite and all. Mind, he's all talk, but when it comes to Saturday arvo, he's a slob in front o' the telly. Rugby, weren't it? Saturday gone? Finn and me was watching with him. Good win." She grinned at Jess, and bagged up a bundle of seed packets for a woman Jess vaguely recognised. "You heard about that man who got shot?"

Jess nodded. "Yeah. He was in here last week. He lives in Ballyfortnum. Lived. That's why I remembered about Finn's dad. Seems someone was unhappy about the way he was farming, and I know he's been draining the bog up there; turning it to grazing land. Another chunk of bog lost."

"Ah." Ella chewed on her lower lip as she rang up yet another purchase of bedding plants. "So Finn's da wants to keep getting peat off the bogs, and yer dead man's wanting to turn it to grazing, and you reckon that's an excuse to nip round and pop a bullet in his head?" She wrinkled her nose at Jess, rabbit-like, and giggled. "C'mon Jess! I know you love a good mystery, but ye can do better than that! Wait till I tell Finn his da's on yer hitlist!" She took a large swig from her coke can, wiped her mouth with the back of her hand, and giggled again. "Nah, sorry Jess. I shouldn't think Finn's da's yer man! Who else have ye got?"

The woman with the bedding plants tutted something about idle gossip, and scooped her purchases off the counter. "Ye young ones. Nothin' better to do than gossip. Ain't no wonder it takes so long to be served around here." She shoved her purse into an over-sized green handbag, turned on her foot with a loud huff, and left the shop. As soon as she was out of earshot, Jess and Ella doubled over with laughter, glad of a moment's reprieve from the steady flow of customers.

Finally, the shop quietened down, the flood of customers reducing to a trickle. Jess closed down the second till. "Phew. Almost done. That was manic. Think it'll be the same tomorrow?"

"Should hope not. Ah, sure, everyone'll be in the pubs."

Jess laughed. Good Friday, while not officially a holiday in Ireland, was a day off for many, and the pubs, in true Good Friday tradition, would be packed. Hopefully Ella was right, and they'd have a calm, quiet day in the garden centre, and she'd get away good and early to be home with her family. Eric, Belinda and the girls wouldn't be arriving until sometime in the early evening, if all went to plan, so Alice would just have to look after herself while Jess worked in the afternoon. *Alice!* She'd all but forgotten her sister was already here.

"You okay here while I go see if my sister is okay?"

Ella nodded towards the front doors. "I think I'll manage. Jack's about to lock the doors, anyway."

A few straggling customers lingered in the aisles and in the yard, but Jack had a great knack of making just enough noise about bringing in the front-of-shop display goods to ensure everyone in the shop knew it was closing time. On cue, he wheeled a display rack through the sliding glass door, and bumped it clumsily-on-purpose into a stack of plastic garden chairs. "Ah feck it!" he exclaimed, and Jess knew if she looked up, she'd see an unmistakable hint of mischief in his eyes.

Trying not to laugh, she ducked out through the back doors and into the yard, where she called, "We're closing in five," to a couple arguing over a pot plant, before scurrying over to the portacabin. Inside, Alice was sipping tea from a mug bearing the logo of a fertilizer supplier, and opposite her, Shay had his feet up on his desk, slurping from a matching mug, in the very picture of relaxation and friendship.

Alice set down her mug and got to her feet. "You done?" she asked, stepping froward to give her sister a hug. "Thanks for the company, Shay. Good to see you again."

Shay swung his feet onto the floor and squeezed around the desk. "You too," he said. "Come again. It was nice to have someone to chat to while my little skivvies worked their socks off!" His smile included both sisters, and Jess was reminded yet again of just how lovely he was, and how glad she was that they had managed to stay friends after she'd messed him about last summer.

"Thanks for minding her, Shay. Mind if I scoot off now? Jack's locked up. Ella's done the tills. I'll tidy the plants again on my way out. Come on Al, you can help."

Having collected Fletcher and Snowflake from Marcus's cottage on their way through the village, Jess and Alice decided to take them for a walk before making dinner and settling down for an evening of catch-up.

"It'll be nice to have a stretch and some fresh air," Alice said.

"Did *you* just suggest a *walk*?"

Alice ignored her sister's amazement and continued as if Jess hadn't spoken. "The train was stuffy and crowded, and although it was great to see Shay and he is very good company, that little office is even more stifling than mine." Alice worked in an office block in Dublin, although Jess still had no real idea exactly what it was she did there. "Where can we walk that is close, not too long a walk, and won't have any murder victims lying around?"

Jess shoved her sister in the ribs. "Oy. I don't find murder victims all the time, thank you very much. I only found one, remember. The rest were nothing to do with me."

"You make it sound like you killed the poor bloke," Alice teased, referring to the poor fisherman Jess had found last year.

"Right, well. We won't go the river then, and we should be fine. Did you bring walking boots or do you need to borrow some?" Jess rummaged in the cupboard under the stairs for her Canadian wellies. "Here, wear these. We'll go down the Gun Club track. It's not far, and less muddy than the farm track."

Alice sniggered. "How am I supposed to have the faintest notion which walk is the 'Gun Club track' and which is the 'farm track'?"

"There's also the bog lane, the bog track, the pub lane, the river—"

"I get the idea. Come on." Alice clipped Snowflake's lead to his collar while Jess fastened Fletcher's, before opening the door and setting off along Orchard Close. "So, which way, crazy track-namer?"

The track leading the Gun Club land was quiet and greening up nicely. As Jess had hoped, it was far drier than the bog lanes or the heavier-used farm tracks. The dogs charged in and out of the trees, knocking the low branches as they leaped through the undergrowth and filling the air with the scent of fresh pine and new spring grass.

As they neared the end of the track, Fletcher barked and dashed ahead, straight up the track, abandoning his carefree weaving in and out of the trees to focus on whatever it was that had got his attention.

"A body!" Alice hissed, in an exaggerated whisper.

"A rabbit more like. Fletch! Come back!"

They rounded the bend to find two of the same shabby farm vehicles Jess had seen last time she'd walked this way. Or at least two very similar vehicles—they all looked the same to her.

"Fletch! Here!" Jess caught him up at the gate, where he'd come to a panting halt and now stood, nose through the bars, watching the activity beyond. She clipped on his lead before he could act on any notions of scrambling through the gate towards the group of men gathered around the bird enclosures.

"Mystery," Alice hissed again.

"Nope. Just the men from the Gun Club. It's a nature reserve."

Alice threw her a disbelieving look.

"I know, I know. I'll explain it on the way back." With Fletcher safely restrained, and Snowflake put back on his lead by Alice, who'd taken charge of the little Westie in the same manner Clara adopted him anytime she saw him, Jess raised a hand in greeting.

Five men ambled towards them, one of whom Jess recognised. Of the other four, one seemed slightly familiar—perhaps an older, greyer, version of one of the men she'd met here last week.

Chapter Twenty-One

"Jess, isn't it? Bumping into you a lot these days!" Billy White strode forwards, breaking away from the group. He held out his hand over the gate. "How're you?" He smiled at Jess and cast a questioning glance towards Alice, including her in his smile.

Jess shook his proffered hand. "This is my sister, Alice."

"How're you Alice?" Billy shook her hand too, then turned to encompass the other four men with a wave. "Matty. Sure, didn't you meet him the last time you were here? This one's my boy, William. And Ethan and C.J." He gestured to each of the younger men in turn—teenagers, really, judging by their lanky limbs and acne-mottled faces.

The three teens mumbled a collective, "How're you?" and went back to whatever it was they'd been doing by the bird enclosures, but the man introduced as Matty stepped forward and rested his arms on the gate. He nodded a hello to Jess and Alice, with a strained smile that didn't quite reach his eyes.

Alice watched the boys go, taking in the surroundings. "Are they chicks?" Her voice was high with a childish excitement Jess would never have equated to her composed, refined older sister.

She stared at Alice with open-mouthed, exaggerated amazement. "Alice! When did you learn what a chick is?"

Alice glared for a fraction of a second, but couldn't keep her attention from the fluffy chicks scrabbling in the nearest netted enclosure for long enough to be properly annoyed by Jess's teasing.

"Want to come and look?" Billy made to open the gate, then tipped his head towards Fletcher. "P'rhaps best to leave him here? Tie him to the gate?" He shot a glance at Snowflake. "That one too, I s'pose. Better safe."

Jess looped both leads around the tow hook of the nearest vehicle, not trusting Fletcher not to pull on the gate and drag it open, and followed Billy and Matty to the cages.

"Pheasants, in these three." As Billy pointed, a cluster of fluffy chicks scuttled away to a far corner and huddled behind their mother. "Grouse, here." He moved to a fourth enclosure. "And partridge, in the far ones." He gestured to more runs beyond the first row.

"Oh they are darling! Look at their little stripes!" Alice squatted down beside one of the cages containing pheasants. She was right; the chicks had dark stripes along their heads and backs, reminding Jess of a clutter of tabby kittens from a long-distant litter of her childhood.

Billy nodded. "The different birds' chicks are quite distinctive, once you look. See these partridges, now?"

Alice tore herself reluctantly from the pheasants, her eyes still on the kitten-striped chicks even as she moved to where Billy stood, gesturing to a group of partridge chicks.

"Oh!" Jess murmured. "Leopards!"

Behind her, the teens, having come closer to share the visitors' admiration of their endeavours at the breeding program, laughed. One of them peeled from the trio and moved to her side. "They are, aren't they," he agreed, "with those little spotty heads. Camouflage. See how all of them are the colour of the grass?" The boy waved his arm around the area, where last year's growth was every shade of palest sandy beige through to warm chestnut; the new green of spring just peeking through at the bases of the old plants. Dead seed heads still adorned the tops of some of the grasses, and clumps of heather had yet to show any signs of new life. The chicks would blend in perfectly.

"Jess! Wouldn't the girls love to see them?" Alice swung to face Billy. "Would it be possible to bring our little nieces to look at them? They're coming for Easter. They'd love to see."

Even as Alice voiced the idea, Jess envisaged laying an Easter hunt trail along the track, culminating in a cluster of chocolate eggs, of course, but also in this collection of adorable fluffballs that would totally enthral the two girls. "Oh! Yes! Could we? They'd love it. We'd be careful, I promise."

Billy exchanged a look with Matty, a silent question asked and answered between them.

Matty nodded. "Don't see why not. Long as you mind them."

"There's a pond." Billy pointed further into the area, beyond the enclosures. "Mind they don't fall in. I'll show you where you can walk, and where to mind yourselves." He pulled a phone from his coat pocket and checked the screen. "Best be quick, now. We need to get moving. Besides, it won't be long till dark. You want to get on?" He directed the question to Matty. "You'll be missed soon enough, won't you?"

Matty shrugged. "Ethan, C.J., come on. We need to get scrubbed up." He nodded to Billy, Jess, and Alice. "Good to have a bit of distraction, all right. See you later, so?"

"Mary'll be in to help. I'd say she's there now. We'll call in around eight. That okay? You sure you don't want us sooner?"

Two of the boys followed Matty to the car parked furthest from the gate, manoeuvring around Fletcher's excited leaps to avoid his muddy paws.

"Da, we should go on, too. Mam's wondering where we've got to." The third boy held up his phone as evidence to support his words.

"I'll just show them the pond, then we'll be away." Billy led Jess and Alice a few yards along a rabbit-track, but gestured after Matty. "Removal this evening. His mam'll be giving out something wicked about him not being there, I'd say. You going along?"

Jess was immediately contrite. She hadn't even considered that Billy White would need to attend Thomas Docherty's removal and wake, or that it was this evening. The body would have been brought from the funeral home to the farmhouse, in advance of tomorrow's funeral, so people could visit the house and family and pay their respects. Thomas, Jess presumed, was currently lying in his coffin somewhere inside the large stone farmhouse, laid out for his friends and family to say their farewells.

"I'm so sorry," she said. "Here we are taking up your time. Don't worry about showing us any more. You get on, but if you're sure it's okay, we'll bring the girls to look over the weekend. Does it matter when?" Before he had time to answer, she realised something else. "Is Matty related to Thomas?"

"His brother. Thomas was the oldest of the four of them. Matty's the next one down."

Jess's mouth fell open. "Whatever was he doing down here, then, at a time like this?" Heat rushed to her face and she clamped a hand to her mouth, trying to stuff the rudeness back in. "Shite, sorry. Who I am to say how anyone copes with grief? God only knows I was a wreck and avoided everyone after Dad died." She glanced guiltily at Alice, who was carefully studying her feet. "I should've said something, though. Offered condolences, at the very least. I'd no idea who he was."

"I'd say he's grateful for the anonymity, truth be said. He came down here for a bit of peace. The boys, too. Ethan's Matty's son. C.J. is Matty's cousin; Colm's lad. They've been at the house all day, needed a breather, Matt said. Didn't see eye-to-eye with Thomas, truth be told. Devastated, of course, that he's gone, but hadn't much good to say about him in life, God rest him. Matty and me, we were in school together, been mates ever since we could walk, I'd say."

Jess was silent for a moment as they headed for the gate. "So, will Matty have to take over the farm?" Fletcher leaped to greet them, and Jess unhooked the leads from the tow hitch and handed Snowflake's over to Alice. "Or did they run it together anyway?"

Billy shook his head, but it was William who spoke up. "No way. Matty hated Thomas's notions of 'farming'." He made quote marks around the word with his fingers, his tone giving away his own thoughts on Thomas Docherty's approach to farming. "Matty lives in one of the new bungalows away on the far side of the farm. He keeps well away from Thomas. Has his own fields, over the other side. Keeps a mix of sheep and rare-breed cattle, so he does."

"Early to guess what'll happen to the main farm, now," Billy added. "But I'd say it's fair enough to predict changes will come, whichever of them steps in."

William's phone buzzed. "Mam again. I'll tell her we're on the way. She's getting in a right state." He tapped at the phone screen, his thumbs moving at lightning speed across the glass, tucked it in his pocket, and swung himself into the passenger seat of the pickup truck. "Come on, Da."

Jess and Alice held the dogs back until the pickup was out of sight around the first bend, then unclipped the leads and let them loose.

"Well," Jess said.

"Well."

"At least we know where to plan the egg hunt."

Alice nodded slowly. "Yes ... and ... Jess? You have another suspect to add to your list, don't you think?"

"Matty? But ..." Jess couldn't think of a but. A younger brother, irate with the older brother, who farmed the family land—vast acres of it, by all accounts—in a way the younger brother vehemently disapproved of ... Alice had a point. He should go on the list.

Chapter Twenty-Two

Jess drove to Ballymaglen via the back roads, to avoid the funeral traffic that would be cluttering Ballyfortnum's village centre. She'd briefly considered whether she should attend the Good Friday funeral, or the wake the evening before, but Alice had talked her out of it:

"Did you know him?"

"No. I met him once in the garden centre."

"Well then, why would you?"

"Don't the police usually send someone to funerals after a murder? You know, to see who's acting suspiciously?"

"Jess! You are not seriously suggesting going just because you're a nosy cow? No."

"But ... what if?"

"Jess! No. Besides, you would be the one acting suspiciously, and then your darling Marcus would put you straight back up there at the top of his list." Alice had laughed, but her tone was serious and Jess had grudgingly agreed it wouldn't be the proper thing to attend the funeral of someone she didn't know just because she had elevated notions of outing his killer.

Instead, the sisters had spent Thursday evening cooking and enjoying the mushroom stroganoff—with a non-fat alternative to cream as a concession to Alice's lingering battle with eating—then enjoying a lazy evening of chat and an old black-and-white murder mystery on Netflix that they only partly paid attention to.

Rather than shortening her list of possible killers, it had grown longer. Once she and Alice had settled on the sofas after dinner, the main thing that had distracted them from the film was the real-life murder mystery. Jess had shown Alice her notebook, and they'd added Matty to the list. And his son, as another named family member, although Jess had protested that he was too young to be a killer.

Alice had countered Jess's emotional response with solid reason: "He's old enough to be in the Gun Club, and if he knew his father was worried by Thomas's actions, of course he could have been capable. Anyone is capable. Look at what happened to that poor fisherman? And that other farmer. And those people in Kate's slimming group. I'll bet you never thought their killers were capable either."

The next thing, the sisters had agreed, was to add names to the other members of the Docherty family they didn't yet know, and simultaneously try to reduce the number of names on the list.

"So add more names to make the list shorter? Yeah right." Jess had tossed the notebook aside and padded to the kitchen to make them both a cup of tea. "Perhaps this is one for the police. Marcus will be so smug," she'd called through to Alice.

"He won't. He's not the type. And it is his actual job, too."

"Hmph," was all Jess had deigned to reply, and that was the end of that conversation.

Until now, when, alone in the car on Friday lunchtime, driving to work on the twisty country lanes with only the radio for company, the list grew and shrank in Jess's mind. Matty definitely had *reason*. He'd looked so old and tired last night beside the bird enclosures that Jess hadn't even realised he was the same man she'd seen there just the week before.

But that would be grief at his brother's death.
Or guilt at killing him.
Could be both.
No one would kill their own brother.

Even as she argued with herself, she knew that last thought wasn't true. Plenty of people were killed by family members. Statistically, wasn't it *more* likely? In which case drawing up a list of other family members was even more crucial. And getting rid of the other names on the list ... She was going round in circles. She needed to start talking to the people on the list, or find someone who knew them, or could give them alibis. She flicked on her indicator and swung left into the garden centre's car park, hoping for a quieter day than yesterday and an early finish.

In the shop, one of her wishes was immediately granted: the shop was empty of customers. Jack lounged on one of the garden benches near the door; a half-drunk mug of tea in his hands. Ella sat on the counter by the till, swinging her legs and slurping from a can of coke, seemingly dragging out the end of a lingering lunch.

"Afternoon, Jess." Jack nodded towards the back doors without getting up. "Shay's somewhere out back. Go on an' find him, so."

She found Shay pottering in the nearest polytunnel, rearranging trays of bedding plants and seedlings and whistling to himself; a sure sign of an easy, quiet day.

"You want to take some of these out and restock the yard? There's a few gaps. These are good to go." He gestured to an array of bright pansies, just bursting from their buds in every shade of purple. "Put them on the front table; prominent. We could do with shifting them."

Jess was doing exactly that when another of her earlier wishes was granted. The low, soft vowels of Cindy's Canadian accent drifted across the yard, countered by another voice Jess knew she'd heard very recently. She stepped around the end of the bench, a tray of mottled violet pansies in her hands. "Hello."

The two woman stopped their chatter and looked up to see who had greeted them.

"Oh!" Cindy's eyebrows shot up in surprise. "You're stocking your garden as well, eh?"

"I work here, twice a week. I'm studying horticulture at college, too."

"They're a pretty colour." Lila Finnerty stepped forward, peering at the plants Jess held. "I was looking for purples."

Jess ushered the women around to where she'd just laid out the pansies. "You didn't go to the funeral, then?"

Lila stroked the velvety petals on a tray of pale mauve flowers. "I'm many things," she said with a faint smile, "but I'm no hypocrite. I know I shouldn't say it about someone who just died, but I didn't like the man. But I did go along. For the family. It was a pretty quick service, all things considered. Think Father J. was rushing it so he'd get a break before the Good Friday mass, if you ask me." Now her smile was wide and genuine, and Jess, knowing Father James as she did, guessed there was some truth in Lila's words.

"You're probably right," she said. "He's said before he's no fan of Good Friday. Too long a service and a strong reek of drink, he described it to me once." She laughed at the memory of Father James confiding in her as he'd tried to cheer her up not long after her dad's death. "Adding a funeral onto that would tip him over the edge. I'll bet he had Mrs Harris knock up an extra-large batch of scones, to help him get through. Maybe I'll pop in later. I've not seen him in a while."

Jess and Father James shared a love of scones, and she knew he'd like to hear how Alice was. He'd not only helped Jess through her father's death and the dark times afterwards, but he'd also listened to her worries and frustrations over Alice as she'd struggled with her eating disorder and all but abandoned her family. He was almost as relieved as Jess that Alice finally seemed to be both recovering and happy. She snapped her thoughts from scones and the vicarage kitchen and back to the women in front of her. "It was a terrible thing, though. Does it not worry you that someone shot a man so close to your houses?"

Cindy and Lila shook their heads in unison.

"Where I come from, there's a crime every five minutes. This is such a quiet little backwater. Your crime rate here is nothing to the drug crimes and vandalism we see in Nanaimo." Cindy paused for a moment; a thoughtful look on her face. "Although murder is more unusual, eh?"

Lila shrugged. "It was clearly personal. He wasn't much liked. We don't lock our doors; never have. I can't imagine whoever went looking for him will be a serial killer, can you?"

Jess shook her head and laughed. "Honestly, even after what happened last year, I still forget to lock my door most of the time. Marcus is always going on about how I should be more careful. Oh!" Heat rushed to Jess's face and she clamped a hand over her mouth.

Lila and Cindy gazed at her with matching expressions of curiosity.

"Well, I've just done exactly what he worries about, and let two more people know my door is unlocked, haven't I?" *And one of you is on my list of people who have reason to kill Thomas Docherty.*

"Even after being here six months, I can't get used to how you people are so casual about security. I can't imagine not locking my doors." Cindy's face registered a mix of horror and bewilderment at the very idea.

"But you live in a city?" Jess asked.

"I think I'd lock up even if we lived in the country." Cindy shrugged. "Besides, there are other problems in the countryside, eh. Sometimes bears get into houses, you know. Better to lock up."

"No bears round here," Lila said with a quick laugh. "I'd never even *think* of locking my door when I'm at home, even if I did lock up when I go out. Which I usually don't." She picked up a couple of pots of salvia and added them to her trolley. "The bees love this. I have a few already, but I'm doing a new border. Have you lavender?"

Jess guided the women to another row of plants, pointing out other purple-flowering herbs along the way. "I don't have much success with lavender," she admitted. "It's far too wet here, I think. Does it grow for you?"

"I keep it pots. Move it around to follow the sun."

"Like to the south of Spain?" Jess said.

"Or at least into my conservatory, sometimes," Lila said with a giggle. "Anything to declare, madam? Yes, four pots of lavender. Do they have passports? Enjoy your holiday!" Lila alternated her voice with each sentence to emulate a thick Dublin accent as she enacted an imaginary exchange with a customs officer.

Jess laughed, picturing the scene. "My mum lives in Spain. I should visit; take my sun-loving plants." She rarely saw her mum, and had no great desire to visit her, but maybe it was time. Doreen had caused a lot of pain when she'd left her husband not long after they'd moved to Ballyfortnum to enjoy their hard-earned retirement. Doreen O'Malley was now enjoying her retirement with a man called Alan, who Jess had met twice and despised, although possibly because of circumstance more than personality. Should she give him a chance? Maybe go over with Alice, enjoy the sun for a week or two? She shook her head and dragged her attention back to the garden centre. "So did you hear anything the night Thomas was shot? I heard some of the neighbours reported shots?"

"Trouble is," Lila said, "it's not that unusual to hear shots." She stooped to sniff a pot of oregano. "And most of them came from him." She picked up the pot and the scent of pizza and pasta wafted into Jess's nose. "Shooting foxes and crows. And that poor buzzard."

"Poisoned, as well," Jess added, watching Lila for her reaction.

"No!" Lila's free hand flew to her chest, clamped in a fist over her heart. "But ... but that's just how Thomas was killed?"

"Yes," Jess said. Either the woman was a convincing liar, with a dramatic pretence of surprise, or she had genuinely not known that Thomas had died in the same way as the buzzard. Jess squinted at her, studying her face for signs of deceit but finding none.

"Which implies ..." Lila let the thought hang between them, clearly reaching the same conclusion Jess had already come to. "Shite."

Lila's realisation and surprise did *seem* genuine, but there was still the matter of what she'd been doing on Saturday, when Cindy had seen her heading up the lane at the dead of night. Sure, it wasn't the night Thomas had died, but if she'd gone that way one night, she could have done it on Monday night too. Had she been casing the joint, as they said in the movies? *One way to find out ...*

"Do you know the other neighbours up your lane? Who is it who has those gorgeous cocker spaniels? And the people next to Billy's driveway? I've seen a man working on an old car—who's he?"

Lila's face crumpled into a frown. "Yes, well ..." She busied herself with rearranging the plants in her trolley. "I've had a bit of a falling-out with them." She straightened up and gave Jess a half-smile, somewhere between amusement and embarrassment.

Cindy chuckled. "Somebody *may* have caused a bit of disturbance on Saturday night." She threw a sympathetic smile at her younger neighbour. "And may have set those 'gorgeous cocker spaniels'—" She shot a glance at Jess as she mimicked her words. "—off into a frenzy of barking that woke the entire neighbourhood."

Jess, delighted by the effortless segue into what she really wanted to find out, laughed. "Ah, yes. You might have mentioned that someone—" She rested her gaze on Lila, a smile tugging at her mouth. "—*may* have been singing in the lane after the pub closed."

Lila laughed again; her cheeks a little pink. "I'd had a few. What can I say?" She held out her hands, palms up, accepting the guilt. "I got a bit merry."

"So did you just forget where you lived?" Jess asked with a grin.

"Hah, no! I'm not that bad. There were a few of us; we'd been in the pub since we came home from the protest ... well, we went up to the farm first; gathered the masses, but after that, we were in the pub till closing. Warmed up by the fire, and a few whiskies on top of whatever else ... and we decided to go and take a look at the bog. I think I suggested showing them exactly what was happening right on our doorstep." She grinned, acknowledging the madness of walking up to the bog in the middle of the night. "The rain had stopped. We thought it was a good idea. What can I say?" she said again, her smile wide and open. "Happens to the best of us. The really mad thing? Most of them are from up there anyway and would know better than me what that fecker had been at, and all we got for our efforts was wet feet!"

Jess raised her eyebrows in an unspoken question: *What fecker?*

"Thomas. Thomas Docherty. Honestly, it's no wonder someone shot the fecker after what he's done." A cloud of anger darkened her eyes. "Sorry, but he feckin' deserved it." She raised her chin and glared at Jess as if Jess might dare to disagree.

Chapter Twenty-Three

After helping Cindy choose a potted plant to brighten the kitchen windowsill in her rented house, Jess walked with the two women to the till. "I can do these," she told Ella, seeing the shop was still devoid of other customers. "Do you want to go make tea?"

The younger girl happily relinquished the till, and Jess stepped into her place to key in Lila's purchases. "So who were you with? On your drunken trip to view the bog in pitch darkness?" she asked as she began to scan the barcodes on each plant pot.

"Hah! Just the usual suspects." Lila grinned, all signs of earlier embarrassment long gone. "Siobhan and Anne Docherty. Emily White. Deiric Shaughnessy. Dom—my hubby. For his sins. Couple of others from further afield. We're trouble when we get together." She laughed. "Throwback to our schooldays. It wasn't quite dark ... Can't have been—we'd have fallen in the drains or something. Maybe I did, come to think ... Found my shoes drenched on the doormat Sunday afternoon; tipped a lake out of them!"

Jess's ears pricked at the mention of two other Dochertys. And a White, too. "White? Is she related to Billy?"

"Younger sister. Not really a White anymore, so. She married a lad from Glendanon. Lives over that way. Spent Saturday on my sofa. Our poor heads, Sunday morning." Lila groaned, clutching her forehead.

"You said before Siobhan is a cousin of Thomas? Is Anne another cousin?"

"Anne? She's Thomas's baby sister. We're all the same age, me an' Shuv an' Anne; grew up together. I didn't live in Ballyfortnum, back then—lived here in Ballymaglen. Me and the girls were always friends, though. That's how I met my Dom; heading over to Ballyfortnum all the time, drinking in the pub with the girls since I can remember."

"So Anne and Siobhan, they were at the protest with you? They want to protect the bogs?" Jess stepped around to the front of the counter to help Lila stash the plants back into the trolley to bring to her car.

"Yeah. They're as pee'd off about what Thomas was doing to that farm as anyone. I don't think anyone in his family approved of what he was doing. Blinded by the money, he was, ever since he turned to full-on dairy and went all commercial. Broke their grandad's heart, Shuv says. She adored him when they were younger; looked up to him; Anne too, but they'd been so angry at him these last few years—" Lila stopped and swung around to face Jess. "They'd never have killed him though. They wouldn't have it in them."

She set the last of the plants into the trolley and held out her hand for the plant Cindy still clutched. "Here, pop that down in here too. I just remembered I need to get some seeds. Won't be a mo." She tucked Cindy's plant into the trolley beside the salvias and went to the end of the nearest aisle, where the seed packets were displayed in neat rows. "Anyway," she called to Jess, a pack of carrot seeds in one hand and a pack of courgette seeds in her other. "I was with them both for a good chunk of Monday night. We'd met up at the farm, for a drink or two. Thomas was there for a bit; we hung out in their big family room for a while, then traipsed across the fields to Shuv's house. Anne's mam wanted us out the way so they could get off to bed. Wasn't even midnight, but I s'pose it was getting close to it, by then. Said we were making too much of a racket. Their grandad was there, too, and Mags—that's Anne's Mam—she said we were keeping him up and he wasn't able for it. He may be about a hundred, but he's hilarious, and was keeping with us drink for drink. Mags was funny." Lila smiled at the memory. "She really wanted to laugh, but told us she really couldn't encourage the old fecker. He's a wicked sense of humour. He'll outlive the lot of us, shouldn't wonder."

"Where does Siobhan live?" Jess asked, trying to place the Docherty cousin.

"Down near the school. God only knows we could've got there easier if one of us was in a fit state to drive! Should've called Dom to chauffeur for us. After all the rain, the fields were sodden. We'd almost had to swim. Shuv got us all dry clothes, once we were at hers. Some point before morning we fell asleep. Her kids were at their other granny's for the night, for the Easter hols, and her man was out on the lash too. God only knows what time he got in. We were dead to the world by then."

Jess didn't know what to say. She must only be a couple of years older than Lila, but felt ancient listening to her stories of drunken nights with her girlfriends. For a moment, a small flutter of sadness tickled her chest. She hadn't kept in touch with most of her school friends, what with having moved from Ireland to England almost before she could remember, and back to Ireland in her early teens; too late to fit in with the well-established cliques in the high school she'd attended in Dublin. "You're lucky," she said, eventually. "I didn't keep in touch with anyone from school."

"Me either," Cindy said, selecting a seed packet of salad greens from the shelf. "I'll take a pack of these, too. They'll grow quick enough that we'll get to benefit before we leave, eh?"

Jess walked with them to Lila's car, where Lila shoved aside various objects from her clutter-filled boot to make room for the array of plants she'd bought.

"Why don't you call in, sometime? I work every morning and all day Wednesdays and Fridays, but I'm home most other times. You'd be very welcome." Lila stared deep into Jess's eyes, and for a moment, Jess had the uncanny feeling that Lila had seen into her very soul, picking up on that brief flash of loneliness she'd felt a few minutes beforehand.

"Thank you. I will," she promised. *I will*, she told herself silently as they drove away. *I will*.

During the forty-five minutes after Lila and Cindy left, only two more customers ambled in. At three-forty, Shay made the welcome call to shut up shop early and enjoy an afternoon off.

Jess hastily scrawled CLOSED EARLY, OPEN TOMORROW AS USUAL. CLOSED SUNDAY, OPEN MONDAY 11-4. HAPPY EASTER! onto a sign to stick on the door, and twenty minutes later, let herself into Number 7, Orchard Close, where Fletcher greeted her with a slobbery doggy-kiss as she kicked off her shoes.

Alice filled the kettle.

Jess retrieved her notebook from the junk drawer, turned to the list of suspects, and drew a line through Lila's name. She then added Siobhan and Anne's names, only to immediately cross them through. "I haven't verified her story, of course, but I believed it," she told Alice as she summarised

Lila's alibi for Monday night and her account of her drunken stroll along the water-logged lane on Saturday. "And it sounds like the three of them can vouch for each other, so it certainly makes them look unlikely, don't you think?"

"Yeah," Alice agreed. "Besides, they all sound completely mad, with all those midnight ramblings. If they were that drunk, they'd not have managed to shoot straight, never mind force-feeding anyone a dose of rat poison."

"That's a point, actually." Jess chewed on the end of her pen. "What was the deal with the poison? Would you think someone put it his mouth after they shot him, or before? Do you think there's any chance of Marcus telling me that?"

Alice shook her head. "Nope. My money says not. Good luck with getting that one out of him."

Jess was quiet for a moment, staring through the French windows to the view of distant mountains beyond the garden. "Alice ... Only thing is? You don't think it's a bit suspicious that Lila said she's definitely not worried about leaving her doors unlocked, even though she lives almost next door to where a man was murdered? Do you think that means she *knows* she's safe? Because maybe she *did* kill him?" She hovered the pen nib over the page, wondering whether to reinstate Lila's name beside the crossed-through original.

Alice thought for a minute. "You don't lock *your* doors. Even after the murders last year. Even when you thought your opposite neighbour had been murdered."

"That was different ... Bert wasn't shot in his own home. Or shot at all. Or murdered." She shuddered, remembering that although Linda's Bert hadn't been shot, another local *had* been, last summer. And just around the corner, too. She shook the thought from her mind. "Okay, I get your point. Maybe leaving her door unlocked is quite normal."

"I'm not sure you're normal. I didn't say that." Alice's tone was teasing and once again, Jess felt a rush of happiness that her sister was here, bantering with her like a proper sister.

"Al, let's go and see Father James before the others get here? I've not seen him in ages and I think he'd love to see you. He'll have had a mad busy day, what with Good Friday and the funeral, so we won't stay long; just a cup of tea and home again." She glanced at the clock on the kitchen wall. "We need to be back for Eric but we've time enough, if we go now." Eric wouldn't get to Ballyfortnum before seven, and the Good Friday mass would have finished by four; the perfect window of time to call in on Father James. *And see if he wants to share those scones.* "Come on. We'll go in the car. Stay here, Fletch, we won't be long."

Fifteen minutes later, Jess's third wish of the day came true.

Mrs Harris set a heaped plate of fresh scones onto the vicarage kitchen table beside a dish of butter and a jar of homemade raspberry jam. "And you'll be Alice." She made it sound like a statement, although the two had never met, proving that the beady-eyed vicarage housekeeper missed nothing.

"Yes, I'm Alice. It's nice to meet you."

"You'll eat a scone." Again, it wasn't a question.

Jess watched her sister with interest and apprehension.

Alice obediently took a scone from the plate, carefully sliced it in two, and spooned on the tiniest dollop of jam, which she spread thinly over the scone without butter. "I'll eat half a scone, at least." She dipped her head in assent, and Mrs Harris returned the gesture as an unspoken conversation was exchanged between her and Alice.

Wow, thought Jess. *She knows it all.* She threw a quick glance at Father James; his own scone slathered in a thick layer of butter and jam, equalled only by that which Jess had slathered on her own, and they, too, exchanged a look of silent understanding. Jess smiled at her friend, and a wave of solid relief, hope, and gratitude washed through her. "Thank you," she mouthed to the priest. "How was the funeral?" she said aloud, and took a large bite of crumbly, jam-smothered scone.

"It's a big family," he said, through crumbs. "And it's always a full house when the deceased is young." He stifled a yawn. "Busiest time of our year, too, Easter. I'll be to bed early tonight."

"You've not been out on your bike much lately?"

"Ah, he has, so," Mrs Harris interjected, her back to the table as she sliced vegetables by the sink. "I've been telling him to wear something more seemly, so I'm right glad you've not seen much of him."

Jess laughed. "They do show a little too much of him!" She flashed a smile at Father James, who grinned back.

"It's proper cycling gear and I—" He lifted his chin, feigning haughtiness. "—am a proper cyclist, I'll have you know."

"Mown anyone down lately?" Jess smirked, referring to more than one occasion when she'd been almost knocked over by him as they'd met on blind bends; her out walking and him whirling around the lanes faster than the speed of Mrs Dunne's gossip, or so it seemed.

He assumed a look of innocence. "No. But I heard you reported the dead buzzard that kicked off this whole unfortunate chain of events and had me working overtime on Good Friday?" His voice was light and teasing; Jess knew he would never complain about the job he loved, and especially about something so serious as a funeral.

She sighed. "Yes. Seems like it. Sorry. You heard, then, that his injuries were exactly the same as what killed the bird?"

The priest nodded.

"So you know that means it must've been someone who knew how the bird died? Who killed Thomas, I mean."

He nodded again.

"So, who knew that, except me?" Jess asked, helping herself to a second scone even though it was dangerously close to dinner time. *Although,* she justified, *we'll be eating late, by the time Eric gets here. It's just a stopgap to stop me starving.*

"I hope for your sake someone else did." Father James stared at her thoughtfully, his grey-green eyes searching hers for a moment.

"It seems the Parks and Wildlife woman told half the village. Well, she told Mrs Dunne—"

"—and that's the same thing." Father James nodded as he finished the sentence.

"She also told half the Dochertys but she doesn't know which ones. Who even lives in the farmhouse, anyway? Did Thomas live in it, or do his parents? Peggy—that's the Parks woman—said she was in the farmhouse, and there were a few people she talked to, but not him."

"Oh they all live roundabout." Father James waved his hand around the table in a sweeping motion, which Jess took to represent the village rather than to imply there was a family of Dochertys huddled beneath the vicarage table.

"Here and there, that's for sure," Mrs Harris muttered dryly. "I'd say if you throw a stone, you'll hit one of them."

Jess laughed. "Or an O'Sullivan."

Alice nibbled at the second half of her scone. "The trouble is," she said softly, studying Father James carefully and without a hint of deceit on her face, "Jessica here is Suspect Number One, since she found the bird, got angry about it, reported it, and, as you say, kicked off a whole chain of events. Which led to a man being murdered. So she really, really has a vested interest in clearing her name." She broke off a small piece of the scone and popped it in her mouth.

Jess bit the inside of her cheeks to stop herself from giggling. Alice really was earning her right to be the newest recruit and oldest member of their childish Lollipop Club.

Father James had no such restraint. He leaned back in his chair and guffawed. "You're almost convincing, Alice O'Malley, and let me tell you it is wonderful that you are here in Ballyfortnum looking so well and making our Jess so happy after all you went through. Your father would be so proud to see you now." His voice became more serious as he held her gaze for a long moment before adding, "Both of you," and turning to include Jess in his praise. "But—" He leaned forward again and folded his arms on the tabletop. "I know for a fact that our Jess is *not* Suspect Number One any more, thanks to that lovely Garda of hers. And what you really mean is, tell us everything you know about the Docherty family. And Jessica O'Malley, you know full well it is neither my place nor my habit to gossip." He met Jess's eyes with a steady, stern gaze and a familiar warmth rushed over her face.

"I ... we ..." She looked up, sheepishly, to see Father James's eyes crinkled with silent laughter, and his mouth twitching as he tried not to smile. "You!"

Over the rest of Jess's and the priest's second scones, while Alice slowly nibbled away at her first one, Father James filled them in as to which of the Dochertys lived where, helped by Mrs Harris when his memory of names or of whose children were whose failed him. "Because," he and the housekeeper said together, "anyone would tell you, so it may as well be us, over tea and scones." He lifted the hefty teapot and topped up their cups. "And, it's nice to chat with friends after a day like the one I've had. Cheers." He raised his cup and clinked it against first Jess's and then Alice's.

Chapter Twenty-Four

By the time they left the vicarage, it was almost six and darkness was closing in. Eric had texted to say he was about an hour away, give or take, and they might as well get a Chinese takeaway when they arrived, mightn't they, in case they got delayed in the holiday traffic.

And I'd spent all day slaving over cooking a slap-up meal, Jess lied in her reply, *but if you insist. Chinese it is. See ya xx*

Happily abandoning the dinner preparations they'd only just begun, Jess and Alice diverted their full attention to Jess's notebook, adding the information Father James and Mrs Harris had divulged, and arguing gently about whether they remembered it correctly.

By their combined reckoning, Thomas's mother and father lived in the main farmhouse with Thomas's elderly grandfather—he who'd shared the news with Mrs Dunne that his grandson was dead. Confusingly, both these men were also called Thomas, although the middle one, the dead Thomas's father, went by Tom.

"Like that helps," Alice grumbled, trying to get them straight.

"Especially once you start adding in the Annes," Jess agreed, drawing arrows to plot the marriages and offspring on a roughly-sketched Docherty family tree, including Tom's mother, now deceased; his youngest sister, and his youngest daughter, all named Anne, if she was correctly remembering Mrs Harris and Father James's somewhat confusing account of the family.

"Which ones do you know?"

"None, really. We met Matty. And his son ... what was his name? And dead Thomas. That's all."

"You can't keep calling him Dead Thomas."

"Can. He is. We can call them Old Thomas, Middle Thomas, and Dead Thomas." Jess giggled like a schoolchild and wrote *Dead* in front of the youngest Thomas's name.

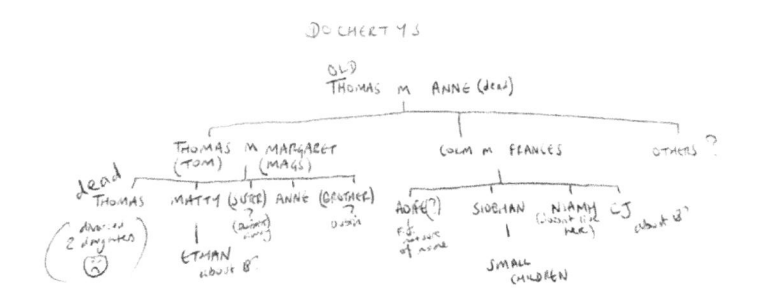

[Hand-drawn family tree diagram labeled "DOCHERTYS": Old Thomas m Anne (dec); their children include Thomas (Tom) m Margaret (Mags), Colm m Frances, and Others?; Tom and Mags's children: dead Thomas (divorced, 2 daughters), Matty (wife?) with son Ethan (about 8), and Anne (Brother?); Colm and Frances's children: Aoife (?), Siobhan, Niamh (doesn't like her), CJ (about 8?), with small children]

The farmhouse, Mrs Harris had told them, was quite strange in its layout since the family had made alterations in the early 2000s. It was built, originally, as a typical stone two-storey, double-fronted, double-chimneyed farmhouse, at least a century ago.

Jess had *not* asked Mrs Harris if she remembered it being built, despite the village rumours that Mrs Harris had lived in the village since time began.

The elderly housekeeper had told the O'Malley sisters as the Docherty family grew and the farm became all "new-fangled", they'd built new, bigger sheds and barns, and converted the old stable block into houses for the sons, who they'd presumed would carry on the farm and help their father and grandfather, in the time-old tradition of so many farming families.

What about the daughters? Jess hadn't voiced the thought, not wanting to interrupt the flow of information Mrs Harris imparted as she drew imaginary lines on the scrubbed pine vicarage table to map out the rough locations of each of the Dochertys.

And then, Mrs Harris had said, in deference to the Irish weather, someone had had the smart idea of building a large, American-style Great Room to join the homes together, and now a huge, glass-roofed sunroom filled in the space that was once a cobblestone farmyard. The buildings made two sides of a square, and the new glassed-in space was used freely by the whole family.

"I can't decide if that's a good idea, or a really terrible one," Jess had said.

Alice was quicker to make up her mind. "Sounds horrendous. How'd you ever have any privacy? Glad I didn't marry a Docherty lad!"

One of them, Father James had told them, agreed. Matty—the brother they'd met at the Gun Club lands—had taken it on himself to renovate an old derelict cottage on the far side of the farm. Father James reiterated what Billy White had already told them: Matty had cut himself off from the main farm, and did his own thing on the seventy-odd acres his father had allowed him to parcel off.

The two converted stable-cottages in the main yard had, until Tuesday morning, been inhabited by the youngest Thomas, and one of the sisters—Anne—who Jess deduced must be Lila's friend Anne. Another sister had married and moved away, and a third brother lived and worked in Dublin. Jess had felt a fleeting pang of guilt and sadness when Mrs Harris revealed that Dead Thomas was a father himself, to two girls who lived in Kerry with their mother and rarely visited.

"Do you think one's called Thomasina?" she said now to Alice as they bent over the pages and added more lines, more names, and more notes to show who lived on or near the farm.

Alice snorted into her mug. "Probably." She sat back and studied their notes. "So. We have the old man, then Tom and Mags, then a sister called Anne. They all live in the farmyard, in houses joined by that sunroom? And then over the fields is Matty, and his family? Which is about fifteen minutes' walk across the fields?"

Jess nodded. "And then there's Tom's brother, Colm, who lives in another house across the fields. I met a Colm the other day, the first time I saw Billy White at the Gun Club. I wonder if that was him. He'd be C.J.'s father—you know, the other kid we saw yesterday? Which would make C.J. Siobhan's brother. And Siobhan was with Lila, so she can be crossed off the list, as long as Lila is telling the truth. And Anne, too. Which doesn't leave many very close to the farmyard, does it?"

Alice tipped her chair forward on its front legs and squinted at the page again. "Guess not."

"But then there'd be labourers. And some would be about good and early, because of milking. Dammit. As fast as we narrow it down, it widens again. I wonder if Marcus has a better idea of what time he died, yet."

"Jess," Alice said, letting her chair legs down with a hefty thud. "Do you actually know *where* he was killed?"

Jess looked at her sister.

"I mean, are you just assuming he was killed at home, or do you *know*?"

After a moment of silence, Jess closed her mouth.

"I guess from you face, you just assumed. Tut tut, Jess, whatever would Marcus say?"

"Alice!" Jess glared, but her heart wasn't in it. She couldn't deny the obvious; that Alice, overdue by some decades, was a *bona fide* member of the Lollipop Club, thoroughly earning her place. "I think," she said, "I will need to make you a Lollipop badge."

She drew what may have been a lollipop or may have been a superbly well-drawn magnifying glass on a corner of the back page in the notebook, took a spice jar from the cupboard to use as a template to make a perfect circle around the design, and carefully cut it out. "I must have a pin in here somewhere," she mumbled, spilling an assortment of clutter from the depths of the junk drawer.

Alice laughed. "Shouldn't you wait for Eric?"

Jess covered the front of the badge with sticky tape to stiffen and protect it, then stuck the safety pin to the back. "Hell no, we've been waiting twenty-five years for this moment, I'm not waiting any more!" She pinned the badge to Alice's chest and stood back to admire her handiwork. "It's a bit floppy, but it'll do for now."

In the Golden Wok later that evening, Jess sat patiently on the red vinyl bench, below a red-and-gold calendar depicting an ornately-drawn golden dog. Beside her, Eric jiffled and squirmed and got up to read the couple of notices on the wall next to the calendar.

"Sorry," he said, catching her look. "I've been sat in the car for about a hundred hours, and can't sit still any longer."

"You shouldn't have come; I could have managed on my own!"

He smirked at her from across the restaurant lobby. "You're so right. I could have been on my second drink by now, sprawled across the sofa ... with the girls bouncing all over me, getting the dogs all worked up, none of them even thinking about going to sleep ..."

Jess flapped the menu at him and he expertly dodged out of reach.

"Well they won't go to sleep until after we feed them, will they? And I fed the dogs already, so it's only your daughters to blame here. And personally, I blame their father. Couldn't you have stuffed them with sandwiches on the way?"

"We did! What do you take me for?"

Jess laughed. "We all know they weren't going to go to bed early tonight. I haven't seen them for ... I don't know, ages. You came at half-term, didn't you. A whole month, then. Don't be so mean to them!"

As the siblings tossed banter back and forth, the shop door swung open, admitting an icy breeze and a petite young woman in a thick red scarf and knitted bobble hat. She kicked the door closed behind her and peeled off the hat, to reveal a mass of dark curls framing a freckled face.

"Peggy?" Jess got up from the bench and stepped towards the new arrival.

"Jess! Fancy seeing you! Here for a takeaway too? Or are you eating in?"

At that moment, the dainty Chinese proprietor stepped up to the far side of the counter, bearing two large brown-paper carrier bags. "Miss Jessica," she said, setting the bags on the countertop.

"Thank you." Jess picked up the bags and smiled at the proprietor before turning back to Peggy. "Takeaway. This is my brother." Jess shoved one of the food bags into his hands, grabbed him by the arm, and pulled him close. "Eric. Eric, this is Peggy. She took the dead bird away. Parks and Wildlife."

Eric's eyebrows shot up to meet his fading red curls. "*That* Peggy?"

Jess nodded. "Yup. *That* Peggy."

He thrust his hand forward. "Nice to meet you. I hear you are as much to blame as Jess here for this new murder she's got herself mixed up in?" His wide grin and sparkling eyes took any harshness out of the words, and Peggy matched his smile with one just as wide.

"Ah. Yes, I'm that Peggy then. Guilty as charged. Nice to meet you. You have to be related to Jess? You look just like each other! If only you had red hair, too, Jess, I mean, but aside from that you could be twins! *Are* you twins?"

"He's two years older. Here for Easter with his wife and kids."

They continued to chat for a few minutes; Peggy doing most of the talking, while Jess and Eric each stood clutching a bag of steaming Chinese food, the waft of soy sauce mingling with garlic, ginger, and the delicious, honeyed scent of sweet and sour sauce.

Eventually Peggy broke off long enough to direct her attention to the food. "I must order. I'm starved! Thank heavens it's a long weekend. I'm whacked. Give me a sec." She turned to the restaurateur and gabbled off what sounded like a well-practiced order, with no need to even glance at the menu."

"Sure thing, Miss Peggy." The woman jotted the order on a red-bordered notepad, and yelled through the saloon doors to the kitchen. "Miss Peggy's usual." She followed this with a string of Chinese, and a disembodied male voice from the kitchen threw a garble of sounds back. The woman turned to Peggy, gave a little bow, and translated. "He says he add extra chilli, like ever, and portion of spring roll for best custom. You welcome." She bowed again.

"Is that just for you?" Jess asked. Peggy had only ordered one dish, with rice, and even with the complementary spring rolls, it sounded very much like a meal for one.

"My partner's gone off away to her family for the weekend. I'm all alone and can't wait for the peace."

"I was going to say come and join us, but if it's peace you want ..." Jess shot a look at Eric.

"Then definitely don't come. There's two noisy and very excited girls and two equally excited dogs back at Jess's place."

"One excited dog. You know Snowflake will be sitting quietly and watching with disdain."

"Well, either way, no peace. In fact..." Eric smiled his most charming boyish smile. "I know we've only just met, but can I come to yours instead?"

"Eric!" Jess nudged her elbow into his side, causing him to scrabble frantically at the bag as it slipped in his arms.

"He's married." She told Peggy.

"And I'm not his type," she countered, her freckled face lit up by her grin. "Your family sounds delightful. Peace is overrated." A cloud of something—longing?—passed over her face, momentarily dimming the bright smile.

"Come?" Jess said. "Really, you'd be most welcome. We're going to spend the evening solving a murder, and you may hold some vital clues."

"If the girls ever go to bed," Eric added. "But yes, do come. Jess said she's only met you a couple of times, but she talks about you like you are already friends."

Peggy, for once lost for words, looked from Eric to Jess and back again, a slight blush disguising her freckles.

Jess's cheeks were warm, too, in embarrassment that Eric had said too much. "It's true, though. I don't have many friends around the village, not who aren't old. It's funny, actually, as since I found that buzzard, I feel like I've met a few new friends."

"Shame they are all on your suspect list," Eric said dryly.

At that, Peggy's excitement almost bubbled over. "I'm a suspect! Wahey! I did get interviewed, come to think, but they said it was routine! They never said I was an actual suspect! What fun. I've never been involved in a real live murder before. Not of an actual person, that is. Loads like your poor buzzard, of course. Ah, thanks a million, Mrs Hui." She reached over the counter and relieved the restaurateur of a brown bag, somewhat smaller than Jess's and Eric's laden ones. "Are you sure?" she said to Jess. "I don't want to impose, especially on your family time. I know how important that is…" For the second time, her expression clouded. She ducked her face to the bag and inhaled its steaming aroma.

That decided it. Jess ushered her out of the door, calling goodbye to Mrs Hui, guiltily realising that she'd never taken the time to learn the woman's name, in all her visits to the Golden Wok over the last couple of years.

She unclicked the locks of her car, and set the takeaway bags on the back seat. "You have a car here, I guess?" she said to Peggy. "So follow us." She caught herself, and chuckled. "You know where I live, of course. See you there in ten. You must come."

Chapter Twenty-Five

Marcus's car was parked on the road outside the house when Jess and Eric got back to Orchard Close.

Inside the house, Fletcher and Bryony were jumping up and down on the sofa in the bay window, awaiting Jess and Eric's return. Clara perched on the back of the same sofa, nose pressed against the glass, with Snowflake tucked under one arm. Marcus stood with his back to the glass, talking to Belinda and Alice. The whole scene was lit like a stage play, held in snapshot by the window frame. Happiness flooded from Jess like water in those overflowing drainage ditches, oozing out at the edges and spilling across her world. *My family,* she thought, as her stomach turned somersaults. "Look," she said to Eric, gesturing to the scene. "It's really not so bad, is it?"

He jostled the takeaway into one arm and wrapped his other around her shoulders. "It's really not bad at all, little sis. Not bad at all."

As Jess stepped forward to open the door, the Parks and Wildlife van rounded the bend.

Peggy shunted it around effortlessly in the tight circle of the 'bag end' of Orchard Close, and pulled up with two wheels on the kerb. She jumped from the cab and slammed the door, sending Fletcher and Bryony into an even greater frenzy of squealing and barking, that could be heard not only outside the house, but probably also halfway to Dublin.

"Come on in." Jess flung open the door and ushered her new friend indoors.

For a few minutes, mayhem ensued, not least caused by Fletcher's daft indecision over who to greet first.

Above the cacophony of noise, Jess did her best to introduce Peggy to the group, but soon gave up. "Sorry, it's manic. You'll work it out fast enough. Follow me to the kitchen? We'll sort out the food and everyone'll quieten down once they have their mouths full." Even as she said it, she realised it was unlikely to be true, but from what she'd already seen of Peggy, she guessed she'd hold her own well enough.

She retrieved a stack of plates from the oven, where Alice or Bel had put them, following Jess's instructions to put them to warm on the lowest heat. Someone had spread a cloth over the table and pulled in the garden chairs to give seating enough for everyone, although by adding Peggy to the mix, they were one short again. "Bel, Eric, will Clara sit on your knee or will I drag in one more chair?" Although with seven chairs already squashed around the table, they'd be climbing over each other to get seated as it was. "I'm not sure there's room, to be honest? Will you cope?"

Jess couldn't remember a time she'd had this many people in her little house, although she was sure that when her dad had been alive, he'd have had plenty of gatherings with the neighbours. Besides, she reminded herself with a shake of her head, it's only one more than Christmas, or last Easter. Last Easter had been the first time Marcus had met her family. A whole year ago. A wave of nostalgia washed over her as she realised it had been an almost identical scenario: A Chinese takeaway; Eric, Bel and the girls. Alice. That time, Marcus had come by to collect Snowflake after work, but ended up staying to join them. That time, too, they'd been discussing murder and mystery, as Jess had tried to come to terms with Bert's death and the dawning suspicion that someone was deliberately targeting Kate's slimming group members and killing them off.

As she remembered how easily Marcus had slipped into her family, he entered the kitchen and pulled her into a hug. "Hello you," he whispered into her hair. "You okay?"

She turned and nodded, and met his lips for a quick kiss before stepping back to introduce him properly to Peggy. "Marcus, this is Peggy. Peggy, Marcus. I don't think you met?" She raised questioning eyebrows to Marcus.

"No, I wasn't there. Hello Peggy, nice to meet you. You met some of my colleagues, I believe. I work at the Garda station."

Peggy flushed and took a step back, dropping his proffered hand as fast as she'd accepted it; a deer, frozen, deciding which way to run. "I ... but ..."

Jess, mortified, immediately guessed what thoughts had flashed through Peggy's mind. "Oh, shite, no! Don't be daft. Yes, he's a Gard, but honestly, ignore what my eejit brother said; you aren't really a suspect, not any more than I am, at least. I promise you this isn't a set up! Honest. Shite, sorry. I should have told you Marcus was here. We ... He's ... I ..."

Peggy recovered her composure and giggled. "Well I gathered *that* much, when you kissed him. Unless it was a Judas kiss ... 'Here, I've delivered your suspect,' like? So I'm not under arrest? Or at least, can I eat my supper first?"

"I'm on his suspect list too, but he doesn't think it was either of us. Besides," she whispered in a *sotto voce* aside to Peggy, "I put him on my own suspect list. He has just as much reason to be on it as we do."

Behind her, Marcus sighed. "Oh Jess. I really, really want to think you are joking about having you own list of suspects, but you're not, are you?" He turned to Peggy. "I'm on your side: can we at least eat first?"

Jess scooped up the carrier bags and transferred them to the table, where she lifted out the foil dishes one by one, studied the scrawled writing on each lid, and set them in a line down the centre of the table cloth. She placed a serving spoon beside each dish, and yelled through to the living room: "Come on, you lot! Food."

For the next half hour, all talk of murder and suspects was forgotten as they shared the spread of Chinese dishes and other news of their lives. Belinda had been promoted. Alice had bumped into Declan—Kate's husband—a few times, and said he was a "changed man" now he was a father. Bryony had come second in the latest class spelling test, and Clara, in the most important news of all, had lost two of her teeth and had a visit from the tooth fairy. For several minutes, the talk had turned to admiring her gap; discussing how the tooth fairy had got into her bedroom, and how the fairy had managed to carry a whole two-euro coin at the same time as flying.

"I've got a wobbly one too." Bryony, not to be outdone, demonstrated the wobble through a mouthful of noodles.

Peggy, amid all the family chatter, was somewhat quieter than Jess had expected, although with everyone talking at the same time, perhaps it wasn't so surprising after all.

"Tell us more about yourself," Jess suggested, in a moment's lull. "I bet you're regretting giving up your peaceful evening now?"

Peggy laughed. "Not at all. I'm a bit jealous, though. I don't see much of my family." She fiddled with her chopsticks, picking at a single grain of rice. "They don't approve of my lifestyle. It's nice to be in the midst of a family." She plastered a smile back in place, but Jess sensed a hint of underlying sadness.

"We don't see much of our mum either," Eric said, deadpan. "We don't approve of her lifestyle."

Jess and Alice sniggered and the mood lifted immediately.

"She's retired disgracefully," Alice explained. "Ran off with a younger man, leaving our dad here alone, not five minutes after they bought this place to retire together."

"Too busy sunning herself and pretending she's not old enough to have us lot," Jess added. "Trying to pass herself off as fifty when Alice is already forty!" She took a gulp of wine and giggled again. "She's oranger than an Oompa Loompa."

Eric began to softly sing the Oompa Loompa song from *Charlie and the Chocolate Factory*, becoming steadily louder as first Jess, then Bryony, then Alice and Clara joined in, until Fletcher got up from under the table and whined mournfully.

"He knows all the words," Jess said.

"He wants to go out," Marcus said. "And I'm not sure I can blame him. Here, boys." He leaned back in his chair to push open the door, and the dogs rushed out into the cold darkness.

"Me too," said Belinda, hands over her ears. "Are we done here? Why don't you go on through to the other room and me and Eric will clear up?"

Eric tossed her a disbelieving look. "I'm on holiday," he complained, but began to stack the plates. "Still, if it means someone else gets these monsters to bed ..." His gaze fell on Jess.

"I will. But not just yet. I've guests to entertain. Come on Al, Peggy, Marcus." She pushed back her chair and stood, adding her plate to Eric's pile. "And you two scallywags, I suppose." She scooped Clara off Belinda's lap and bundled everyone but Belinda and Eric into the living room, where she collapsed onto the sofa with a giggling Clara tucked under one arm, pulling Bryony down with them. "Why don't you two run speedy-fast upstairs; get into your PJs; choose a book, and clean your teeth?" She tickled Clara's belly. "Oh, I forgot, you don't have any teeth. Wash your face, anyway. It's as orange-saucy as an Oompa Loompa."

With that, the girls burst into giggling song again as Jess flapped her hands to shoo them towards the stairs. "Go on, Loompas, off you go. I'll come and read to you in a bit. If you pick a good book."

"Auntie Jess only has good books," Eric called from the kitchen doorway into the suddenly-quieter living room.

"We kept all our old mystery books," Jess explained to Peggy. "They're up on the landing. The girls love them."

"We all love them, to be honest," Alice said. "Eric, did you notice anything?" She peeled herself off the sofa and padded to the doorway, where she stopped in front of Eric, facing him. "Look."

"What?"

"Look harder, stupid."

"Sauce on your face? Oh!"

"Yep. Jess let me in. Finally."

"Oy!" Jess said, an edge of childish petulance creeping in. "You make it sound like we kept you out. You never wanted to be in!"

"But I'm in now, and that's what counts."

Peggy and Marcus watched the exchange with identical expressions of confusion crumpling their faces.

Peggy raised her eyebrows at Marcus, who shrugged.

"They're all mad, here," he said.

"It's a daft old club me and Eric had when we were kids," Jess said. "And Alice was too snooty to be in it. She never played with us. Me and Eric were the best detectives in the country. Countries. England and Ireland. We lived in England when we were younger. But we were still great when we moved here."

"Best in the world," Eric agreed, still standing in the doorway, a tea towel hanging by his side.

"If you aren't going to be any help," Belinda said from somewhere behind him, "you may as well go and sit down. You'd better make up for it tomorrow, though."

Eric dropped onto the sofa beside Alice; Marcus having moved to sit with Jess on the sofa in the bay window, once she'd banished the children. Peggy sat demurely in the single armchair, but when Alice and Jess curled their legs up under them, she did the same, looking instantly more relaxed.

"So," Eric said. "Two things. One. How is Alice in the club when she hasn't given me the password? And two, what she did do to deserve being let in after all this time?"

"One," retorted Alice, "what is the password? I bet you don't even know it yourself. Two, I pointed out to our baby sister that she needs help from a better detective than you two, since she'd overlooked a crucial piece of information in a murder inquiry."

Marcus coughed. "A better detective?" He poked Jess in the ribs. "And what exactly am I, then?"

"You are the kind that won't tell us anything," she answered primly. "Whereas we—" She gestured to her siblings with a smirk. "—are the kind who gossip."

Chapter Twenty-Six

Aside from a brief interlude while Jess tucked Clara and Bryony top-to-tail into the narrow bed in the smallest bedroom, and read them a chapter of *The Mystery of the Disappearing Cat*, the evening passed in a buzz of chatter and banter, much of which the three adult members of the childish Lollipop Club kept focused on the Mystery of the Murdered Farmer.

"The Well-deserved Demise of the Ignorant Tosser, we could call it," Peggy said with only a trace of humour and a far larger helping of ill-disguised truth. "Don't get me wrong, no one has the right to take a life, but ..." She tailed off; Jess and Alice already nodding agreement.

"An eye for an eye," Belinda said. "Isn't that what this is about?"

"You know," said Alice, tapping her fingers against her lips, "if we weren't grown adults, and far above such idiocy, I'd suggest we make badges for Bel and Peggy too. Not Marcus, though." She flashed him a sidelong grin. "What with him being a policeman. Sorry." She stretched across

Jess, who now sat sandwiched between them, and patted his knee, though whether in apology or sympathy, Jess couldn't tell.

"You never told us why Jess let you in?" Eric waved his glass towards his older sister.

Alice turned to face him. "Oh, yeah. Miss Amateur Detective Jess here has overlooked a crucial point." She shifted her focus back to Marcus, leaning over her sister again to address the policeman in an over-exaggerated conspiratorial manner. "She *assumed* something." She widened her eyes and clasped her hands to her open mouth, which Marcus returned by gasping, clutching at his chest, and giving Jess a most withering look.

"Assumed? O'Malley, I am so disappointed in you." His tone was that of a headteacher reprimanding his cleverest student for failing a test. "I can't believe it." He shook his head slowly, sighing. "So tell us, what exactly did you assume?"

Jess hung her head, pretending shame.

"*Where* was Thomas killed?" Alice asked, leaning around Jess once more to talk to Marcus.

He rolled his eyes. "Oh, damn you. You know I'm not allowed to discuss cases with any of you."

A mutual groan of protest filled the room as Eric, Alice, and Peggy all protested at once. Belinda stretched her long legs out across Eric's lap and watched them all, her eyes darting from one to the other like a cat might watch snooker balls on television.

Jess knew Marcus well enough by now to wait it out. He'd be weighing up what he could or couldn't say, and planning exactly how he would share the information, if and when he decided to share anything.

"I think," he said after a pause in which Jess almost offered to get him an early slice of Easter cake as a bribe, "if you had asked Mrs Harris or Mrs

Dunne, either one of them would have speculated that he was found in the hay barn, but I can't comment. Sorry. I'm really not allowed to tell you any details in case it compromises the case. It's a shame that so many in the village already know the things you don't." He patted Jess on the knee, in the same condescending manner that Alice had patted his leg just moments before. "If only you were a better detective, eh, O'Malley. You know what, though?"

She met his eyes, waiting.

"You could always leave the policework to the police." His voice was deadpan, but his eyes crinkled into the creases she loved so much, and she punched him lightly on the leg.

"If only they could solve anything. If only they hadn't needed me to step in the last two times anyone was killed around here." She mimicked his even tone, but couldn't hold back the first laugh as they locked eyes in a silent battle of wills, each trying to maintain the pretence of a serious, composed demeanour. She leaned in to drop a kiss on his mouth, butterflies pulsating in her stomach. *I do love him.*

"Not killed in the house, then?" Alice shook her head slowly, echoing Marcus's feigned disappointment in Jess's detective skills.

Jess drew away from Marcus. "Not in the house." She shrugged, apologetic at her rookie error.

"But—" This time it was Peggy who spoke, defending her new friend. "Jess did wonder who exactly *was* in the house when I went steaming up there on Friday to talk to them about the buzzard and remind them that birds of prey are protected, and let them know they were very much on our radar."

Jess nodded, grateful for the reprieve.

"And it is important," Peggy said to Marcus, "because I told them explicitly what the post-mortem showed. The buzzard's injuries, I mean. I even showed them some photos. I had pictures on my phone, and wanted them to see exactly what he'd done. And because the pictures weren't great, which was annoying, I also kind of demonstrated—I stood there in that huge big room that joins their houses together, and I remember that I poked at my arm to show where he'd been shot. I had a tender spot there, later, I poked myself that hard! The pellet wounds, the poison, I told them all of it. The fecker. That absolute fricking *toss*." She waved her arms as she spoke, reminding Jess of a large, angry bird flapping its wings, although her rising voice didn't *quite* reach the shrill tones of a screech owl. "And that means that every person who was there had a very clear knowledge of the injuries—"

"Which were replicated in Thomas's murder." Jess flashed a grateful smile at Peggy, who sat forward in the armchair, feet on the floor again, elbows on her knees and chin cradled in her now-stilled hands.

She looked like a little pixie, with her delicate features and freckled nose; not at all like someone who could go into such graphic details of gunshot wounds and poison, or who became so animated mere seconds ago. "I really laid into them," the pixie went on, her voice now level and calm. "I was so angry."

Jess caught Belinda's disbelieving stare. "Honestly, when I first spoke to her on the phone—" She inclined her head towards Peggy. "—even then, she *oozed* anger. I was terrified of her. I thought she'd be this massive powerhouse. Ten foot tall, at least."

Belinda shook her head.

"I know, right," Jess agreed. "You'd never think it."

Peggy grinned as she absorbed the teasing. "It's a job that brings out the worst in me," she admitted. "I see some terrible things."

"So," said Alice, taking in the room but settling her gaze on Marcus, "here in this room you have two angry women, both of whom said they'd kill the fecker, and both of whom knew exactly what happened to that bird, and who strongly suspected that particular farmer of doing it, based solely on Jess's opinions about him having cut down a tree or two—"

"I—"

"Hang on, I'm not done." Alice held up her hand to stop Jess's protest. "And you also know that neither of them did in fact kill the fecker—"

Marcus nodded but Eric spoke up. "Do you though? Do you actually know that? I mean is my little sis really in the clear? And—" He cast an apologetic look at Peggy. "—sorry Peggy, but we don't really know you, do we? And, well, we know we're not supposed to 'assume'—" He made quote marks in the air around the word. "—so let's get your alibis out and firmed up, before one of you does, in fact, get yourself arrested?"

Heat rushed to Jess's face. Sure, Marcus was sitting here beside her, and sure, her family knew they were seeing each other, and yes, she was all snuggled up against him, but ..."

"I was with Jess," Marcus said, squeezing her shoulders with the arm he had draped around her. "Luckily, she has a real live policeman to vouch for her. Glad to be good for something."

Everyone laughed, although Peggy sat a little stiffly, as if waiting for bad news.

"And Peggy, well, she has an alibi too. I can safely confirm she is not a person of interest, otherwise she would not be sitting here." His soft, dark eyes sought out Peggy's green-greys, his smile reassuring and kind as she visibly relaxed again.

"You lot! It's a fricking roller coaster being here. Every time I start to chill out, you make me wonder if I'm here under false pretences and you're just trying to catch me out." She sighed, and sat back into the chair, tucking her legs under herself once more. "I guess I should go home, if I'm allowed to leave the vicinity?" She flicked the question at Marcus, but it was Jess who answered.

"Don't go yet, we love having you, and no one here thinks you killed anyone."

"Even though we've been stalking the Chinese takeaway for days," Eric lied, his voice light and teasing. "Waiting for you to turn up. I'm amazed Jess can fit through the door; she's eaten that many prawn crackers—oy!" He ducked as Jess flung a cushion across the room. It hit Belinda square in the face, sloshing her glass of wine down her top.

"Oh shite, sorry Bel."

"Right you lot, more wine." Belinda glared first at Eric then Jess as she got up and went to the kitchen to sponge off the spill and refill her glass.

Jess followed her, half-contrite, half-laughing. "I'm sorry Bel, but he's such a brat." She opened the fridge to retrieve the white wine. "Peggy," she called through to the living room, "do you want to stay? There's room on the second sofa, if you want a drink? What does everyone else want?"

Peggy declined the offer of alcohol, and the sofa for the night, and by the time Jess had made cups of tea for Peggy and herself, Peggy was explaining her alibi to the others in her typical excitable, exclamation-filled way. She'd been called to the far side of the next county on Monday afternoon; roped in to help with a herd of deer that had strayed onto the motorway and brought traffic to a standstill. It had been late into the evening by the time they'd rounded them to safety, so she'd ended up in a hotel for the night. Her partner, Julie, had come out to join her, because, "Who in their right minds doesn't take advantage of a night in a hotel?" and they and two of Peggy's exhausted colleagues had got drunk enough to be noticed by the manager, who verified none of them had left the hotel until long after breakfast the next day. "I'm not sure we'll be allowed back," she said with an elfin giggle.

Marcus laughed. "I cannot confirm or deny whether the manager said anything of the sort. Although the officer who went along did say he wasn't offered coffee because the machine had broken. Perhaps it was over-worked at breakfast on Tuesday? But that would only be an assumption, and we don't make those."

Jess snuggled back onto the sofa between Alice and Marcus and let her head fall against his shoulder. "Are you staying tonight," she whispered, and felt a pit of disappointment lodge in her throat when he shook his head.

"I have to be up early. And I don't think any of you would appreciate that, somehow." He stroked her upper arm, his fingers soft through her jumper.

"Peggy?" Alice said. "I don't suppose you *can* remember any more about who might have been in the farmhouse that day, can you? Now you're not in the bright lights of the police station, nursing a hangover?"

Beside Jess, Marcus stiffened slightly. Jess put her hand on his, silently willing him to let the conversation continue. *Wait,* she willed him. *See what she says.*

He met her eyes, nodded, and stayed silent, although his arm remained tense around her shoulders as Peggy began to speak.

All right, Marcus matters more. Jess held up her hand. "Hang on, wait a min." She turned back to Marcus. "If you're not staying, I assume—oh shite, there I go again! But anyway. I assume you mean you're heading off quite soon, otherwise you might as well stay? Am I right?"

He sighed. "Yes, sorry."

She nodded. "Well then, would you be happier if Peggy waited until you have gone and the Lollipop Club can confer without you, and then we won't compromise you."

On the other sofa, Eric sniggered and she shot him an icy stare, which he returned with an over-blown nod and wink.

"Feck off," she mouthed to her brother, then put her mouth close to Marcus's ear and added, "Not tonight, anyway." She dropped a kiss on his ear, stood, and dragged him to his feet. "I'm sorry then, but I'm throwing you out. You go and get your beauty sleep and we will solve your case for you. Are you bringing Snowflake?"

The Westie lifted his head from Eric's foot and tilted it to the side, one ear cocked. "Well," he seemed to say, "are you?"

Chapter Twenty-Seven

Jess's lingering farewell to Marcus at the front door was eventually interrupted by Eric and Alice nagging her to hurry up or they'd all fall asleep. Or worse, solve her mystery without her. She reluctantly let Marcus out into the night; watched until he rounded the bend out of sight, then softly shut the door and stood in the empty hallway for a moment to savour the imprint of his arms around her.

Eric called her again. "Come on, you. We've almost solved *everything*."

"Life. The universe ... all of it." Belinda added.

With a sigh, Jess padded back to the living room and shoved Fletcher out of the seat Marcus had just vacated. "Shift over, you, that's my space now."

Fletcher obligingly wriggled over to the middle of the sofa, and Alice eased her feet under his warm belly.

Jess jumped up again. "Hang on. I'll grab my notebook. Anyone need a drink while I'm up?"

Ten minutes later, Peggy nursed a fresh cup of tea; Alice a mug of hot water, and Jess, Eric, and Belinda each clasped a topped-up glass of wine.

Jess flicked her notebook to a new page, pointed her pencil at Peggy, and said, "Consider this your initiation. You need to describe everyone who was there in the minutest details. We'll make those sketches like they do in the police."

Eric snorted into his wine. "We do want half a chance of finding out who they are, Jessica."

Alice ran a finger across her lollipop badge. "You know, I genuinely don't know if you intended this to be a magnifying glass or a lollipop. I really can't tell. Maybe just write notes?"

Throwing each of her siblings a glare that would freeze lava, and with a huff matched only by Fletcher's deep breathing, Jess rested the point of her pencil on the paper, looked up at Peggy again, and said, "Go."

Following Peggy's train of thought reminded Jess of one of the mazes she used to solve in children's puzzle books, where you had to untangle several balls of string by following the entwined lines.

Every now and then Eric would throw in some unhelpful comment about how great Barbara or Pam from the Secret Seven were at remembering details, or how even Bets from the Find-Outers could tell if someone was old or young.

"Everyone looked old to Bets," Jess said, as she crossed through yet another line of descriptive details after Peggy changed her mind for the umpteenth time. "She was only about seven."

Belinda pushed her wine glass into Eric's hand and swung her legs off his lap. "Give me a sheet of that paper," she said to Jess. "Have you another pen?" She got up and went to the kitchen, returned with a pencil, took the page Jess had torn from the notebook, plonked back down beside her husband, and took a large swig of her wine. "Okay," she said to Peggy.

"Close your eyes. You are arriving at the farm. You what? Knocked on the door? Talk us through it."

As Peggy spoke, Belinda coaxed her to recall what she'd seen, and who was where in the room; her pencil scritch-scratching as Peggy talked.

"Who spoke to you first?"

"The woman. She answered the door. She was covered in flour. She yelled at the dogs to shut up."

"Dogs?"

"Couple of collies. Old and cantankerous but more bark than bite. They barked like mad but didn't come close enough to bother me. Wonder if they were working sheepdogs, once. They lay and listened quick enough when she told them to shut up."

"Good. And this was the farmhouse door?"

"Yes."

"Did you go in?"

"We stood on the doorstep for a bit, then she dashed in saying something would burn, and I kind of followed her in, and she took something off the stove—big old Aga thing, it is—and set it on the side and wiped her hands and seemed a bit surprised I was there, and then she took me into that big room with all the glass and it's feckin' lovely, so it is, and I said about how much I liked it and there was the old fella sat in the corner—oh!"

"Old fellow?"

"Yes. 'That's Da,' the woman said, and I thought he was asleep, but he was just staring out the window and it was all stormy black clouds closing in on us, although it had been nice enough earlier in the day, and the other woman came in and said it couldn't just stay dry for five minutes could it, and she'd hung washing out and all as it was all right half an hour ago." Peggy finally paused for breath.

"Okay," said Belinda, "so there was another woman. Where did she come from?"

"From?"

"You said she came in."

"Oh, you're right. There was another door. It's weird, that room. It sort of joins the main house with an old row of outbuildings, only they've been converted. She came out from the second one. The one further from the farmhouse. It makes a kind of square. Here, let me see?"

Belinda held the page towards Peggy, who took it from her and squinted at it for a minute or two.

"Pass me the pencil." She sketched new lines over Belinda's pencil marks, providing a non-stop commentary as she worked. "Door there, and there. Old fella there. Window ... sofa ... Woman comes from there ... man comes in from there ... door ..." She stopped drawing, peered at the sketch, added another few strokes, and handed it back to Belinda before turning towards Jess. "So there were the two women, the old bloke who didn't say a word, and the other man who came in from the same house as the first woman—the main farmhouse, that'd be. She called him Da, the old fella, that is, and he must have been eighty if he were a day. Older, maybe. He was just sat there, didn't seem to take any notice that I was there. And then the other woman, and she called the first one 'Mam,' come to think, and she'd be about our age, I'd guess." She encompassed the room with a wave of her hand and Jess added *daughter, 30-40?* to the bottom of her new list:

old man
man and woman (old man's son/daughter?)
daughter, 30-40?

"Just the four of them?" Jess asked.

"In the house, yes. Just four. Funny how I thought I couldn't remember, but I *am* quite sure. Now, I mean. I can picture it quite clearly. The man and woman would be Thomas Docherty's parents, I'd guess. The younger woman rolled her eyes and cursed a lot when I told her why I was there. The man—not the old one, the other one, he just seemed like he'd heard it all before. He's not a small man, but he had a small manner, if you know what I mean? Like he was tired of life, somehow, you know? He had a kind face, and a good head of hair. Grey, but not fully grey. He sighed and said he'd be sure to tell him but no good it'd do. Sad. That's how he was. Sad. The woman didn't say a lot—the older woman, I mean. She kept muttering about getting back to the kitchen. Sixties? Late fifties? Hard to tell—I'd say they would be younger than they seemed, if that makes sense?"

"You said 'in the house'? Did you see anyone else, not in the house?" Belinda took another sip of her wine, then leaned forward to reach for the paper.

"The dogs started up again when I left the house; made an awful noise, but I'm used to that, in this job. Another dog ran up as I was heading for the van. Braver than the collies, this one. Black Lab. Reminded me of your fella." She threw a glance at Fletcher, sprawled on his back with his legs in the air, his head against Jess's thigh, and tail on Alice's lap. "Well-bred, not neutered, a gun dog, I'd bet. Fine-looking boy. I stopped to pet him." Her face pinked slightly and she ducked her head. "He reminded me of your fella and I said as much to the man who came up to retrieve him. So that'd be someone else who'd know you'd found the bird. Oops. My mouth. I'm sorry."

Jess waved away the apology as she scribbled *man with black lab* on the list. "Doesn't matter. But did you tell him about the bird? More than me finding it, I mean?"

Peggy's blush deepened. "Probably." She glanced up at Jess, guilt clouding her elfin features, then jolted forward on the armchair as if stung; her eyes wide and clear. "Wait! No, I didn't, it was the younger woman. She'd followed me out, and when I said the dog was like yours and did he know you, and you were the one who'd found the buzzard, that's when the woman stepped up and said that her feckin' eejit no-good brother had shot the poor thing and that was why I was there, telling them about it. And then he said, 'Ah for feck's sake Anne,' and she said, 'I know,' and they just looked at each other and shook their heads like they had a problem child on their hands and not a grown man."

"Anne?" Alice said. "So the younger woman was Anne. But you crossed her off the list already, look." She leaned across Fletcher and flipped back a couple of pages to find Jess's earlier list. "There. She's the one you said was with ... what was her name? Lila. And Siobhan. She knew how the bird had been killed, but if your Lila one is telling the truth, she has an alibi. Who was the man, I wonder? The one with the dog, I mean. I think we can assume—yeah, yeah, but Marcus isn't here, so don't give me that look!" She grinned at Jess before turning back to Peggy. "It looks like you met Thomas's parents. And his sister. And the old man must be the older Thomas."

She took the book from Jess and turned to the roughly-drawn family tree they'd made earlier that afternoon, and jabbed each name with her finger as she said them aloud. "Old Thomas. Middle Thomas. Mags. Anne. And the old man sounds like he's not exactly with it?"

Jess shook her head. "If he's Old Thomas, Mrs Dunne said he's the one who told her Dead Thomas was dead. Said he walks down to the shop most days. Maybe it's not the same man?"

"Maybe," Alice shrugged. "Is there anyone else that old on the list? I don't remember Mrs Harris or Father James saying about anyone else that old ... Anyway, seems more important to work out who the other man was. The one outside."

Jess stared vacantly across the room, not looking at anyone or anything, almost remembering something. *What was it?* "Tell me again what you said about him, Peggy?"

"Erm ... he'd a cap on ... Checked shirt under scruffy jacket ... jeans?"

"No, not that ... what did you say before? Go back to the dog?"

"Black Lab, like Fletcher, only the right way up?" She nodded at Fletch, still belly-up on the sofa, dead to the world.

Jess rubbed his tummy and he opened one eye. "Go on."

"Stockier than Fletch. Well-toned, great condition." She gave Jess an apologetic glance. "He is too, I mean, but this one, he had the look of a stud dog. A gun dog. A perfect specimen of the breed."

Jess sat forward, jerking Fletcher awake and causing him to leap off the sofa, wagging his tail. "That's it! Gun dog. I bet he's the one I saw at the Gun Club. Fletch! Stop wagging, you're making a draught! Sit down." She thought for a moment, racking her mind for who had been at the Gun Club that day. Billy White. Three other men. Black Labrador. Border Collies. Matty. He'd been one of them, hadn't he? "Matty was there that day. The dog could be his."

"He didn't have a dog with him yesterday," Alice pointed out.

"True. There were two other men too. Can't remember their names ... Conor? Colin? One of them might have been something like that." She studied her list, running her finger down the names. "No one here with anything like that. Oh! Colm! The other could've been Colm. He's here, look." She traced the lines on the family tree with her fingertip. "Okay, so Colm's an uncle of Dead Thomas. Brother of middle Thomas—Tom. I wish I could remember what he'd looked like." She twirled her empty wineglass in her fingers. "But," she said, almost to herself, "he was definitely older than Billy. One was old and leaning on the cages. The other had grey hair too, I think. He must've been one of those two. Did your man with the Lab have grey hair."

Peggy shrugged. "Don't know. He had a hat on. Wouldn't think he was really old, though. He moved easily enough when he came to see what the noise was about."

Jess put a question mark next to Colm's name and wrote *Black Labrador?* before turning to the newer list and writing *maybe Colm Doherty?* beside *man with black lab*. "So we definitely have five people at the farm who all knew I reported a dead buzzard, riddled with pellets and poison, which Dead Thomas may or may not have killed, but everyone seems to think it likely." She tapped her pencil on the page, scanning the names. "And you said there was someone in the shop? When you told Mrs Dunne?"

"A man." Peggy shrugged. "Don't ask me to describe him. I've really no clue. Sorry."

Chapter Twenty-Eight

Saturday passed in a lazy mix of eating, reading, and board games. It was, as the forecast had predicted, dry, and while not exactly bright, not exactly dull either; what Jess called a 'nothing day'. No rain, no sun, no wind, no colour in the sky. Too lethargic—or hungover—to go out, Jess had decided it was time to teach Bryony how to play Cluedo. Together with Alice and Belinda, they played endless rounds throughout the morning until Bryony had enjoyed at least one turn as each different character, causing a lot of confusion as everyone tried to remember who they were each time.

Eric and Clara took Fletcher and Snowflake for a muddy walk up the bog lane that ran through the farmland to the east of Orchard Close, and returned filthy. The dogs, much to their disgust, were shut in the garden for the rest of the afternoon, to clean themselves up before being allowed in the house.

Marcus, at work, texted to say he'd be done early and was happy to cook a curry for them all, and how were their heads? Jess answered the last part first, with a sad-faced emoji and a couple of kisses, followed by *Curry! Yes please! Someone will probably help you, if you're lucky.*

※

Before they knew it, the evening rolled around; the spicy aromas of cumin and garlic still hanging in the air. The girls were tucked up in bed, and the adults sprawled across the living room in a sluggish haze.

"We're not drinking tonight." Jess smothered a yawn with the back of her hand. "We won't enjoy tomorrow if we all feel as bad as we did today."

"Speak for yourself." Alice hadn't had half as much wine as anyone else, and had spent the day least afflicted, just a little tired. Peggy hadn't left until almost two, and even after that, the three O'Malley siblings and Belinda had chattered for almost another hour before finally calling it a night.

"We have to decide who's laying the trail." Jess usually took charge of the egg hunt, but as they weren't using clues this time, any one of them could set out twenty minutes ahead of the others to scatter the chocolate eggs along the track.

"You or me should lay it, and the other of us go with the girls?" Alice suggested. "Since we know where to go?"

With that, the decision was easy. Jess and Eric would go ahead and lay the trail; Alice, Bel, Bryony and Clara would follow.

Marcus didn't commit to either team, suspecting he might be called to work, even on Easter Sunday, as the murder enquiry was still unsolved and pressure mounting. "No one likes to know a killer is uncaught. Although," he said, rubbing the day-old stubble on his chin, "no one seems particularly worried about this one. Except my bosses. But the local community doesn't seem to be very concerned, nor his family. We'd usually have the family breathing down our necks, but there's nothing." Deep lines crumpled his forehead. "It's a strange one."

"Do you think it's because general consensus is that he deserved it?" Belinda asked. "No one deserves to be murdered, though, not really."

There followed a heated debate as to whether some people, did, in fact, deserve to be murdered, which turned into an even more heated game of Trial by Trolley, in which each team had to choose which fork of the train track the runaway train—or trolley, as the game called it—should take, by virtue of whether the people on one side were more deserving of life than those on the other side. Those on the losing team would lose any characters placed on their side of the fork; mown down violently by the errant train.

Eventually, the game petered out, and the conversation turned once more to whether one man's life was worth more than a vast wildlife habitat.

"The thing is," said Jess, "even though I was—am—furious to see that a farmer or anyone can decide to uproot ancient trees; acres of woodland; miles of hedges, and do whatever it is that's been done to make sections of the bog into grazing land, and even though I said he should be shot, I wouldn't actually kill him, would I? Most people wouldn't. I mean, take Billy White. He said the same thing, but does that mean he'd actually kill him? Or Lila Finnerty. She said it too. And Peggy. So many people said they'd kill him ..."

"And one of them did." Alice shuffled the cards and tidied the game into its box, but left the game board on the small table they'd pulled into the middle of the living room. She picked up a counter and set it on one side of the track. "That's Thomas."

She picked up a handful more counters and dropped them onto the track on the other side of the railway's fork. "That's all the wildlife that's been killed or displaced. All we need to decide is who was driving the train, and which way they'd steer if they had to choose." She picked up the train counter. "That's you, Jess. Which way will you go?" She studied her sister, who in turn studied the board for what felt like several silent minutes.

"I honestly don't know," Jess finally admitted. "When you lay it out like that, it's numbers. All those counters versus a single one. That should make it no contest. But when you think of it as do you run down a woodland or a person, well, that's different. But on the face of what's on the board, I'd probably take the track with fewer counters." She plucked the marker that represented herself driving the train, and drove it along the track into the Thomas counter, knocking him from the board and onto the carpet.

"But," Belinda said, "it's not about choosing one or the other, is it? It's about revenge and retribution. If you replace the Thomas counter with a pile of money, and now you have woodlands and nature and wildlife versus a towering pile of money, there will always be people who choose the money. And now someone else, who wasn't even driving the train, wants to punish that decision."

They all looked at Belinda.

"When you put it that way, it definitely sounds wrong," Eric said. "Even if the money-grabber is in the wrong, it's not up to just anyone to punish that."

Marcus, who'd said little any time the topic swung back around to Thomas Docherty's murder, spoke up. "And the catalyst was clearly Jess's buzzard, but there is no proof whatsoever that Docherty was responsible for killing the bird. Which means a man has been killed on no more than speculation and gossip. Assumptions."

For a long moment, the room was quiet again as they weighed the truth of Marcus's words.

"He has precedent, though?" Alice suggested. "People do *know* that his intensive farming and land-grabbing has impacted the land there."

Jess nodded. "And there is plenty of proof that it's his farming methods that have led to the woodland and trees and hedges being lost. Even if he didn't do the physical labour, he must have initiated it, since he farms the land and makes the decisions regarding that land?"

"Actually," said Eric, "that's a good point. Peggy said there's still a father and a grandfather. Why *is* Thomas in charge?"

"Well the old one is about three hundred years old," Jess said with a chuckle. "So I guess he's not able for it." She frowned. "The other one though …" She let the sentence tail off and turned to Marcus. "Do you know why Tom—the middle Thomas—doesn't run the farm?"

Marcus wrinkled his forehead and narrowed his eyes.

Jess watched as he battled with what he could or couldn't say. She rested her hand on his leg. "What is already common knowledge in the village?" she asked.

His face relaxed and he laid his hand over hers. "Common knowledge in the village is that the grandfather, the oldest Thomas, loved the farm and farmed until he was almost eighty. I've met him a couple of times in the shop, or walking on the lane. His face changes when he talks about the farm." Marcus rubbed his chin with the back of his fingers. "Hmm. That's not it, not quite. It's more that his face lights up when he talks about how the farm was in his day. He is, unfortunately, yet another who vehemently disapproved of Thomas's farming methods. He's always happy to spend a few minutes talking about the farm he remembers as a boy, and how it used to be, twenty, thirty years ago. He talks about the badger setts, and the deer he'd sometimes see grazing alongside the sheep. The acres of trees and flowers his mother loved."

"No sheep there now," Jess said. "And I doubt a deer would bother. There's nothing there for them, and your man would probably have shot any that did turn up."

"If someone hadn't shot him first," Alice reminded her.

"But what about the other one? Dead Thomas's father?" Jess said. "Surely once his own dad gave it up, it would fall on him to take it on? That's what I don't get. Why did Dead Thomas run the farm, and not his dad?"

Marcus sighed and shifted in his seat. He wrapped an arm around Jess's shoulders and she tipped her head to rest against him for a moment. "It seems," he said after another moment of deciding what he could share, "that he may have been bullied out."

"What do you mean?" Belinda asked. "By his son?"

"Maybe bullied is too strong a word. But the younger Thomas seems to have had very clear ideas about how to improve the farm. From a commercial point of view, that is. At first, his father went along with the suggestions, as they increased the income and made good use of the land. When younger Thomas suggested converting from a mixed farm—sheep and cattle—to pure dairy, his father agreed. It would refine the work; mean they could focus on the one thing. Thomas brought in a local businessman—kind of a silent partner, if you like. This man funded the changeover from sheep to dairy. Thomas paid him back long ago, and bought him out. Financially, the changes were a big success. Tom could see that."

"And then," Alice guessed, "he started to take it further? Increase the grass productivity by taking out non-grass areas."

"And keeping the animals in sheds, so they wouldn't hinder the growth of that grass?" Belinda added.

Alice leaned down from the sofa, plucked the Dead Thomas counter from the carpet, and twiddled it between her fingers. "And as he turned more land over to grass, and could feed more cattle, he built more—or bigger—sheds, and got more cows, and needed more grass, and so on ..."

"So every last inch of land needed to produce grass," Eric added.

Everyone's eyes turned to Marcus. "That's about the level of it. As you've seen—" His eyes flicked briefly to Jess. "—he's removed almost every tree from his land, and has been gradually reclaiming land from the bog, too. He would have seen the bog as waste land, no good for anything. I doubt he saw anything wrong with taking it for grass."

"But his dad did? See something wrong, I mean. His dad didn't like it?" Eric sat forward with his elbows on his knees, one hand cupping his face as he spoke to Marcus.

"That seems to be the gist of it," Marcus said. "And I'd imagine he was caught between his father and his son, too. Wanting his son to do well; succeed. But mindful of how much he was upsetting his father in the way he was doing it."

"Marcus Woo!" Jess sat up straight, pulling away from his arm to stare at him in feigned incredulity. "Did you just 'imagine' something?" She made the quote marks in the air as she laughed. "Isn't that near as dammit to assuming? What kind of policeman are you anyway?"

He batted her arm and raised his other shoulder in a half-shrug. "A bad one, sitting here joining in with gossip and speculation about an ongoing case. You'll get me fired one of these days."

"Then you could stay home and cook curry for me every day," she said quietly into his ear. "Not so bad, huh?"

"Jessica O'Malley, I will happily make you curry or anything else whenever you like, but if I get fired, we will be eating nothing but potatoes dug from the garden." His voice was stern; the tone Jess thought he must use with difficult and non-compliant interviewees or suspects, but the lines around his eyes were crinkled with silent laughter.

"Ahem," Alice swung her legs to the floor and got up. "Just reminding you two that we are all still here. Anyone want a drink? I'm going to put the kettle on and get that notebook of yours. We've a damn fine motive for Thomas's father to have killed him, not that I'd want to believe anyone could shoot their own son."

Chapter Twenty-Nine

Not long after eleven on Easter Sunday morning, Jess tugged on her walking boots and wrapped her fingers around the handles of the plastic bag containing about a hundred tiny, jewel-like foil-wrapped chocolate eggs, each one about the size of a grape. "You sure you don't want us to bring the dogs?" she asked Alice and Belinda through the open living room door. "Will you manage?"

Alice threw her a withering look. "We are quite capable, you know. Besides, we'll let them loose as soon as we get to the end of the track. They'll soon catch you up."

Jess nodded, unhooked a spare lead from the coat pegs by the door, and stuffed it into her pocket. "Better take this, then, just in case." She glanced apologetically at Marcus and then at Snowflake. "I haven't another, but he'll be okay anyway. He's a *good* dog. Ready?"

Eric, already standing outside on the path in front of Jess's blue front door, jiffled impatiently from foot to foot. "Some of us have been ready for ages."

Marcus tugged up the zip of his coat and followed Jess out to join Eric on the path.

Rather than immediately setting off down the road, Jess squashed her face against the glass of the living room window, pulling faces and waving to her nieces. Both girls sat perched on the back of the sofa with Fletcher between them, his paws on the windowsill, threatening to unseat Clara with his madly-wagging tail. Jess held up her hands to Belinda, who stood watching them go. She flashed up all ten fingers, closed her hands into fists, and opened them again. "Twenty minutes," she called through the window. "No sooner. Be careful on the bend."

Belinda made a shooing motion with her hands. "Go on," she mouthed.

Jess, Marcus, and Eric strolled along Orchard Close, three abreast, Eric walking in the empty road and Jess and Marcus hand in hand on the pavement. The street, as usual, was quiet and still. Above them, in a patchy blue sky, the sun was determinedly trying to break through the clouds, although the air was fresh and cool.

At the junction of Orchard Close, they turned right, heading towards Tractor O'Sullivan's farm and down the hill beyond, falling into single file as the road bent sharply to the left, then falling into step beside each other again as they joined the grassy track leading to the Gun Club lands.

"Oh," said Eric, stopping abruptly in the path. "I've been here before."

Jess looked at him quizzically. "You have?"

"Yeah. Dad brought me down here once or twice. Clay shooting."

Jess's mouth hung open. "I never knew that." It sounded like an accusation. "When?"

"Dunno. Ages back. Probably not long after Mum left?"

"Don't ask me! I didn't even know, so I'd hardly have a clue. I never knew you'd even been shooting. Were you any good?" She rummaged in the bag for the first handful of eggs. "We'll leave them obvious to start." She placed four of the shiny chocolates in a line, and made an arrow head with four more, pointing forwards along the path. "Let's put a twig arrow too; so they know to look for both." She plucked sticks from the edges of the track, and added another arrow beside the egg arrow.

As they hurried along the track, they alternated stick arrows with small clusters of chocolate eggs, usually leaving these at the edge, out of the way of feet, but easily visible. "I don't want to hide them," she said. "I don't want us to miss any. We'll need to check, on the way back. Be sure we don't leave any rubbish." She pulled out her phone to see if they were making good time. "Come on, they'll be well on the way by now. We need to speed up."

Some fifteen minutes later, they rounded the final bend and arrived at the gate; the trail laid behind them and the bird enclosures in front.

"Should we hide?" Jess peered into the thick entanglement of pine trees that edged the track. "It's a bit prickly."

"That never stopped you before." Marcus turned his dark eyes to her and pulled one half of his mouth up into a smile that said, *Remember last summer when you led me into the trees by the river?*

She held his look, her stomach flipping as she recalled the touch of his fingers when he'd brushed a scattering of pine needles from her hair. She'd spotted something in amongst the trees, and gone in to see what it might be, and they'd followed a trail from the riverbank to a field of startled cows, ducking under branches and tripping over brambles on the way. *That was the beginning,* she thought. *The beginning of me realising how much I liked you.*

Eric leaned on the gate. "I suppose we should. They'll expect it, after all those arrows." Last Easter, they'd only laid clues around the house, leading the girls from room to room and on into the garden for the ultimate prize of a larger Easter Egg each, but other times, when the family got together in summer or autumn, they'd go off tracking in the woods. On these outings, they'd lay elaborate trails with sticks, ferns, or anything else they could use. These tracking games always ended with the seekers looking for the hidden trail-layers. Eric pushed himself off the gate and started towards the trees. "Come on then."

Before Jess and Marcus could follow, two things happened. First: the sound of an engine as a vehicle approached, still out of sight beyond the curve of the track. The second: a flurry of excited barking, and a large black Labrador flew around the bend and launched himself onto Jess, knocking her off balance and onto her bottom on the grassy track.

Eric, quick-thinking even while doubled over with laughter, pulled out his phone to snap her picture.

Marcus, trying not to laugh, held out a hand to tug her up.

A shabby black farm vehicle chugged into view, creeping towards them slowly, partly in deference to the rough track but more in deference to Fletcher, who was running in idiotic circles, charging from Jess to the approaching vehicle and back.

"Fletcher! Come here. Sit!" Marcus put on his no-nonsense policeman voice, evidently feeling sorry for Jess, whose efforts to catch her errant dog were hindered by yelling at her brother to stop laughing.

Fletcher slithered to a halt, tongue hanging out and panting like a steam train, allowing Marcus to grab his collar; take the lead from Jess's pocket, and clip it on.

The pickup drew up beside the gate, where the driver cut the engine and climbed out, closing the door on a second black Labrador and trapping it inside.

"How're you," the man said, stepping around the car. "Your sister said you were up here, and your dog led the way. He's friendly enough, I'd say." With that, he opened the passenger door and signalled for his dog to jump out.

The Labrador lifted a leg against the wheel, then ambled towards Fletcher, who was straining at the lead, desperate to say hello. The two dogs sniffed around each other for a minute while Jess threw surreptitious glances towards the man.

"It's Colm, isn't it?" She asked, with some hesitation in her voice. "Sorry, I know you were here the other day, but I'm hopeless with names."

"That's right. And you're George O'Malley's daughter." The man nodded, his smile warm and friendly. "Marcus, good to see you." He dipped his head, then turned to Eric. "Eric O'Malley. How're you? Been a few years, I'll say." The man's tone was even and unsurprised, although Jess's mouth hung open as Eric held offered his hand.

"You were here when Dad brought me to the clay pigeon shoot? You did well to remember me. I don't think I'd have placed you. Nice to see you again."

Jess swung her head from her brother to Colm and back. For the second time in half an hour, her brother had surprised her, although judging by his face, he was just as amazed as she was. As if sensing her bewilderment, he turned to her and shrugged. "I didn't remember, it was ages ago." He turned to the man again. "I can't believe you remember me, to be honest."

The man chuckled; a deep, booming laugh. "You'd be hard to forget, after that first shot you fired." He turned to Jess with a large grin. "Your brother here was so taken aback by the kick of the first shot he tripped over his feet and landed on his arse. Was a right picture, I tell you. Gave us all a great laugh."

"Well," said Jess. "And you had the cheek to laugh at me. Does Bel know about this? Does Alice? Do the girls? Just you wait till they catch us up."

"Ah, that's your wife, the dark girl? I guessed the other was your sister, once she said you were up here. They'll be your little ones, so? They'll be wanting to see the birds? Matty said there was a chance you'd be up here and to watch out for children on the track. I'm just in to throw feed out for them, but it'll wait for the kiddies. I'd say they'll be around that bend in just a minute."

"Daddy! Auntie Jess!" Right on cue, Bryony raced around the final bend, a myriad of plaits swinging free from her pushed-back hood.

Behind her, on shorter, slower legs, Clara gave chase, Snowflake jogging beside her, matching her pace. "Wait for me, Bryony, wait for me."

"They'd love to help," Jess told Colm. "Billy said it would be okay to look in the cages, as long as we are careful, but if they can watch you feed them, better again. They'll love it. Bry, Clara, come here. Did you find all the eggs? I've something to show you, now you've reached the end of the trail. Look."

Bryony flung herself into Jess's outstretched arms, and Eric swooped Clara into a spin.

"Spin me too, Auntie Jess, spin me," Bryony yelled, her mouth far too close to Jess's ear. "We found loads of chocolate. Who's that dog? What's in those cages? Can we see?"

Jess obediently swung her niece in a full circle before dropping her to the ground. "Show me the eggs after? This man is about to feed some birds. He says you can watch. You have to be gentle and quiet though, or you'll scare them. Where's your mum and Alice? Did you lose them in a ditch? Did the Easter Bunny bounce them into a puddle?"

Before Bryony could answer, Fletcher barked and pulled towards the track, and Alice and Belinda strolled leisurely around the corner, chatting, laughing, relaxed, and in no apparent hurry to join the others. For the millionth time since last spring, Jess was flooded with the hope that Alice really was better, and filled with a gooey warmth that her sister had finally, finally, decided she wanted to be a part of the family.

"Al," she called, "come on, bring Bel. Colm is going to feed the birds. Come on."

Alice and Belinda quickened their pace, and as they neared, Alice threw Snowflake's lead to Marcus, which he caught deftly in one hand, his other still restraining the over-excited Fletcher.

"I'll wait here with the dogs, shall I?" he said to Jess, who threw him a grateful kiss.

"Guess it might be easiest, if you're sure you don't mind?" She took Bryony's hand, and led the excited child through the gate after Colm. "Quiet now, Bry, shh."

"We have to do a quick check of the fencing, first." Colm addressed his words to Bryony, who gazed at him with adoration in her nearly-black eyes. "It's a very important job."

"Are you a farmer? I'm Bryony and I'm eight years old. I don't think I want to be a farmer always, not when there's all sheep poo, but I like it when the animals are cute. Are there animals in those cages? Are there foxes? I like foxes a lot, but my daddy says we can't even have a dog because me and Clara are enough work. That's Clara. She's six but she's a bit scared of foxes."

"Not." Clara sat on Eric's back, peering over his shoulder, surveying the scene. As they neared the enclosures, she wriggled free and tiptoed towards the birds, eyes wide. "They're birds, silly. Look. Aw, they are so cute. There isn't a fox, is there? Or a wolf." She looked at Colm, searching for reassurance that no predators were lurking in hope of making the chicks their Easter dinner.

"Not round here," Colm assured her with a smile. "Would you like to help me check there are no big holes in the wire?" He gestured Clara closer, and showed her how to walk around each enclosure, making sure the fencing was intact.

"Wow." Belinda's voice was high with surprise. "She's usually such a shy little thing. Bryony, you could help?"

Bryony was bouncing from one pen to the next, flitting between them like a bumblebee searching for the best flower, and unable to settle on any. "Look! Look Mummy! Look Auntie Jess! Look Auntie Alice! Just look at all the little chicks!"

Once Colm, with Clara's questionable assistance, had checked all was well with the enclosures, he strode back to his pickup to retrieve a sack of feed, the Labrador at his heels. He rummaged in the load bed for a moment, then held up a paper coffee cup bearing the logo of the large petrol station on the road to Lambskillen. "This'll do. Here." He used the cup to scoop feed from the sack, and passed it to Clara, who held it in both hands as carefully and proudly as she'd carried the frankincense in the school's Christmas nativity play Jess had sat through for an hour and a half last December.

"Is it for the birds?" Clara asked, her face serious and her hands steady, in sharp contrast to her sister's gleeful dancing and jumping.

"Bry, calm down, you'll frighten them," Belinda warned, taking her older daughter by the hand. "Shh. Come and see."

Once Colm had instructed Clara on how to scatter some food for the birds, and then let Bryony take a turn, he managed to catch one of the chicks. He cupped it gently in his hands as each of the girls stroked its downy feathers and Eric snapped photos on his phone. Enthralled by the soft chick, even Bryony quietened, and as Colm set the bird down to scuttle back to its flock, the two little girls squatted, side by side, dark heads touching, and followed the chick's progress as it scuttled around the pen.

The adults stood back, watching, and Jess once again felt a surge of happiness as she breathed in the fresh spring air in the midst of her family. Noticing Marcus watching from the gate, a feeling of contented bliss bubbled in her and burst. She left the others and went to him. "Aren't they sweet?" She leaned into him, the gate between them, and he kissed her hair. "You okay?" she asked, guessing he'd be thinking of his own little daughter as he watched her family enjoying Easter together.

Colm gathered up the bag of feed, swung it over his shoulder, and came to join them. "You forget what they're like, when they're small. My youngest is eighteen. A lifetime ago."

"I think we met him. Is he C.J.?" Jess asked, suddenly remembering the hasty introductions Billy had made on Friday, and the family tree in her notebook. "I'm sorry for your loss, by the way. I'm sorry; that should've been the first thing I said. How is the family coping?"

Colm set the sack down. "Ah, you know. It's never an easy thing, is it? Tom's broken up, of course, and poor Mags ... I suppose time will help them heal." A flash of sorrow darkened his face, and he shrugged. "You never know when it's your time, I suppose." He shot a glance at the girls. "Makes you grateful enough for what you have, while you have it, that's for sure."

"I think you must be the man who the Wildlife woman met last week?" Jess said. "You probably heard; it was me who reported that buzzard." She held out her hands, palms upwards. "I'm so sorry. I just thought I was doing the right thing, reporting it, but it seems to have caused a horrible chain of events. I'm so sorry."

Colm held her gaze. "You can't possibly go blaming yourself." His tone was soft, but firm and steady. "My nephew made some mighty bad choices regarding that farm, and there's many were grateful to you that Parks woman came to give him a kick up his you-know. You weren't to know it'd be more than a scare. You didn't pull the trigger. He did that to himself, and now look at the mess he's caused. I hate to admit it, but I can't say we were all that surprised, after the shock of it. He'd not made himself popular. Young eejit." He thumped the top of the gate gently, once, twice, then picked up the feed bag and headed for his pickup. He stashed the feed in the load bed, called a thank you to Bryony and Clara for their help, and reminded them to have a look at the pond: "There'll be frogspawn by now, most likely." He whistled for his Labrador, wished them all a happy Easter, climbed into the driver seat, and shunted the pickup around to drive away down the track.

"Strange," said Jess, as she and Marcus watched him drive off.

"What is?"

"Two things, really. One, he told me I didn't shoot Thomas, which is true, but he said it without any emotion or doubt, even though I'm the person who started the whole thing. The other thing ... well, it seemed weird that he never once said they'll be glad when the person who killed Thomas is caught. He didn't say it when he said Thomas's parents are upset, and he didn't say it when he said he knew it wasn't me. And I just would've thought he would. It was almost like ... either he didn't care who did it, or ..." She squinted at Marcus, letting him finish her thought.

He gazed into her eyes, causing a flutter in her belly. "Or he knew who it was."

Chapter Thirty

With the Easter miracle of Jess having remembered to set the oven timer correctly, the waft of roasting beef greeted their return.

Jess opened the oven door, and a blast of beef-and-rosemary scented steam swirled into the kitchen and warmed her face. She slid out the roasting tray bearing the joint and set it on the counter to rest, shut the door and started on the vegetable preparation; Alice and Eric sitting at the table pretending to offer help.

In the living room, Marcus and Belinda chatted over the heads of Clara and Bryony, who lay sprawled on the carpet with a pile of books. Every now and then, when the adult chatter lulled, a snippet of *The Mystery of the Disappearing Cat* drifted into the kitchen.

"I loved this one," Jess said to no one in particular. "I always wanted a Siamese cat, after that. Here, one of you peel carrots?" She passed a peeler and chopping board across the table. "They're in the fridge."

"That's the one where they painted the cat's tail, right?" Eric said, his head inside the fridge as he retrieved a bundle of fat carrots.

"If only all mysteries were so easy to solve," Alice said, staring out at the garden, a frown wrinkling her forehead. "If it's nice tomorrow, we'll take a walk along your lane? You can show me what this farmer was up to that caused everyone to dislike him so much that no one, not even his family, seem to care very much that he's dead."

"We could all go, if we stay another night," Eric said. "Bel," he called to his wife, "do we have to leave today or can we stay and help Jess solve this mystery?"

"Jessica O'Malley?"

"Uh-oh." Jess swung round as Marcus padded into the kitchen behind Belinda. "That's his policeman voice," she said to Eric and Alice in a stage whisper half-hidden behind her hand. "Watch out."

"You wouldn't still be sleuthing, would you? Do you *want* to get yourself shot?"

"I thought we'd all agreed that no one is likely to shoot anyone except Thomas? And he's already been shot, so that makes us pretty safe?" Jess flashed Marcus a triumphant smile. "You said yourself that no one seems to care."

He pulled out the chair beside Alice, angled it so he was facing into the room, and sat. He pinched a baton of carrot from the chopping board and bit into it with a crunch. "They might, if they think they'll get arrested and locked up. If you start snooping around, you'll be asking for trouble."

"Jess doesn't bother to ask," Eric smirked. "Trouble just finds her."

"Talking of trouble ..." Belinda ruffled her oldest daughter's braids as Bryony wriggled past her and flung herself at Jess, her vibrant beads clattering as she moved.

"I'm hungry, Auntie Jess, can I have more chocolate?"

"No," Belinda answered. "You've had far too much already. You can't possibly be hungry. And no, we really can't stay, much as I'd love to. Sorry. You'll have to solve this one without Eric." She winked at Jess and threw Marcus an apologetic smile. "Sorry, Marcus," she said in a tone oozing with false sympathy, "but perhaps if I take Eric away, they won't get anywhere. After all—" She took two large strides across the kitchen floor and draped an arm across her husband's shoulders. "—he's forever telling me he was the one who solved all the mysteries when you were children, and I can't imagine he's exaggerating at all." She dropped a kiss on the top of Eric's greying-orange curls. "Not one tiny little bit, right, Jess?"

"You brat! See if you get any Easter cake. He was useless. Useless, I tell you. And now I have Alice to help, we'll prove it."

Marcus groaned and put his head in his hands. "Jess," he mumbled into his palms. "Can't you just leave it to us?"

"Us?" she said, in her brightest, breeziest tone. "Us, you say? Does that mean you'll help?" She wrapped her arm around his neck and planted a loud kiss on his head, mirroring Belinda's gesture to Eric. "Oh, thank you!"

With the sole exception of Marcus, everyone erupted into giggles.

"Bry," Eric addressed his eldest daughter. "Can you draw Uncle Marcus a lovely picture of a magnifying glass? Make it about this big." He held up his forefingers, about two inches apart. "Not too big, or it won't make a badge."

Bryony scampered from the room, leaving four adults giggling in her wake and one doing his very best to look serious and official, despite the telltale crinkles at the corners of his eyes and the lips clamped firmly together in a very suspicious manner as Jess gazed adoringly into his eyes.

"Marcus," Alice asked, in her sweetest, most innocent voice. "I don't suppose you'd be a love and tell us what time the poor man died, at least? Or who is still on your radar for it? It would save us so much effort."

"No, Alice, I will not. Not until it's officially public knowledge." He pretended to glare.

Jess caressed the back of his neck, hoping he realised they were teasing. She really didn't want to get him into any trouble at work, however curious she was to find out who else had been so incensed by her discovery of the buzzard that they would kill over it. "I know we said yesterday that me finding the bird, and everyone hearing about it, was the catalyst, but really, I wonder if that was just an excuse? Or a final straw. Almost like a reminder that Thomas was causing so much environmental damage."

All eyes turned towards her.

"What do you mean?" Belinda asked.

"Well, as we said, no one could actually prove it was down to Thomas that the buzzard died, could they?"

Four heads nodded agreement.

"So maybe someone was already up to here—" She raised her hand from Marcus's neck and held it high above the table. "—with him, and already teetering on the edge of doing something about it, and when they heard about the buzzard's injures, it gave them the idea of *what*."

Four heads slowly nodded agreement.

Marcus pulled her onto his lap. "I hate to say it, but go on."

"And we know it has to be someone who knew about the buzzard—"

"—but that's quite a long list," Alice said.

"And—" Eric paused, waiting until he had everyone's attention. When he continued, his words were balanced and certain. "—someone who was at the farm a lot. Not someone who only visits occasionally."

Everyone turned to face him.

"Why?" Jess asked.

"What did Peggy say? Think about it. What did she say happened when she first arrived to give out about the buzzard?"

"The woman—who we assume was Thomas's mother—" Alice threw Marcus a quick smile as she said the word 'assume'. "—was baking? She was covered in flour?"

Eric shook his head. "Come on, Lollipops! Something else. She said the dogs—"

"—barked!" Jess and Belinda finished the sentence together.

Eric beamed at them in the indulgent manner of a proud parent. "Yes. Marcus, maybe you can't answer this, but have you considered whether the farm dogs barked in the night the man was killed, or around whatever you know to be the time of death?"

The heads turned to Marcus, who was nodding slowly.

"And," added Jess, "you might want to try to find out who else on the list—outside the family who live there, I mean—the dogs do or don't bark at. Do they bark at every visitor? Lila, Billy, Colm ... for example ... or are there some people who are regular enough that the dogs know them and don't bark?"

Marcus sighed and shifted Jess's weight.

She glared at him. "I hope that sigh wasn't implying I'm too heavy for you." She got off him, scooped up the chopped carrots, and tipped them into a pan of water.

"No." Marcus stood up. "Not at all. You lot are impossible. Give me a minute." He opened the French doors and stepped out into the garden. He left the door open just long enough for the dogs to follow, then closed it, dulling any sound he might make as he pulled out his phone, pressed a few buttons, and held it to his ear. He turned his back to the kitchen, and walked to the very edge of the patio, as far from the house as he could get without stepping onto the grass in his socked feet.

"Those stones must be freezing," Alice said. "Should I toss him some shoes?"

Jess shook her head. "No, he'll think we're trying to hear."

Eric smirked. "We are."

Jess grinned at him. "True, but still no. I really don't want him to lose his job, believe it or not." Heat rushed to her face. "I really like him, you know." She opened the fridge door in pretence of looking for something, grateful for the cool rush of air on her flaming cheeks, and the barrier it made between her and her gawking siblings.

"We know, Jess. We like him too." Belinda reached out and patted her back. "He's lovely, and you—" Jess envisaged her sister-in-law giving Eric a strong warning stare. "—must not badger the poor man. We do want him to *stay* with our Jess, don't we."

In the sudden silence that hung in the kitchen, Jess rooted in the fridge for a bit longer. When she couldn't hide any longer, she pulled out a jar of horseradish sauce, pretending it was what she'd been looking for all along. She set it on the counter then rummaged in the icy drawers of the freezer to extract a bag of peas.

Outside, Marcus still had his back to them, although he was now pacing the short width of patio. Jess smiled softly. He *always* paced when he was talking to the station. Although this time, she suspected he was also trying hard to keep his feet off the chilly slabs as best he could without coming back inside or sitting on one of the cold metal garden chairs. She'd never known him to sit still while talking to his colleagues.

At last, he tucked his phone into his pocket and stood motionless, gazing out across the garden for a few seconds, before finally coming back inside. "Brr. I might just change my socks." He rubbed his feet on the doormat, looking innocently around the audience of expectant faces. "What? My feet are freezing. It's cold out there."

"I'll find you some socks." Jess laughed. "And if that's not the very most domestic thing I've ever said to you, I don't know what is." Her face flushed once again and she scarpered from the room to run upstairs and root for the promised socks, almost tripping over her nieces as she dashed through the living room.

"I've nearly done it, Auntie Jess," Bryony called after her as she ran up the stairs two at a time, towards the sanctuary of her bedroom.

"I'll look when I come down," she promised from halfway up the stairs, puffing a little as she neared the landing.

On the bed, Marcus had dumped an overnight bag, unzipped and spilling its contents over the duvet. She retrieved a pair of warm walking socks and stood in the quiet of the room for a few minutes, holding them to her chest. *I like him so much.*

Back downstairs, Jess pretended to step on her eldest niece's back as she lay on her tummy colouring the picture. She rubbed Bryony's back gently with her foot and Bryony rolled over in the way Fletcher did when he wanted a belly-rub, and grabbed her aunt's leg.

"Finished."

"Goody. He can have two presents then. A badge and some socks. Lucky Marcus."

Bryony giggled as Jess tugged her to her feet, still clutching the drawing, and the two went hand-in-hand to deliver the gifts.

Jess threw Marcus the socks, extracted the scissors from the junk drawer, and carefully snipped the magnifying glass picture into a neat circle. Just as she'd done with Alice's badge a couple of days before, she covered this new one in a layer of sticky tape before rummaging in the drawer again for another safety pin. "Dammit. I can't find one." She pulled another inch or so of sticky tape from the roll, folded it over on itself, sticky side out, and handed it back to Bryony. "Go and stick it on him, we'll find a proper pin later."

Bryony danced across the kitchen to where Marcus had reclaimed his seat and was peeling off the cold, damp socks. With the careful precision of an eight-year-old performing a solemn and important ceremony, she pressed the Lollipop Club badge carefully and firmly onto the very centre of his chest.

Jess snatched up her phone to capture the moment, and the room was filled with laughter once more as she handed round the image on the screen: a bewildered Marcus, a damp sock in one hand, with a glaring white circle in the centre of his jumper. The light had reflected from the sticky tape, making it completely impossible to tell whether the badge design was that of a magnifying glass, a lollipop, or something else entirely.

"Thank you Bryony, I'm honoured to have such an important and beautiful badge," he said, straight-faced and kind. "Would you like one of my wet socks?"

Bryony squealed and darted from the room.

He looked around at the others. "I suppose you lot *do* want something in return. And not wet socks. Okay ... None of the Docherty family said anything about the dogs barking that night. Of course, they may have not thought it important enough to mention ..."

"If they bark a lot, it mightn't be something they'd even think about," Jess agreed.

Marcus nodded. He waited a beat, watching her. "None of them said the dogs barked. But in Margaret's statement, it is noted that she clearly said she was surprised the dogs *hadn't* barked, with all the disturbance. She is noted as expressing some disbelief over it. She said, and I quote, 'How could someone have shot him? The dogs would have barked. It can't be true. I don't believe you.' I've asked them to follow it up."

"Margaret?" Eric asked.

"Mags, I suppose?" Jess went to the stovetop and lifted the lid to check the vegetables. A cloud of steam drifted across the room.

Marcus nodded. "Yes. Tom's wife. Thomas's mother."

Jess set the lid back on the pan and opened the oven door, slipped on a pair of oven gloves and removed the roast potatoes, setting the dish on the counter beside the beef. The scent of rosemary and sage filled the air.

"Or daughter-in-law, depending on the Thomas," Alice said. "Now everyone shift off this table and let's get it set for dinner. It must be *nearly* ready; it's already two o'clock and that smell is even making *me* feel hungry."

Chapter Thirty-One

Eric and his family left shortly after the washing up was done, with promises to visit again over the May bank holiday weekend.

Not long after Eric left, Marcus took Snowflake home for a night in his own cottage, "... to pretend I still live there and to give you two another evening to yourselves."

Jess had a sneaking suspicion what he *really* meant was that he didn't trust the sisters not to go on with their snooping, and he wanted no part of it.

If that *was* what he thought, he was right.

After a quiet Sunday evening spent relaxing in front of the TV, Alice eschewed a fourth night on the sofa to take the bed Eric and Belinda had vacated. The house's second double bedroom looked out over the garden, towards a view of greening fields, open bog land, and distant mountains, and the only reason Jess didn't use it for herself was that she still thought of it as her father's room. As she and Alice wrestled with changing the sheets, they made plans for Easter Monday. Plans that very definitely included a visit to, if not exactly the scene of the crime, at least the very near vicinity.

On Monday, Jess and Alice managed to lie in until Fletcher's increasingly persistent demands for his breakfast and a trip to the garden eventually dragged them from their beds at almost ten o'clock. Over a lazy breakfast, they made last-minute amendments to the day's plans, adapting to suit the almost-blue sky and welcome lack of rain.

The day, they agreed, was just about warm and bright enough to take Fletcher for a good long walk, so they bundled a flask of tea, a package of hastily-made sandwiches, a couple of bananas, and a handful of chocolate eggs into a backpack. Wrapped warmly into coats and scarves, they tugged on their boots—Jess in her walking boots, Alice in the borrowed Canadian wellies—and set off.

"It's a long walk," Jess said, for the umpteenth time. "I hope it's dry enough, or we'll be scuppered. Are you sure you don't just want to drive down there like we first planned?"

Alice shook her head. "A long walk will do us good. Come on."

So, at about quarter to one, they set out towards the river, planning to follow the riverbank eastwards until they joined the bog at the end of the lane beside the pub. In summer, the path was firm and easy, but at this time of year it would be rough going. If the land was still waterlogged, the bog would be difficult to cross—maybe impossible—in which case they'd need to retrace their steps and rethink. They'd argued for a while about starting in the other direction, so they could at least ensure they'd reach their ultimate goal: the pub lane, but didn't want to be walking along that lane while it was still lunchtime. That, they were certain, would be a bad time to catch anyone out and about, or to call at anyone's house if opportunity arose. This way around, they could stop for a sandwich beside the river, and reach the pub lane closer to three.

"A perfect time to casually pass by and be invited in for a cup of tea," Jess said. "We'll decide who when we get there!"

She had only walked this full loop a couple of times in all the time she'd lived here. Those times, it had been the middle of summer, when the land was drier underfoot, but the deluge of the previous weekend had subsided, so while she guessed the land would be soft, hopefully it was no longer waterlogged.

Brisk bursts of March winds through the week had done a lot to dry the worst of it, and the river path, so far, was pleasant enough. On the easterly side of the Glendanon road, the land was more open than the west side, with vast stretches of bare black earth reaching as far as the eye could see. This part of the bog had been farmed for garden peat, although production had slowed over the past year or so and there were encouraging signs of nature creeping in at the edges. Between the farmed area and the river, there lay a width of scrubland, which later in the summer would be blooming with wild mint, rare orchids, and a host of other more common flowers. Now, just as March gave way to April, the land was windswept and the greens still muted and wintery even where the stalks and stems of mixed grasses were long and unruly. On the high banks of uncut bog, the heather was still rough and brown. By August, it would be a blaze of purple, honey-scented flowers, and buzzing with insects.

Fletcher, bounding ahead, sought out the driest paths, and the sisters picked their way through the ditches and clumps of grass in his wake.

When they clambered up onto the higher ground, Jess eased the picnic blanket from her backpack, spread it across the heather, and sank onto it with a contented sigh. "It's so lovely up here." She lay back for a moment, watching the clouds scud across the pale blue sky.

Alice did the same, lying the other way around, her mud-splattered boots pointing towards the river and her reddish-brown hair swirling over the blanket to blend with Jess's darker curls. "It is."

"Al," Jess said, still watching the sky. "I meant to ask while Eric was here. Have you thought any more about what we should do with the house?" Before giving Alice time to answer, she went on. "Only, I want to stay here. I like it here. We should talk about that. I'm not sure I can afford to buy you out, not yet."

Alice propped herself up on her elbow and tuned to her sister. "We did talk about it, a bit, me and Eric. A while back. We're in no rush. We like coming out here too. If we sold it, we wouldn't be able to."

Jess gave her sister a sidelong glance, not turning her head, and raised her eyebrows.

"I know, I know. But I do, now. I wish I'd come more often, you know? Before Dad ... before he died. But ..."

Jess moved her hand up to reach for Alice. Not able to reach her sister's hand, she settled for touching her head, caressing her face for a second until Alice jerked away.

"Oy! You poked my eye!"

Jess sat up. "Oops, sorry. But yeah, I know. I'm glad you're here now though." For so many years, Alice had stayed away, in out of hospitals and therapy, trying to win the battle against her eating problems. Jess stared down at her sister's face, searching for the old signs and finding none. "I'm so glad you are well, Al. Please, *please* stay well this time?"

Alice pulled herself up into a sitting position and swivelled her legs around, careful not to get her muddy boots on the rug. When she was facing the same way as Jess, she leaned her head onto Jess's shoulder. "It's going well."

For a long moment they sat in silence, gazing out over the bog.

"That's one reason why we decided to not worry about the house yet, actually. Eric thinks it's good for me to spend more time out of the city. And with you. He's probably right. We have a lot of catching up to do. For now, Jess, we want to leave things just as they are. You take care of the house, and we get to visit when we want to!"

Jess laughed. "Not too frequently! It's great to see you, but ..."

"Do you think it's serious with you and Marcus then? Will you move in together?"

Jess shrugged. "I don't know. It's only been six months."

"You've known him a full year. It was there from the start, Jess. Everyone could see it but you. You're made for each other!" She elbowed Jess in the side. "He's lovely. Make it work."

"Bossy!"

"I mean, try to make it work. I mean, we hope it works because we all adore him and he makes you happy, and it's nice to see you happy. Eric told me you weren't very happy for a long while after Dad died, and I didn't even notice and I am so, so sorry, Jess. I owe you this time. Be happy." She pulled out the package of sandwiches, and slowly, deliberately, unwrapped them, handed one to Jess, and took a large bite from another. "Eat. Then we'll get on. Or we'll still be sat here at nightfall and have got nowhere in solving our mystery."

Despite one particularly soggy section, where Alice had almost lost one of Jess's beloved Canadian wellies, and after hopping around madly while Jess tugged the stuck boot free from the mud with a rude-sounding slurp, then dissolving into doubled-over giggles for a few minutes at the thought of Alice having to hop all the way back to Orchard Close on one foot, they finally reached the rough-but-solid earthen track that would eventually lead them to the tarmacked stretch of the pub lane.

Fletcher, muddy from nose to tail, and still the cleanest of the three, bounded ahead with inexhaustible energy.

Jess and Alice, in need of a breather, leaned against a five-barred metal field gate, contemplating the sterile grass of the Dochertys' farm.

"That's it." Jess pointed across the fields to the far left of where they now stood. "That's all that's left of the old woodland. And that—" She gestured along the lines where the electric fencing sectioned the grass into evenly-sized, rectangular paddocks. "—is all that's left of miles of hedgerow, and more birds and insects than you'd ever be able to count. I haven't seen any bees yet this year, come to think."

"Bit early, still?"

"Hmm, maybe. No buzzards, either. Well, hardly any. There was a time I'd come out walking down any one of these bog lanes and see at least one buzzard. Usually a pair; sometimes even a group. A wake, apparently. That's what they're called, in a group." She cast a sidelong glance at her sister. "Now it seems we're having a wake *for* them. At least that one I found, anyway." She flashed her sister a half-smile. "I came down here last summer with Sheelagh Flannery, remember her? You met her in the woods that time we were tracking with the girls? And then …" Jess shuddered and let the sentence tail off, not wanting to dwell on what had happened to Sheelagh.

Out of sight but not out of earshot, Fletcher barked.

"Dammit! Where is he? Fletcher!" Jess pushed herself off the gate and jogged towards the sound of increasingly frantic and increasingly distant barking. "Shite! Fletch! Come here!"

A way along the lane, Fletcher leaped joyously around a pair of dogs, one black, one golden, and ignored his mistress completely.

"Fletcher! Come!"

Still taking no notice, the three dogs ran in circles, ducking and bouncing, first one way then the other, all barking madly, their tails wagging hard enough to blur.

Jess slowed to a brisk walk as she drew closer, panting and hot. "At least they are friendly," she called over her shoulder to Alice. "The little brat. He *usually* comes when I call him." It wasn't strictly true and she doubted Alice believed her. "Fletcher! Come here!"

At last, the errant Labrador turned towards his mistress's voice. He threw a look at his new friends, as if to say, "Come on, I'll introduce you," and the three of them charged to meet her, clods of wet mud flying from their feet and coats as they ran.

By the time they reached her, it was too late to bother with clipping on Fletcher's lead. The dogs were happily playing, and if she caught him up now, she'd still have the other two to contend with. Instead, she strode onward to meet the owners, hands outstretched and an apology on her tongue. "I'm so sorry. We weren't paying attention. I'm really sorry. They are gorgeous! I saw them the other day when I came by. You live just beyond Dochertys' gate, yes? I'm Jess. Jess O'Malley. I live up by the park." She waved in the vague direction of Orchard Close, far across the fields and out of sight.

The girl held out her hand. "I'm Ciara. Ciara O'Brien. And this is Rory. Rory Gallagher." She was younger than Jess, mid-twenties, perhaps, with dark-blonde hair scraped back in a high pony tail that swung as she talked. Rory was a similar age; tall, with a short almost-beard and thin-framed glasses. He nodded at Jess, smiling as the dogs careened around their feet.

"And this is Alice, my sister."

Alice, who hadn't bothered to speed up to help Jess catch Fletcher, sauntered towards them as if she hadn't a care in the world. "Hi," she said. "Jess was just showing me what's happened to the farmland. And the bog. We walked miles, round by the river."

Jess sent her a sideways look of mild surprise. Alice was not usually so chatty with strangers, but here she was again, garbling like an overflowing stream. Perhaps she'd had a point when she'd said time out here in the country was changing her. She used to be so reserved. Perhaps this was another sign that she was finally beating her illness. *Please let it be true*.

Rory Gallagher nodded at Alice's words, a frown clouding his face. "He's made a right mess of it, that's for sure. We've kept out of it, to be honest, but the neighbours have all been furious about it all."

"It's wrong to say it," Ciara added, "but no one seems sorry he's dead. It's a right bit of drama."

"What do you think happened to him?" Jess asked, hoping to sound as if she had no idea that her actions in calling Peggy had started anything.

"What Jess really means is 'who?'" Alice chipped in. "We heard he'd been shot. But do they have any idea who it was?"

"No one's saying much, to be honest. The Gards were round again on Friday, but we couldn't tell them a thing. Didn't see anything. Might have heard a shot, but we couldn't even be sure of that, to be honest." Ciara slipped her hand through Rory's arm. "Only thing that was a bit out of the ordinary was that the milk lorry had a puncture at the end of the lane, down near the pub."

"Blocked the road for a bit while he changed the wheel. I was late to work," Rory said. "Only by a few minutes. He was quick enough, once I got there."

Jess exchanged a look with Alice. "What time was that?"

Ciara didn't hesitate. "He comes down the same time every morning. Could set your clocks by him, my mam would say. Bang on six, he comes past; starts the dogs off. Every. Single. Morning. You'd think they'd be used to it by now."

"It's okay in the week, when we're up for work, but it would be nice if he didn't come at the weekends." Rory smiled at Ciara with the loved-up look of a puppy dog. "But you wanted the dogs, and you know you wouldn't be without them." He grinned at Jess and Alice. "I would, at six o'clock every Sunday morning. Do without them. Not gonna lie. And again at six-fifty, when he comes back past again."

"And it was definitely Tuesday he broke down?"

"Yes, because when we got home, and heard about Thomas being dead, we joked that it would have stopped the killer escaping."

"Does he go to both the farms?" Alice asked.

"Over the road first, to Billy's." Ciara pointed back the way she and Rory had come from, towards Billy White's farm. "He's quick there. Billy hasn't many cows. Then he's at Dochertys' a while longer."

"It's not that we're nosy," Rory said with a laugh, "but you notice, when these two are barking their freaking heads off every time he passes."

"It's only the milk lorry they bark at." Ciara ruffled the head of the golden one, now jumping at her jeans with muddy paws. "They don't mind the postman."

Jess chose not to mention that they'd barked incessantly when she drove past the other day. Or that Fletcher was idiotic enough that he still barked at the postman even though Gerry'd been delivering their mail for as long as she'd lived there. "What time do you leave for work?" she asked Rory instead.

"About half-seven, usually."

"So he was only stuck there half an hour or so, then?"

"Yeah, he'd trouble with one of the wheelnuts, or he'd have been done and away. I gave him a hand. It only took a few minutes after that. He was calmer about it than I'd have been."

"True fact," Ciara said, beaming at him like love's young dream.

"I wonder did he see Thomas, or was Thomas already dead by then?" Jess asked, again trying to keep her voice level and curious rather than nosy and snooping. Not that Marcus would think there was much difference between curious and nosy, not when it came to Jess and murder investigations. She smirked at the thought of Marcus telling her to butt out, and hid her grin beside a hastily-raised hand.

"Oh, no, he was killed after that." Rory's answer was instant and sure. "He said he'd been talking to him."

Chapter Thirty-Two

Jess glanced at Alice, but kept her mouth shut. *Let him talk, then we'll talk about it after,* she hoped the look said. *This really narrows down the time frame.*

"Said Thomas had seemed mighty chipper that morning, considering it was still so fecking dark. Said something about how nice it'll be from next week, when it's light by six once the clocks change. Tommy, that is, not Thomas, that bit. Me too. It's so much easier getting up in daylight."

"True fact," Ciara agreed.

"Tommy?" Jess said. "Which one of them goes by Tommy?"

"Ah, no, he's the milk driver. Tommy Dolan."

"Feck's sake," Jess said. "Is there anyone round here not called Thomas or Tom or Tommy?"

Ciara laughed. "Not many. And the ones who aren't are mostly called William. What with Billy and his son and Willie Keegan."

"Who's Willie Keegan?" Jess was following the names with all the success of trying to find her way through a dark maze in a thick fog.

"Fella opposite us, sort of. Next to Billy White. He's away to his mam in Galway for Easter. Went off last Saturday, missed all the excitement, what with that hippy one dancing up here on the lash Saturday night and then that Docherty brat getting himself shot." Ciara giggled and clasped her hand to her mouth. "Shite, sorry, I know he's dead an' all, but ..."

Rory butted against her with his hip, knocking her off balance. "Ciara! What would your mam say? No one deserves to be shot." He grimaced in mock annoyance; the smile in his eyes giving away his real feelings towards his girlfriend.

"Mam'd say the same. Some people do deserve it." She shrugged. "I can't be sorry. He *was* a brat. Everyone said it."

Fletcher, impatient with standing still, jumped up at Jess, planting his filthy paws on her coat and licking her face.

She stumbled backwards, almost tripping over the golden spaniel, regained her balance and clipped on Fletcher's lead. "I guess that's our cue to get on. Nice to meet you both. Enjoy your walk."

"You too." Ciara's smile was wide and infectious, and Jess found her somehow endearing, despite, or perhaps because of her blunt honesty. Mind, she was only echoing what everyone else had said, anyway. Was no one upset that Thomas Docherty had died? She was beginning to feel quite sorry for the poor man. He'd seemed nice enough, that day she'd met him, weedkiller purchasing aside.

As soon as they had moved far enough away to be out of earshot, she grabbed Alice by the arm and stopped her in the middle of the lane. "Did you hear that? So that means he died after, what, sevenish? And Marcus said before that it was before daylight, so that's only about what, half an hour or so? What time did it get light on Tuesday? That really narrows it down. And it should be easy to find out exactly who was near the farm at that time!"

"And if no one could get in or out of the lane ..."

"It must be someone who was already this side of the milk lorry!"

"Does Marcus know this?"

"He must ... it's his job. He must know ..." Jess pulled out her phone to call him, then tucked it back in her coat pocket. "We'll stop at his on the way past. We're only about ten minutes away."

"We're that close already? Wow. I've kind of lost my bearings. So where are we now?"

Jess pointed across the empty green fields to the distant house. "That's the Docherty farmhouse, there. And that—" She swung around to point to the farm on the other side of the lane. "—is Billy White's land. You can't really see his house, behind the hedges."

The strip of bare earth on the Dochertys' side, marking the ghosts of hedgerows, was gloopy with wet mud. The ditch between track and verge on Billy's side brimmed with water, but this week, at least, it remained within the confines of the ditch, rather than spilling out across the road. The dandelions, resilient, bloomed bright against the mud-stained grass, and a sprinkling of daisies lay like an unfinished dot-to-dot drawing, leading from the start of Billy's land all the way to his gates. Among the bare thorns of the hedge, new green buds were just thinking of opening, and beyond, in patchy glimpses through the branches, scruffy, cloud-like sheep grazed peacefully while lambs danced between them.

"I've never been to either farm," Jess told Alice. "If I could think of an excuse, we could call up to one or the other, but I really can't! I'm really not *that* nosy, or insensitive, despite what Marcus thinks."

"Shame," Alice said, peering through the straggly hawthorn at the lambs. "I see what you mean about the difference between the farms, though. Even as a city girl, I can see a clear difference. It's a bit of a mess, where that other hedge must've been, but I suppose it'll be covered by grass soon enough?"

"Yes, but without the hedge, or any trees, there's poor drainage, and nothing to stop the rain washing the field into the road anytime it rains." Jess laughed. "Listen to me sounding like I know about land management. I am learning a bit, on the course, but honestly, we're not really covering agriculture. It's more horticulture. Plants and pretty flowers." She glanced at Alice. "I might add on a module, though. Maybe do a dissertation on all this." She gestured around them, encompassing the land on both sides of the lane. "That's a way down the road yet, though. I'm only six months in."

"There's time enough," Alice said. "I'm so happy you've found something you like. You always were such a drifter."

Because I was too busy worrying about you to think about what I wanted. Jess bit back the retort. It didn't matter anymore. Alice was here, and better, and that was what counted.

They passed the driveway to Billy's farm, and the house that Ciara had said belonged to a William Keegan. The man with the car, Jess presumed. "He's off the hook, anyway, if he's been away all week."

"So that's Dochertys' driveway?" Alice nodded to the lefthand gateway.

"Yes, and that's where that couple live, who we just met." Jess pointed to the next bungalow. "Their dogs do bark at more than just the milk lorry, by the way. They barked their bloomin' noisy little heads off when I drove down here on Friday morning!"

Alice chuckled. "Who's next?"

As they meandered towards the village, Jess pointed out the rest of the houses, echoing Marcus's commentary of the previous Sunday afternoon, when the lane was still underwater and they'd turned back before reaching the farms.

At Cindy and Walt's rented house, the driveway was empty. No smoke puffed from the chimney and the curtains to the front windows were closed.

"Perhaps they went away for the weekend," Jess said, trying to recall whether they'd mentioned plans for the Easter weekend when she'd seen them in Finbar's. "Looks like it."

Lila's garden was already a riot of glorious spring colour, with crocuses, daffodils, and hyacinths crammed into every border. Tulips, not yet in bloom, promised a new burst of colour through the coming weeks. Each side of the front door, stood a pot of the lavender Lila had bought after the funeral on Friday afternoon, and Jess could easily visualise the cottage garden in full bloom later in the season. It would be beautiful by the time judging began in June for the annual National Tidy Villages awards that Ballyfortnum not only always entered, but held trophies for as reigning champion in several categories. Lila clearly loved to garden.

"I wonder if she knows Henry," Jess said to Alice. "Her gardening style is more natural than his but their gardens are equally well-tended and she must know as much as he does, by the look. If they don't trade seeds and tips, they should do!"

"Who's Henry?"

"Oh, Al! You do know who Henry is! Dad was on the Tidy Village committee with him. I know you don't know anyone else I've mentioned, but Henry is Elizabeth's husband, and I know I've talked about her enough times. She's the one who nearly died last year, remember? We'll pass their house after Marcus's, see if you can guess which it is by the garden. It's the nicest garden in the village." She cast another look at Lila's garden. "Maybe joint nicest."

Jess pulled out her phone to check the time. "I was going to suggest calling to see if Lila is home. I only met her twice, but I think I like her. I don't think we've time, though. Not if we're stopping at Marcus's and still getting home before your train."

"Actually," Alice said, as they continued walking, leaving Lila's house behind them, "I thought if you don't mind, I might stay another night? Go home tomorrow? Work won't mind; I'm owed some holiday and I told them I might take Tuesday and Wednesday off anyway. Would that be okay?"

A surge of happiness flooded through Jess and she looped her arm through Alice's. "Of course you can! I'd love you to." They reached the corner and turned onto the main village road, beside the pub. "Shall we stop for a drink? It's nice enough to sit out the front for a quick one. Watch the world go by."

"Okay, but I'm not sure we'll see very much world going by, not here in Ballyfortnum." Alice fell into step behind Jess and unzipped the backpack to pull out the picnic rug. They stopped beside one of the picnic tables outside the pub, where Alice shook open the rug and spread it over the wooden bench. "Here. Give me Fletch and you can go in. I'll have a tonic water."

When Jess came out of the pub, she was clutching two glasses, a bottle of tonic water, and a bottle of lager. Behind her, Lila followed through the door with a half-empty pint glass and a man she'd introduced to Jess as "my Dominic." Jess gestured to the picnic table with her lager bottle. "This is my sister, Alice. Alice, it's a good thing we didn't knock on Lila's door. She's here."

Lila slid onto the bench opposite Alice, and her husband slid in beside her. "Sláinte," she said, raising her glass. "Happy Easter."

They made small talk for a while, about Lila's garden, the weather, and how they'd spent the rest of the Easter weekend. Lila's husband was big, booming, and sported a bushy, black beard that reminded Jess of Robbie Coltrane's Hagrid. In fact, overall, if he'd have been wearing a long brown overcoat, it would have been an easy mistake to think they were one and the same. His rugged, earthy manner complemented Lila's long skirts and hippyish image perfectly, and it wasn't long before he had them in stitches with an anecdote about an incident at his work.

"Whatever do you do?" Alice asked, wide-eyed and giggling like a child.

"He's a bouncer," Lila said.

"Of course you are," Alice said. "It was either that or a Hell's Angel."

"Can't I be both?"

Lila slapped a hand on the table. "No you feckin' can't! The neighbours are only just putting up with us without you roaring up on a Harley!"

"I'd say they already have no hope for us, sweetheart. Especially those of us who go serenading the whole street at the dead of night."

"We heard about that," Jess said, taking a swig of lager straight from the bottle. "But seems she's not the only noisy one around. We just met some of your other neighbours and it wasn't you two they complained about." She smiled and sipped at her drink, waiting for them to ask.

They didn't disappoint. "Oh? Who? And who were they complaining about?"

"The young couple with the spaniels. Ciara and ... and ... What was his name?"

"Rory," Alice said. "And they said the milk lorry disturbs them every morning at some ungodly hour."

"It doesn't really bother us," Lila said. "Although it was stuck outside our house for a bit one of the mornings this week. Burst a tyre."

"It did?" Dominic's bushy eyebrows lifted into his thicket of hair.

"He slept through it." Lila's face twisted into a wry grimace. "He'd sleep through an earthquake, after a late shift."

"And your drunken singing." He smirked through the beard but his eyes were full of laughter.

"You wish."

"I made him a cuppa, he was there so long," Lila said. "And then Rory came along and fixed it in a jiffy. Wouldn't have put him as a handy one, have to admit. Think old Tommy was a bit mortified. He'd been at it for ages."

"I got so confused when Rory said the milk guy is called Tommy, too. What with all the Thomases up at the farm," Jess said. "Sounds like milk-driver Tommy must've been one of the last people to see Thomas before he was killed." She picked at the label of the bottle, peeling it from the cold, damp glass.

"How'd you figure that? He was already dead by then," Lila argued.

"No, Rory said the driver said he'd been talking to him when he got the milk? At about half-six. And he was out of the farm again before seven. Because that's when he got stuck with the tyre. That's what Rory said, isn't it?" She looked to Alice for confirmation.

"Yes." Alice nodded and plucked the slice of lemon from her glass. "What was the word he used?" She sucked at the lemon. "Chipper. That was it. He was talking about how it would be light at that time from next week, after the clocks change. He said the driver said Thomas was mighty chipper—"

"—considering how dark it still was," Jess finished.

"Or considering his age," Lila said. "Tommy was talking to *Old* Thomas. Not the younger one."

Jess looked from Lila to Alice and back. "Oh," she said. "Dammit."

Chapter Thirty-Three

Alice sucked at the lemon slice. "One step forward, two steps back." She dropped the lemon back into her empty glass. "Shall I get us another?" She gestured around the table and stood up. "Same again?"

Jess stood too. "I'll just nip to the loo. Would you mind hanging onto Fletcher for a minute?"

Dominic held out his hand for the end of the lead, and rubbed Fletcher's ears. "She'll only be a minute. Stay here with me," he said as Fletcher tried to follow his mistress into the dim interior of the pub.

Inside, once the door swung shut behind them, Jess grabbed Alice by the arm, stopping her progress to the bar. "How come she is so sure he was already dead? Isn't that a bit suspicious? It's like how confident she was that she could leave her doors unlocked." She stared at her sister, willing her to agree. "I think she knows more than she's letting on."

Alice tilted her head a fraction and smiled slowly. "Jess, sweetie, why do you think I suggested we have another drink?" she said, as if she were talking to a very small child who didn't yet understand the world.

"Oh." Jess gave her sister an approving nod, and headed for the toilets.

Back in the pub lounge, she lifted two of the drinks from the bar, nodded to the landlord, and followed Alice outside, where Fletcher's efforts to fling himself at her were thwarted by the rapid response of Dominic.

"Wow, I can see why you're a bouncer, with reflexes like that. Anyone who can stop a Fletch-jump that fast must have no trouble evicting drunks from a nightclub, or barring entry."

Laughter rippled around the foursome as Jess and Alice resumed their places at the picnic table.

Alice didn't waste any time quizzing Lila as to how she knew Thomas was already dead when the milk lorry left. "How can you be so sure?" she asked, peering intently at Lila over her glass.

"I didn't even know he *was* dead, when I was talking to Tommy. I just know it was Grandpa Docherty he'd been talking to. It was later, in the shop. Mrs Dunne said he'd been killed in the night."

"But," Jess protested, "if it was still dark at six, six-thirty, or whatever time the milk lorry was there, that *was* nighttime."

"She said Old Thomas had told her he'd been discovered after the milk lorry left, because it was the milk lorry had roused the farm, what with the dogs going silly. Noisy brats, those dogs; bark like crazy anytime anyone who's not family turn up. He'd had to go out and meet Tommy himself, he said, because Thomas, who's usually up and ready, was nowhere to be found."

"Who'd milked the cows, then?" Jess asked.

"No idea. They'd have a couple of labourers, I think. And the family'd be involved."

"Except Matty," Dominic said.

"Except Matty," Lila agreed. "He's his own farm across the fields, ever since he and Thomas fell out over it."

Jess and Alice exchanged a glance. "Fell out over how Thomas was farming, you mean?" Jess asked, taking another glug from her bottle.

"He never did like how Thomas was managing things. They came to blows over it a few years back. That's when their grandpa divided up the land and their da withdrew from it all. The final straw, it was, for poor Tom. He'd never loved the farm like his da had, if you ask me. He was only too glad to take a step back and let the lads get on with it, I'd say."

"You'd have thought the cows would've been making a lot of noise, if they were late to get milked," Jess said, remembering how, when another farmer had died the previous summer, the labourer had calmly continued with the milking while his boss lay dead in the farmhouse. "Cows don't like to wait, apparently."

Lila shrugged. "I don't know about that. Only that Mrs Dunne said Grandpa Docherty had seen off the milk lorry, gone off to search for Thomas, and found him dead in the haybarn with a hole in his chest." For a moment, she stared silently at her drink, wiping at the condensation with her thumb. After a long pause, she shook her head as if to clear its thoughts, took a long draught of the Budweiser, sighed, smiled, and said, "Drinks on a lazy bank holiday with new friends. What could be better?"

Maybe not calmly discussing yet another murdered neighbour as if it happened all the time, Jess thought, her mouth twisting into a wry smile as she remembered Marcus chastising her: *"This is becoming a habit, O'Malley."* At the thought of Marcus, her smile widened, and she lifted her glass. "New friends," she said, clinking her half-empty bottle against Lila's. "It is nice to be sitting here, especially after we walked so far. Our legs will feel it when we start off again."

Alice, quiet through the last few minutes of conversation, had been staring at nothing in particular, deep in thought. When she finally spoke, she pulled the talk back to the murder: "It was the grandfather who found his grandson? Is that what you just said?"

"That's right, that's what Mrs Dunne said. And although she's an awful gossip—"

"—she's usually right." Jess finished, to Lila's nodding agreement. "When I saw Mrs Dunne on Tuesday morning, it was only about … I don't know, maybe around eleven? Before lunch, but not stupid-early either." She glanced at Alice as if Alice might know, despite not having been there. "I was with my friend Kate, and her baby," she mused aloud to herself. "She got to mine around half-nine … quarter to ten, probably." Had they set out straight away? No, she decided, they'd chatted in the kitchen over a drink first, and Kate had changed Della, then said if they walked, she'd fall asleep for a bit. It can't have been much before eleven before they set out. "We called to Elizabeth, on the way back, and still got home for lunch." With a start, Jess realised the others were gaping at her as if she'd lost her mind.

"Sorry," she said with an apologetic chuckle, "I was trying to work out the timings. If I saw Mrs Dunne at half-eleven, and Old Thomas had been in the shop already, and he'd found his grandson shot dead only that morning, at what, seven, seven-thirty … well, I'm just surprised he'd pop to the shop and casually buy the newspaper! That's all." She grinned across the table at her new friend, and then at her sister. "It's like our dad used to say: 'There's none so queer as folk'. Remember, Al? I think he picked it up from an old colleague when we were in England."

Alice's smile was wide, her eyes bright as she tipped her head back and laughed. "Oh my God, yes! He'd say it in this thick northern accent, and we'd giggle because he'd said queer and didn't know its meaning had evolved!"

"You'd giggle," Jess corrected her. "I was too young to have any idea what it did or didn't mean, back then!" They lapsed into silence, each lost in memories of their dad for a moment.

"It's true enough," Lila said. "It did seem a bit odd, only ... well, maybe it wasn't *that* odd. I speak to the old fella most days, when he comes by. He's walked to the shop every morning since we've lived here, and every morning before that too, according to Anne. I saw him the other day, and said as much—that I'd have thought he might have had a day off, after the shock of finding Thomas—but he said the day he doesn't walk to the shop for his ciggies and his paper will be the day he's dead and lying in the churchyard with his Anne. His wife was called Anne, too." She raised her eyebrows at Jess, who nodded.

"Yes, I think I knew that. And fair enough, I suppose. Routine's good after a shock, too." Jess drained the rest of her bottle and looked at the sky. "We should really head on. It'll get dark soon enough, and we were going to stop and see Marcus."

Alice prodded Jess gently on the ankle with the toe of her boot. "Because you don't see enough of him."

Heat flared on Jess's cheeks, but Lila laughed. "He's all right, is Marcus," she said. "Don't mind her. You see him all you like."

"Oh, don't worry, she does," Alice teased.

Jess, despite her fiery face, laughed with them. "I do." She smiled and stood up, pulling Alice up with her. "Come on you, give me that picnic rug and let's get on, or we'll be walking in the dark or begging Marcus for a lift home and then you'll see even more of him because I'll tell him to stay."

Alice peeled the picnic blanket from the bench, rolled it up, and stuffed it into the backpack. "You know I don't mind. I like him too." She turned to Lila and Dominic. "He's good for her. Keeps her out of trouble and sticking her nose into murders." She paused for a fraction of a beat. "Oh, wait. He doesn't, does he? Nice to meet you both. See you again, I hope." She gathered the empty glasses, shoved the pub door open with her knee, and disappeared inside only to return a minute later, empty-handed, to meet Jess outside the door.

The O'Malley sisters crossed the road and headed towards Marcus's cottage, leaving Lila and Dominic huddled together on the picnic table, still nursing the remainder of their drinks in the last dregs of the weak afternoon sun.

"They seem nice," Alice said, as they strolled along the narrow pavement, elbows bashing against each other. "You're making friends here, Jessie."

Jess smiled. "She is nice. But is she or isn't she still on our list?"

"Hmm ... Off, I think? Don't you?"

"I'm not sure. She seems a bit too complacent, don't you think?"

"Doesn't everyone? Isn't that what we keep saying? No one seems very upset. And—" Alice stopped abruptly, causing Jess to step into the quiet road as she fell off the kerb. The sisters stood face-to-face, Fletcher tugging at his lead, confused as to why his mistress was suddenly not so eager to get to Marcus's.

He whined as if to say, "Come on, Marcus is there. And Snow. Let's go!"

"And what?"

"She said the dogs bark at her when she goes to see her friend at the farm. I say she's off the list. I think we're looking for someone in the family."

"I think so, too, Al. I think so too."

Chapter Thirty-Four

Before they reached Marcus's cottage, Alice stopped again, knocking Jess off balance for the second time in a few minutes.

"What now?" Jess asked.

"The backpack. Did you pick it up?"

She hadn't. To Fletcher's utter bewilderment, Jess and Alice turned around, and the three of them retraced their steps back to the pub. Lila and Dominic were as they had left them, but a pair of woman now stood beside the picnic bench, chatting to the couple. One, auburn-haired and wrapped in a long brown coat, stood straight and upright as if she'd studied ballet since childhood. The other, in a black puffy jacket, her hair short and black to match, had one knee on the bench and waved her hands animatedly as she talked. As Jess and Alice approached, the short-haired woman picked up the backpack and waved it at them. "This'll be yours, then. You must be Jess?"

"Thanks." She reached out and took the bag. "And yes. Seems like everyone knows who I am!" She offered a small smile. "I've no idea who you are though. Sorry."

"Anne. Anne Docherty. Nice to meet you Jess."

"Siobhan," said the auburn-haired woman. "Also Docherty. Lila said you'd be back for the bag."

Lila laughed. "I hoped so, or we'd have had to hunt you down at that gorgeous policeman's house."

Dominic batted her arm. "Mind yourself!"

She smirked at him. "A girl can look. I'll bet you do, at the club." She snaked her arm around his neck and butted him gently with her head. "I was telling the girls you should join us for a girly night soon. What do you think?"

A warmth spread through Jess's belly. "I'd like that a lot," she said. "Thank you." As Alice kept reminding her, it was about time she made some friends her own age around here, instead of hanging out with the oldies in Orchard Close all day. Working at the garden centre, starting her new course, and meeting Marcus had started the ball rolling, but none of that offered her a network of girlfriends to hang out with for the odd evening of drinks and gossip and fun, especially now Kate had Della and wasn't around so much. She'd warmed to Lila instantly, when they'd met in the greengrocer, and the two newcomers' faces were open and friendly, too, although despite their layers of makeup, both women looked tired and panda-eyed. "I'm so sorry for your loss." Jess smiled gently at each in turn. "It must have been a great shock. I met Thomas just last week."

The dark-haired one—Anne—gave Jess a sad smile. "Thanks. It wasn't as much of a shock as you might think, though. Eejit that he was. He'd upset enough people that someone was bound to bump him off one of these days. It was only a matter of time." The harsh words were softened somewhat as tears filled her eyes. She brushed them away with the sleeve of her coat. "Stupid, stupid eejit."' Her voice broke into a sob, and she groped in her pockets in search of a tissue.

Jess rooted in the backpack and found a small travel packet of Kleenex. "Here."

Anne peeled one from the pack, wiped her eyes and blew her nose. "Sorry," she said, sniffing. "He was an absolute fricking idiot but he was still my brother."

Alice stepped closer and rested her hand on Anne's back. "I know," she said softly. "We've a brother, too. He's mad daft at times, but we'd not be without him."

Anne sniffed again and offered Alice a watery smile. "It's hard to believe he's gone. I just keep wishing and wishing I'd not stayed at Shuv's that night, and then maybe I'd have heard him get up like I sometimes do, and got up to help him, or to say something, or just to …" She shrugged, searching for words. "Just to … see him one more time." She gave a hollow, broken laugh. "Who am I kidding? I never get up. It's always too dark and too cold, and he's made it so none of us want to help him anyway, even if there was something we could do. He doesn't—he didn't—need any of us to help with *our* farm anymore." She laced the word *our* with bitter venom but her face was a picture of sorrow as she stared at each of them for a moment, fresh tears spilling down her cheeks.

Funny, thought Jess, how the loss of their traditional ways of family farming seemed to cause her more sadness than the loss of her brother.

"Even when I do—did—hear him, I'd turn over and go back to sleep. I could have—" She dabbed her eyes with a balled-up tissue. "—maybe I could have … I don't know … stopped whatever happened, or at least said something nice to him." She held Alice's eyes for a moment. "I could at least have said something *nice*. And I wasn't even *there*."

Siobhan slipped her arm around her cousin's waist. "We all wish we'd said something nice, but we can't change it now, hon. He was what he was and you can't beat yourself up."

"We all heard that shot and I didn't even open my eyes. Didn't even move. I just thought nothing of it, and went back to sleep."

"Hon, it mightn't even have been a shot. We said that. When we all sat there nursing our coffees and moaning about the state of our heads, and Lila said did ye hear a gunshot or was I dreaming it, and the rest of us said, you weren't dreaming, but so what, because we're always hearing shots over on the farms. Or it could've been anywhere; anyone popping off a shot somewhere. We couldn't have *done* anything."

Anne sniffed loudly into another tissue, straightened her back, and took a deep breath. "I know. I do know. Now, what are we drinking? Are ye staying for another, now you're here?"

Alice and Jess shared a silent conversation:

What do you think?

We could?

No, we haven't time.

Shame though. But no, we really shouldn't.

Jess shook her head. "We'd really love to, but we can't. Another time, though. Please."

As they started to walk away for the second time, Lila called them back. "Oh, wait! Anne, Shuv, Jess had a question about Tuesday. She wondered why the cows hadn't kicked up a fuss when they hadn't got milked."

Oh my God. "Lila! That's hardly important. I'm so sorry. It was only a stupid thought, because … well, because …"

Lila waved away the apology. "No, it was a valid question. Jess said last year, you remember, when O'Sullivan died, the fella who found him called the Gards, then went off to do the milking, and she'd remembered it because it seemed such a weird way to handle finding your boss dead."

Jess was sure they could've toasted marshmallows on her face, but the women didn't seem offended.

"Christ, yeah, you're so right." Anne said, still watery-eyed but smiling through it. "And if they *had* been late to milk, they absolutely would've been raising hell, but they don't get milked till eight. That was one of the few *good* changes Thomas made!"

"The only one," Siobhan muttered.

"Huh?" Anne's explanation had done nothing to clarify the situation for Jess. "But you said the milk lorry came at six every day?"

Anne and Siobhan laughed together. "And so he does," Anne agreed, "but it's yesterday's milk he's taking. He comes twice a day; morning and afternoon. Takes the evening milk in the morning and the morning's milk in the afternoons."

"Oh," said Jess. "Makes sense, I suppose. I just assumed ..." She let the thought tail off as Marcus's warnings about assumptions echoed in her mind for the umpteenth time.

"Would anyone be up, aside from Thomas, when the milk lorry comes?" Alice asked gently.

"We'd all be *awake*. The dogs bark their heads off. Bark at fricking everyone who doesn't live there."

Siobhan nodded agreement and spoke over her cousin. "The feckers even bark at me and my lot, and we flipping lived there for years till we all spread out across the fields and away."

Anne acknowledged the remark with a wry smile. "Wouldn't be long after I hear Thomas crashing about; the milk lorry arriving. Our houses are converted from the old stable block, and we've only a partition wall between us. Stone on the outside, paper-thin on the insides. You could hear him fart."

A ripple of quiet laughter punctuated the sombre mood.

"He wouldn't be the quietest, when it comes to farts," Siobhan said to more laughter.

"Thomas, or the milk man?" Dominic said dryly, causing more giggles.

"Both, probably. Fricking men," Anne said, her smile fading once more as she carried on with her account of early mornings on the Docherty farm. "Once Thomas is up and moving about, I don't go properly back to sleep, just drifting, you know. Trying to convince myself I *might*. I'd hear him go out the door—he never did get the hang of leaving quietly, and I'd turn over and try to sleep, but there's not time enough between him going out and the milk lorry rocking up." Her eyes welled. "It's been really strange this week, without the door slamming. Of all the things to miss! He'd get up about six, to be ready for Tommy. Every day without fail." She sniffed into the tissue, reached across the table for Lila's lager, and took a large swig from the bottle.

"Then the fricking dogs kick off at half-past, once the milk tanker turns into the yard. Da always said we should be glad they don't start up their noise when Tommy turns into the driveway, up on the lane. Gives us four extra minutes of quiet, so it does, Da reckons." She gave a small chuckle through her tears. "Thomas is always—was always—out there waiting in the sheds." She blotted her face with the crumpled tissue. "Mam said they barked a mad long time that morning. Of course, we found out later it was because Tommy—that's the milkman—couldn't find ... couldn't find

Thomas." She looked from Alice to Jess to Siobhan, a raw flash of pain shooting across her face. "He couldn't find Thomas, so he tried to rouse someone else, and Granda would be an early riser, even now, so he was the first one up. Old fecker still likes to keep farm hours, in the mornings, even though he's not needed. So he dealt with Tommy and the milk dockets." Anne took a deep breath and another large swig of Lila's Budweiser; smoothed out the tissue only to crumple it again. "And then," she said softly into her hands, "and then Granda found him, after." She looked up at them now, and said in a clear, steady voice with only the faintest remnant of a tremor, "Granda found him after the milkman had left. He'd been there all the time."

Alice patted Anne's shoulder.

Jess reached over and squeezed her hand. "I'm so sorry," she said.

Dominic, who'd quietly left the table while the women were talking, returned bearing a tray of fresh drinks. He set the tray on the table, picked up a tumbler containing an inch of golden whiskey, and pushed it into Anne's trembling hands. "Got you this. Go on; it'll help."

She downed it in one, set the glass back on the tray, and picked up the glass of red wine. "Thanks, Dom. Sorry, I'm not usually such a wreck. It catches me by surprise, every now and then. He was a shyster, but he was our shyster. You fecking brat, Thomas Docherty, ye feckin' brat." As she said his name, she held the glass in a toast, flicked her eyes to the sky, then took a large mouthful of the wine to wash down the whiskey. "Jess, Alice, it's good to meet you. We'll organise something soon, yeah? When I'm not so morbid and dramatic."

For the second time, Jess and Alice said their goodbyes, crossed over the road, and headed towards Marcus's cottage, Fletcher subdued and confused by the coming and going, and for once, walking sensibly and not behaving like an errant toddler.

"Well," said Alice.

"Well," said Jess.

"The poor girl."

"Can you imagine if Eric ..."

"Don't!"

"But we do at least *like* Eric, most of the time ..."

"True."

"I wonder if it makes it harder, though?"

"What?"

"If Eric ... well, you know ... we'd most likely have said something nice enough to him, I mean, but Thomas ... well, it seems everyone's last memory is being annoyed with him."

"See what you mean ... yeah, that'd be hard enough, I'd guess. Poor family."

Jess unlatched Marcus's gate, unhooked Fletcher's lead, and let him run, barking, to the door to announce their arrival.

Marcus opened the door in jeans, a checked shirt, and socks, and Jess burst into tears and threw herself into his arms.

"What the ...?"

Through sobs, Jess spluttered out incoherent words, which Alice translated.

"We just met Anne and Siobhan Docherty. Jess is feeling sorry for them, because the last memories they have of Thomas are bad ones, and she's feeling grateful for Eric. Make her a cup of tea and she'll calm down. Hello, by the way. Hello Snowflake."

Marcus held Jess until her sobs subsided, then turned her around and pushed her gently towards the conservatory. "Go on; go and sit down. I'll make that tea."

Chapter Thirty-Five

Emotional outburst over, Jess sat beside Marcus on the wicker sofa in the conservatory, drinking her second mug of tea. Alice, ensconced in one of the matching wicker armchairs, clasped her hands around a steaming cup of hot water. Fletcher, finally tired out from his long walk and a romp around the garden with his Westie friend, snored gently on Marcus's feet.

Jess sighed, leaned into Marcus, and closed her eyes. "I'm not sure we'll have the energy to walk the rest of the way home. Feels like hours since we left."

Alice sniggered into her tea. "That's because it is. Our two-hour walk has already taken us four hours. It's ten past five already."

Jess's eyes flew open. "It is? Shite. Well then we either need to leave soon, or you," she said, turning doe-eyes on Marcus, "will have to run us back. What'd you rather, Al? Walk or car?"

Alice smiled lazily at Marcus. "I'd think that's really up to Marcus."

"You know me." His eyes crinkled as he answered Alice, steadfastly ignoring Jess's puppy-dog hope. "If there's food on offer at the end of it, I'll drive you. No dinner, and you can walk."

Jess sighed again. "I'll cook. If you don't mind something easy. I'm all out of effort after yesterday, and from being out for longer than we'd planned now. Freezer-food do you both?"

"I suppose I can rustle up something here, otherwise," Marcus said, with a half-hearted frown. "I suppose I do owe you, after yesterday's feast. And then I'll run you back after? You not going home today now, I presume?" He directed the last question to Alice, and Jess dug him sharply in the ribs. "Ow! What?"

"Presuming again ... that'll get you into trouble." She smiled sweetly at him, and he planted a kiss on her upturned nose.

"You're not going home today, Alice, I deduce with my extensive and refined detecting skills, given that the last train to Dublin left, ooh ..." He leaned back on the sofa and peered around the doorway to glimpse the kitchen clock. "About seven minutes ago."

"I'll get the lunchtime train tomorrow. Thought I'd have one more night of playing at detective with you country folks. Actually ..." Her tone became more serious and she glanced at Jess with an unvoiced question.

Jess inclined her head a fraction, the answer as silent as the question: *Go on, you may as well tell him; I'm too knackered to talk.*

Alice nodded. "Actually, we've made some pretty good progress. It's amazing what an hour at a pub on a Monday afternoon can reveal."

Marcus held up his hands. "It was bad enough when it was just one of you." He glared at Jess in mock-irritation. "Please don't tell me you've been out snooping around the Dochertys this afternoon?" He put his head in his hands and groaned. "You have, haven't you? Is it too late to rescind the offer of dinner and move back to Lambskillen where all was quiet and peaceful and no one ever tripped over quite as much murder as you seem to?"

Fletcher lifted his head and gave Marcus a sympathetic yawn.

"You can come with me, Fletch. You can keep Snowflake company. And perhaps, without you to drag around the village, Detective O'Malley won't feel so inclined to walk so far and won't find so many dead bodies."

Jess wriggled her toes against his thigh, poking him until he squirmed away and pressed his hand over her feet to hold them still. "One," she said, glaring, "Fletcher stays with me, unless you're offering to bath off all this bog muck, in which case you're welcome to him. Two, yes, it's too late to back out of dinner. Three, I guess that means you have absolutely zero interest in who we saw or what we learned, so we won't tell you. Off you go to the kitchen. Go cook!"

Alice, from the chair across from them, with her legs curled under her, Snowflake asleep on her lap, and absolutely no intention of getting involved while her sister and Marcus argued over who would cook, snorted into her mug.

About three seconds later, Jess leaped to her feet. "Shite!"

Alice and Marcus, with identical confusion on their faces, said in unison, "What now?"

"Nothing exciting. I just need to grab a pint of milk before the shop shuts. Back in a sec." With that, she shoved her feet back into the muddy walking boots she'd discarded on the doorstep, said, "Stay," very firmly to Fletch and Snowflake, and ran out the front door, slamming it behind her.

Mrs Dunne was mooching around the shop, straightening shelves and pushing a broom across the floor. She looked up as the bell over the door tinkled, confusion wrinkling her brow. "Jess, love. You're just in time. Milk, is it you'll be wanting?" She tilted her head towards the fridge where two lonely cartons sat beside a single packet of cheese. "You're in luck. I'm almost out till the morning. You had a good walk with your sister, did you? And a fine catch-up with that hippy-dippy one from up the lane."

Jess didn't bother to ask how Mrs Dunne knew all this. Instead, she asked something else that had been bothering her. "Mrs Dunne?"

"What is it, love?"

"You know when Old Thomas came in last week and told you his grandson was dead? Well did he seem even a *tiny* bit upset?"

"Ah now, love, course he were. Us old folks, we just don't show it in the way you young ones do. He'd have been sorry enough, I haven't a doubt in my head. Just because he was just the same as always, and a spring in his step you'd not equate with a man of his age neither, doesn't mean he wasn't grieving. Sure, he was still in shock, I'd say. Couldn't believe it yet, most likely, and that'd be why he'd not seem to have a bother on him, wouldn't you say?" She leaned on her broom and surveyed Jess with curiosity. "Mind you, now, he weren't much different any other day since, neither. Some folks just get on with their lives. Maybe there isn't much he hasn't seen, what with him being ninety and then some. You can leave the money there on the counter if you've it right."

Jess did as she was told, and made for the door. As the bell tinkled again, she paused, turned, and asked Mrs Dunne another question. "I may've asked you this already, I can't remember, but you know when Peggy—the one from Parks and Wildlife came in?"

Mrs Dunne grunted, taking up the broom and swishing it under the edge of the fridge unit. "Aye. What about her?"

"Do you remember who was in the shop when she came in? A man, she said."

"A man, was it?" She reached under a shelf stacked with teabags and instant coffee, and retrieved a scrap of paper.

Jess rolled her eyes, sensing Mrs Dunne, never one to hold back on gossip, was playing with her. "Who was it?"

"Who, love?" Mrs Dunne pushed the little pile of dust and debris along the shop floor, swept it around to the side of the counter, bent from her waist and scooped it into a dustpan.

This time, Jess was certain she heard restrained laughter in Mrs Dunne's voice. "The man!"

"It was Gerry, love. Just our Gerry." She straightened up, dustpan in hand, and beamed, as cheeky as Bryony or Clara when they were causing mischief.

Gerry the postman. Of course. Jess chuckled. "Oh, is that all? No drama there then." She turned to leave. Again, she stopped. She spun on the ball of her foot and added, "But it does explain how every single person in the entire village knew about that blooming buzzard. Anyone you didn't get to, Gerry had covered. You two are incredible. I don't know why you bother to sell newspapers, to be honest with you. You should write your own." She threw Mrs Dunne one last smile and left, the bell over the door announcing her exit into the fresh, light drizzle she hadn't noticed when she'd entered the shop a few minutes earlier.

Back over the road, she set the milk on Marcus's doorstep so she wouldn't forget it, and slipped in through the door without letting the dogs break out into the garden. "You've been out all day, Fletch; stay in now and stay dry."

Marcus and Alice had been busy: the aroma of frying onions and turmeric wafted into the tiny hallway and drew Jess into the kitchen. Marcus stood over the oven, stirring a shallow pan, and Alice stood at the little kitchen table, chopping a red pepper into neat slices. "Thai red curry," he said. "Take it or leave it."

"Mm, yum. Take it, of course." She pinched a piece of pepper from Alice's chopping board, popped in her mouth, and wrapped her arms around Marcus and rested her head against his back. "Mmm. Thank you. Shall I help?"

By the time they sat balancing scalding dishes of fragrant jasmine rice and the steaming, eye-watering mound of chicken and vegetables on their laps, Alice and Jess had almost brought Marcus up to speed with the account of their walk.

"We met the Cocker spaniel couple. They seem nice. So young!"

"They made me feel quite ancient," Alice agreed. "We also learned that absolutely everyone in this entire village is either called Thomas or William."

"Did you talk to the milk lorry driver?" Jess asked, blinking back tears as she bit into a particularly fiery piece of red chilli. "Was he any help to you?"

Marcus peered over his own steaming plate, but said nothing.

"We've narrowed it right down for you." Jess ignored his feigned disinterest. "Anne Docherty confirmed what Lila said, about them all being at Anne's from about midnight. And she confirmed that the dogs bark at everyone who isn't the family."

"Well," Alice corrected, "everyone who doesn't live there, which includes some of the family. Remember? Siobhan said they even bark at her and her lot, even though they used to live there?"

"I wonder who's included in 'her lot'?" They'd look on the list when they got back to Orchard Close, but Jess wasn't going to mention that to Marcus.

"Okay you two, is there any single other thing you would like to talk about?" Marcus said. "How was the weather out across the bog? Did you meet any sheep?"

For the next half hour or so, as they ate, they talked about how different the high bog—the uncut, unfarmed parts of the bog that were left to a natural, wild state—was from the lower, farmed acres of black, sodden peat. Although Jess carefully avoided any talk of the murder, the topic of the sterile farmland followed naturally as they relayed the route of their walk, and they mused for a while over whether the Dochertys would revert back to a less intensive way of farming, and whether Tom would take a more active and decisive role once more.

"I hope they replant some of those hedges, if nothing else," Jess said. "I'm going to find out what would be a suitable mix of native species, just in case. I'll ask on Monday, when I'm back in Kildare."

Alice nodded. "Shay'd know, otherwise?"

"I suppose he would," Jess agreed. "I think it's the wrong time of year to plant, though. Think they'd need to wait till winter comes around again. Bit late, now, for this year."

"I hope Old Mr Docherty sees a change before he's gone," Marcus said. "The old should die happy, not with their final memories being filled with family arguments and discord."

"Ah, sure, he's years in him yet," Jess said. "That's what everyone says! I'm not sure I've ever even seen the man, but I imagine him to look even older than Jack at the garden centre and Mrs Harris combined. A little, wizened man, hunched over a cane." She laughed. "I know, I know. He can't be like that because everyone says he's sprightly and agile, but still."

Marcus set down his fork on his plate, and smiled sadly. "Unfortunately, it seems he won't live forever. Don't go spreading this around now, because he doesn't want everyone worrying about him and feeling sorry for him, but he's not as well as he lets the village believe. He's advanced lung cancer. I suppose some of the family know, but he's not told most of them. His days are numbered, poor old fellow. He's stoic about it. Lived his life, he says."

Jess stared at Marcus in surprise. This was so at odds with the image everyone portrayed of the old man. "Why would he hide it? You'd think he'd want to be cared for?"

Marcus shook his head. "The opposite. He likes his independence. Thinks they'd stop him doing anything; coddle him. Said he may as well be dead anyway, once that happens."

Alice sighed softly. "Ah, the poor man. Lila said that, didn't she? She said the day he doesn't walk to the shop will be the day he's dead. I guess that's why he still walked down there even after finding his grandson dead. Probably made his own death feel a whole lot closer. It makes more sense now, I think."

"Still buying the cigarettes, though," Jess said with a quiet, sad laugh. "Funny how people do that."

"He doesn't smoke them," Marcus said. "When John went up there to interview him, Mags said it's the habit of buying them he can't break. She'd distribute them to other smokers in the family, she said. I imagine she's one of the few who knows how sick he is, given she'd be the one who runs the house. I don't know." He shrugged, and stood to gather the empty plates. "You really must not repeat this, not to anyone. I'm telling you this as my partner and friend, not as any part of the investigation."

At his words, a rush of warm happiness turned somersaults in Jess's chest. Their relationship had grown and grown, but he'd never referred to her as his partner before, not in her earshot, at least.

He smiled his crinkle-eyed smile, and her insides melted as she followed him to the kitchen, leaving Alice alone in the conservatory. He set the plates on the worktop, filled the kettle, and then they stood, wrapped in each other's arms as the kettle rumbled to its boil behind them and visions of Marcus moving into her house in Orchard Close vied for space with the tingling sensation of their kiss. Would he? Could he? Should he? It had only been a year since they'd met, but he felt so *right*.

Chapter Thirty-Six

An hour or so after Marcus left Orchard Close to go to work on Tuesday morning, Jess and Alice dragged themselves out of their beds and sat down to breakfast.

Jess, in fairness, had got up with Marcus, but had made herself a cup of tea and brought it back to bed after waving him off from the living room window. Overnight, the weather had turned wintery again and sleety rain battered the road. She'd stood, huddled in her dressing gown, Fletcher beside her with his paws up on the back of the sofa, and blown Marcus a kiss as he'd pulled away, thoughts from the evening before still churning in her mind. Should she invite him to move in? She'd ask Alice about it.

But first, they had more pressing matters to think about. She pulled her notebook from the kitchen drawer and flicked through the pages until she reached the Docherty family tree.

"If we take what Siobhan said about the dogs at face value," she said to Alice, "we can cross off everyone on her branch of the family. So that's Colm off the hook."

"And Lila said they bark at her, too," Alice said. "And we know they bark at the milk lorry, and they barked at Peggy, and if they bark at Siobhan and Colm and all them, then let's do a terrible thing and temporarily eliminate everyone who doesn't live in the houses in the farmyard. It's applying a bit of assumption, but we won't tell Marcus!"

Jess took up her pencil and drew faint lines through almost all of the Dochertys on the list. "What about Matty?"

Alice chewed her lip. "I think," she said carefully, "we could cross him out, faintly, like you're doing there—" She leaned across the table and poked at the list with her finger. "—because we can apply the same logic. If the dogs bark at Siobhan, let's tentatively apply that logic to Matty." She got up, padded around the table to stand behind Jess and peer over her shoulder, heads touching, as they scanned the rest of the names. "And Billy White can go too. Let's take them all out, just for now ... see who that leaves."

"But that only leaves Tom and Mags." Jess shook her head. "And I can't believe any parent would murder their own child. It doesn't make sense." She flipped back through the pages. "Have we missed something?"

"Besides," said Alice, "they gave each other an alibi. They were together, in bed, asleep, until the milk lorry came. According to Anne."

"Although she wasn't actually there, so doesn't actually *know*." Jess sucked the end of the pencil. "Let's put Matty and Colm and Billy back in for now? Although I can't really believe it'd be them either. They all seem so *nice*."

"You said Thomas seemed nice. But you also said you'd kill him."

"He was nice. If you overlook that he was buying enough weedkiller to decimate the whole of Ireland."

"What about the gun? And the poison?"

Jess picked up her phone and typed out a text. *Hi, can I ask a favour?*

The reply was instant: *You can ASK*

Can you look something up for me?

"Who are you texting?" Alice frowned at Jess's lapse into silence while she focused on the phone.

"Shay. Hang on. I'll tell you in a min."

What?

Did Thomas Docherty buy a load of poison recently? Or ever?

Give me an hour.

She stared out of the French doors to a brighter sky than that of earlier that morning. "The rain's stopped. Let's go for a walk while it's dry. Head down to the Gun Club, in the hope one of them is there? It's a bit of a shot in the dark, but—oops!" She giggled, hand to mouth. "Poor choice of words! Which train are you getting?" She glanced at her phone to check the time.

"It doesn't matter. I called in to confirm I'm taking tomorrow off too, so no rush. Last one's at six-forty. Tomorrow'll do, at a push. Good idea. Let's go. If no one's there, at least we get to see the chicks!"

∞

The track was quiet and empty, and as much as they'd have liked to bump into any one of the Dochertys, Jess and Alice enjoyed the gentle, easy stroll after yesterday's mammoth trek, regardless of its lack of murder suspects.

The dogs gambolled like spring lambs, leaping from side to side across the track in erratic zigzags.

At the end of the trail, Jess looped the dogs' leads to the gate post so she and Alice could meander among the bird enclosures, watching the chicks scratch and scrabble at the ground or follow their mothers on single-file circuits of the perimeter fence.

Jess's phone vibrated in her pocket. She pulled it out and read Shay's text:

He ordered in the special order stuff. About a year ago. That what you wanted to know?

Thanks. Yes. Talk later. Might call in when I take Alice to station.

She's still here then. Becoming a country girl! Say hi. See you x

"Shay says hi. And that Dead Thomas bought lots of poison last year."

In the pond, thick clusters of shiny frogspawn sparkled in the sun's thin rays, which were trying their best to break through the lingering grey cloud. Pin-prick shoots of bright, fresh green grass poked through the damp earth, all but hidden under the dead, browned grass of the year before. Scattered across the entire area, bright spring flowers shone like confetti in a churchyard.

"Look, Alice, cowslips. Aren't they lovely." Jess pointed with her foot to the pale-yellow blooms. "And the gorse is really yellowing up. Mind you, there's been blooms on the gorse since January, in some places. Smell it—see if it reminds you of summer holidays."

Alice obligingly stuck her nose against the golden spray of coconut-scented buds. "Mm. Summer and Clara's hair."

Jess laughed. "I said that to Bel! It's the coconut oil she uses. I love the smell of it."

"You think you and Marcus will have kids?"

"Alice! We only just got together! Besides, he already has Lily."

"You're good together. You think you'll get to meet his daughter one of these days? Do you *want* to meet her?"

Jess was saved from answering, or from any further inquisition, by Fletcher. Still tied to the gatepost, he started to bark. Softly at first, in a low, rumbling grumble, then again and again, until he erupted into a full-volume, gatepost-tugging frenzy.

"Fletcher! Quiet!" Jess hurried towards him, praying he wouldn't dislodge the post. "Shh, I'm coming. Quiet!"

As she reached the gate, a familiar, scruffy pickup rounded the bend in the track. At the wheel, Colm raised a hand in greeting. Beside him, his teenage son sat on the passenger seat, and behind him, the handsome black Labrador, with his head fully out the rear window, tongue lolling. They slowed the vehicle to a halt in front of the gate, threw open the doors, and jumped out.

Jess cast Alice a look of triumphant surprise: *See, I told you it was worth a shot.*

Alice raised an eyebrow and fired back a look of her own: *So now they're here, what do we want to know?*

Jess released Fletcher from the gate and, still holding his lead so he couldn't run off towards the bird cages, let him greet his fellow Labrador. "Hey, how're you both? We were just peeking in at the chicks. Hope that's okay?"

Colm nodded. "You're grand. Long as you're careful. And keep away when it's shooting. You're all right at this time of year, mind. All quiet?" He nodded in the direction of the birds.

"Seems to be. There are cowslips by the pond. Nice to see."

He nodded again. "It's a haven for all sorts. Lizards and newts, in summertime, if you're lucky. Any tadpoles yet?"

Jess shook her head. "Not that we could see. Lots of frogspawn. How's everything with the family? We met Siobhan yesterday. And Anne."

"Bearing up. Well as can be expected. Right, C.J.?" He ruffled his son's hair.

"Right enough." The boy threw an awkward smile at Jess and Alice and ducked away towards the bird enclosures.

"There was a rat, by the cages," Jess lied, in a sudden flash of inspiration. "Would you put poison down to keep them away?"

"Ah no, not a bit of it." Colm went to the back of the pickup to pull a sack of feed from the load bed. "Could do without the rats, and the fecking crows, but we can't be leaving poison around. You'd not know what might get hold of it. The birds, for instance. Like that buzzard of yours. We don't use poison on any of the preserved lands." He lugged the sack towards the cages. "Come on, you may as well help. Hook that dog of yours on the tow hitch. He'll be grand enough there."

Jess did as he said, then followed him to the pen she remembered him saying housed grouse.

"We don't just throw them feed when we come. We go around the wire, check for holes. Someone comes every day. If it ain't rats getting in, it's mink or pine martens. Little feckers. We'd set traps, sometimes."

"To kill them?" Jess heard the note of surprise in her question. "Aren't they protected?"

"Martens are; mink are nothing but a nuisance. And no, we have to use humane traps. They look similar, martens and mink, if you don't know, but one's native and the other is vermin. Escaped into the wild, or let out, from mink farms. Kill anything they find—hens, game birds, even domestic cats. Nasty little things. Martens are vicious too, but seeing as they're endangered and protected, we have to release them if they end up in the traps. It's illegal to disturb their nesting ground, too. It's a fine balance, right enough."

"So would you poison the mink, once you've caught them?"

"No, we'd shoot them. It's the most humane way. Instant. They stay in the trap, enjoying their last meal."

"Does your son shoot?" She nodded over to where the boy was striding around the far enclosure, poking at the fencing with his boot from time to time to test it held firm.

"Clay pigeons, only. He's not interested in shooting vermin. Can't say I blame him. I don't like to do it, either. It's the only way, though. It's the law, for culling. Needs must."

"But ..." Jess hesitated, wary of going too far, upsetting this man who'd just lost his nephew. "So ... I know guns have to be kept locked up, and you need a licence, but I work down in the garden centre in Ballymaglen, and anyone can walk in and buy poison."

"Not in big quantities. If you want a lot, you'd be ordering it special. The sort you'd get off the shelf, that's not what you'd use anywhere but domestic houses and the like. If you've a real problem, you'd be looking for something more potent altogether. In most cases, folks'd call in the professionals, once it's more than just a mouse or two in the attic or a rat in your greenhouse."

"What about up at a farm? Would most farms have problems with mink? Rats? Mice?"

Colm bent to push at a section of the chicken-wire, revealing a tiny tear near the ground. "See this? Something's been at it. C.J.! Grab that bucket of fencing tools?" As his son ambled back to the pickup, Colm gestured to Jess to start around the enclosure in the opposite direction to him. "You go round that way. Test the base, but scan for holes all the way up. Most of these animals are great little climbers."

Jess nodded and did as he asked, looking up, down, up, down, pressing her hand against the wire near the ground with every couple of steps.

"If what you're really asking is, 'What happened to Thomas?' you'd be right. There's poison enough up at the farm. More than any of us approved of him having. Liberal with it, he'd be. Like anything he's done to that farm. If anything got in the way of his notions of how to bleed every inch of that land dry, he'd see it gone." He stopped at the far side of the cage, straightened, and looked directly at Jess, his weathered face serious as he met her eyes. "It was a great lump of rat bait, stuffed in his mouth, they said." He watched her through the wire, coughed, and spat at the ground. "They said it in fancier words, of course, but by the time it got passed along, it got uglier, as stories do. You want the details?" His words were accusing, but his tone was not. His voice was gentle, as if he acknowledged Jess's right to curiosity.

"When I found the buzzard," she said, "it looked peaceful and unharmed. Just dead. But then I gave it to Peggy—she's the one from Parks and Wildlife—and she pulled its wings open and showed me where it had been shot. An old wound, healed, mostly, in one wing, then a newer spray of shot scarring its breast. She was surprised that hadn't killed it, I think. I didn't look very carefully, when I found it. Didn't know what to look for, or see anything obvious, under its feathers."

Colm nodded. "So I heard."

"And I'd asked her to call and let me know what happened, after she took it away. I wanted to know. I wanted to know why I haven't seen so many buzzards in the last few years; where have they gone? I hadn't really considered it, before I found that one. Just assumed they flew off to live somewhere else, once their trees have been felled. But after I found it, I realised maybe they all died. You know?"

"I do."

"But when Peggy phoned, she said it also had traces of poison, and that's what would've killed it, in the end. She said it most likely consumed something that had been poisoned—a mouse, or suchlike. It would have been slower, not so able to hunt, once it had been injured. Might well have picked up something already dead."

"And then," Colm rounded the corner of the cage as Jess reached the end of her side. They faced each other briefly at the opposite ends of the next side, then in silent agreement, continued to check the fence. "Thomas was found shot in the shoulder and the chest, with a lump of rat bait shoved in his gob."

"Yes." She kept her focus firmly on the fence as he moved nearer. For a moment, a flutter of fear ran through her.

"Jess?"

She didn't look up. *Where's Alice?* She squinted through the enclosure. Alice was far on the other side of the row of cages, chatting to C.J., who was holding a battered white bucket and a roll of chicken wire.

Colm stopped. "Jess. It's okay. I don't mind you asking. I can see it'd unnerve you, with him having the exact same injuries. Don't be worrying yourself."

"Colm?" She addressed the words to the chicken wire fence of the grouse enclosure. "When you go to the farm, do the sheepdogs bark at you?" She held her breath, waiting for his answer.

She didn't wait long.

His laugh was throaty and deep. "Do those feckers bark at me? Is there any fecker they don't bark at? More bark on the pair of them than in a whole fecking forest of trees." He laughed loudly at his own joke and Jess immediately felt her shoulders relax, the brief moment of fear draining as she laughed with him. *It's not him. I never thought it was, but it's not him. Thank God for that.*

Colm's laughter faded as he coughed, spat, and coughed again. "They bark their fecking heads off. Only that Mam won't hear of it, or I'd shoot the pair of them as fast as any mink." He laughed again, then stopped abruptly and threw her an apologetic look. "Don't mind me. I'd not shoot a dog. They're just doing their job. There's only five people they don't bark at—" He broke off, a startled expression crossing his face as he remembered afresh. "Four, now. I keep forgetting. Tom, Mags, Anne, and Da. They even bark at Matty, Patrick, and Sarah."

"Patrick and Sarah?"

"Thomas and Matty's other brother. Lives in Dublin. Sarah's the other sister. Next one down after Matty. And they all lived there with those dogs, once. Soon as they moved out, that was all it took. Now, any time they go home, the dogs start up. Daft feckers."

"Colm?" Jess stood and faced him. "Who do you think did it?"

"I can't say that, Jess. I can't say. Only thing I will say is, it'll come out soon enough. Soon enough. And when it does, it won't matter anymore. No one else will come to any harm, that much I can promise you, so stop your worrying and your asking, and help me check this next pen."

Chapter Thirty-Seven

By the time they'd helped Colm and C.J. feed all the birds and check the fencing, the rain had started again.

"Hop in," Colm said, as Jess unhitched Fletcher from the tow hitch and Alice retrieved Snowflake from the gatepost.

"Thanks," Alice said, "but we'll be okay to walk. I'm off home to Dublin tomorrow and I won't get to walk in the country again for ages. A bit of rain won't hurt us. Thank you so much for letting me help. I never did anything like that before."

He looked her up and down. "Aye. You're stronger than you know, Alice O'Malley. I'd reckon your da'd be proud of you. You've come good. Now, are you sure you don't want to hop in?"

Jess and Alice exchanged a glance: *How does he know?*

"Thanks," Jess said, with a smile, "but we'll walk it. Can I help again, Colm? I'd love to get involved. As long as I don't have to shoot. I wouldn't do that."

"We'd love to have you. Any of George O'Malley's kids are always welcome, you know."

"I don't shoot, either. You don't have to," C.J. called through the open passenger window. "There's plenty you can do here without guns, you know." He glanced up from his phone screen to give her a shy smile.

Jess and Alice stepped back to the gate and waved as the pickup trundled off down the track and out of sight.

"You're staying another night, then?"

"That okay?"

"Of course."

"I'm not cramping your style with your lovely policeman?"

A warm blush spread up Jess's neck, but she ignored it. "A bit. No, silly, of course not. Al, do you think it's too soon to suggest he moves in?"

Alice cast a sidelong look at her sister. "No. Yes. Maybe. I don't know. A bit?"

"That helped. Thanks." Laughing, they lengthened their steps in unspoken agreement as the rain came down harder; matching each other stride for stride as they paced the track.

"I think," Jess said, "I know what happened to Thomas."

"You do?"

"Yes. I'll tell you when we get back. I can't walk this fast and talk at the same time."

∞

By the time they got back to Orchard Close, the rain was pelting icy sheets, and even the dogs were miserable.

Jess led them in through the garden gate at the side of the house and into the kitchen, so they'd only drip rain all over the tiled kitchen floor and not the carpets. She kicked off her boots and slung her sodden coat over the back of a chair, a puddle of water already pooling beneath. "Yuk."

She ran upstairs to grab towels for their hair and the dogs, throwing two of the towels to Alice as she returned to the kitchen. "You do Snow? Come here, Fletch." She grabbed his collar and set about briskly rubbing him dry before he shook all over the kitchen.

It wasn't until after they'd showered, got into dry clothes, made tea, and set a pan of soup on the hob to warm, that they finally sank onto the sofas and continued the conversation Jess had begun as they speed-walked through the woodland trail trying not to wish they'd accepted Colm's offer of a ride after all.

"I think," she said, "that if everyone is telling the truth—including the killer, actually—then there is only one person it can be."

Alice tipped her head to one side and raised an eyebrow. "One person is usually all it is. I never did think a whole gang had done it."

Jess frowned and stuck her tongue out. "You know what I mean." She sipped her tea. "Although given the level of dislike the poor man had around here, it could easily have been a community effort." She bent her head over the mug to take another sip, and peered at Alice through lowered lashes. "I think it kind of was, to be honest. Sort of."

Alice slurped at her peppermint tea; its scent drifting with the steam that rose from the mug. She leaned forward with her elbows on her knees and the hot mug clasped between her cupped hands. "Huh?"

"I think he was killed as a favour to the family. That makes it sound a bit psycho, but I can't think how else to word it."

"Go on."

"I think the person who did it was trying to put the farm right. Allow the rest of the family a chance to undo all the environmental damage that Thomas has done; to go back to farming it the way it used to be farmed. Less intensive, more organic." She sipped and swallowed; the tea still too hot for larger gulps. "Not organic in the new sense—just more natural, I mean. Organic like farming used to be way back before weedkillers and forced growth and big sheds full of sad cows under artificial lights, never allowed to graze on all that grass. Plastoturf, Billy called it, and it reminded me of that toy farm set we had, remember?"

Alice shook her head. "Kind of. Not really, but I get what you mean."

Jess laughed into her tea. "It's the opposite, really, because those toy figures were old-fashioned and the smaller animals came attached to grass, and the sheds were too small to fit a huge great dairy herd inside anyway. Dad made us a bigger shed, but Eric always parked the tractor in it. I don't think it occurred to us to put the animals in it, now I think of it. We made fields out of all kinds of stuff ... paper, cloth, books ... We'd use whatever we could to make the fields as big as possible—like the edge of the sofa to make an extra side and save fencing. I wonder what happened to that farm ..."

"Oy. You're drifting. Did you have a point to make here?"

"Oh, yeah, sorry. I miss those old days, sometimes, when me and Eric just played all day. So anyway, if we've learned anything at all about Thomas Docherty, it was that he had no regard for nature and that everyone around him disapproved, right?"

Alice tipped her head the tiniest fraction. *Yes. Go on.*

"And he's a massive family?"

Go on.

"And the land's already been divided because Matty couldn't work to Thomas's ideals, and vice versa?"

Go on.

"And Tom—Thomas's dad—was unhappy, but caught between a rock and hard place."

"Or at least between differing family values."

"Exactly. Imagine how hard it must be if your elderly parents and your adult children want such fundamentally different things that one of them will suffer if the other gets their way? I think it must be a bit like …" She let the thought evaporate with the steam from the tea, not wanting to upset her only-recently renewed friendship with her sister.

Alice, however, was taking their newly-established relationship seriously. Studying Jess closely for a long, silent moment that stretched between them like the string on a tin-can telephone, she seemed to hear Jess's thoughts regardless of the silence. "Like when parents give all their time to one child, and their other children become sad and resentful?"

"Or sad and lonely, perhaps." Jess nodded slowly, meeting her sister's eyes and seeing that, perhaps for the first time, Alice recognised the pain her illness had caused her family. "Ah, Al, it wasn't that bad. At least me and Eric had each other. No wonder we went off solving all those mysteries! It was better to be out spying on other families than being at home watching you slowly disappear. Never mind that disappearing cat mystery—we could never solve the Case of the Disappearing Sister. Or the Mystery of the Shrinking Sister, or whatever." She stared at the steam as it swirled in front of her face, searching for patterns, but finding only abstract changing wisps.

"I'm sorry." Alice spoke so quietly Jess wasn't sure if she'd imagined it.

"I know. And you're better now. Just for God's sake stay better this time. For *our* sakes."

Fletcher leaped to his feet and charged into the hall, barking and wagging and making sure that everyone in the entire street knew someone had arrived at the front door.

Jess threw Alice an inquiring glance.

Alice shrugged one shoulder. "How would I know?"

Chapter Thirty-Eight

With a sigh, Jess pulled herself up from the sofa and padded into the hallway. A blurry, warped figure stood at the door, obscured by a large umbrella, the frosted glass, and rivulets of rain. "Shut up, Fletch. It's only Linda. Get out of the way so I can let her in."

"I just took these out of the oven. Thought you'd like a few. Tell Alice they are fat-free so she can eat plenty. Hello, Alice, love," Linda called through to the living room as she stood dripping at the front door.

"Come on in? Kettle's hot. Have a cup with us. I was just telling Alice who killed Thomas Docherty."

Linda passed the tin she was clutching to Jess so she could close her umbrella. She stood the soaked brolly on the doorstep, slipped off her shoes, hung her dripping coat from the doorhandle, and followed Jess into the living room.

Alice stood to greet her with a warm hug. "What's in the tin? Smells good." Alice cast a sidelong glance at Jess. *See*, it seemed to say, *you can trust me. I'm interested in food.*

Jess prised off the lid as Linda said, "Rock buns."

"Ooh," Jess and Alice said in unison.

"We were just talking about when we were children," Jess said, "and now you've brought us rock cakes! We used to make those with Mum." An image of herself as a child, small enough to balance precariously on a chair; Alice taller and pig-tailed; their mum, a mass of dark curls piled on her head and a cheerful apron tied around her waist. Jess, carefully stirring a mass of gloopy batter in a bowl; licking a wooden spoon. Alice, dolloping spoonfuls onto a baking sheet, meticulously making sure they were the same. Startled by the memory, Jess put a hand to her mouth. "We used to do it together. Both of us? I didn't make that up, did I?"

"I remember," Alice said.

Once Jess had made Linda tea, and Alice had fetched plates and set a fruity, knobbly rock bun onto each, the three women settled themselves in the living room.

Linda perched daintily on the edge of the armchair and studied the two younger woman sprawled on the sofas in front of her. "And how, may I ask, would you know who was responsible for that poor young man's death?" Linda's voice was solemn, as the topic warranted, but her eyes sparkled with curiosity. "Have you been investigating again? Your Marcus will have you shot—oh!" She giggled like a child into her wrinkled, liver-spotted hand. "What an unfortunate choice of words."

"I'm fairly certain it must have been the grandfather. Old Thomas."

Linda's eyes widened; her mug of tea held frozen in place half-way to her lips, and Alice's mouth hung open, the piece of cake she'd broken off dropped back to the plate.

Alice recovered first. "Yes! It makes sense, doesn't it," she said slowly.

Linda shook her head and set the tea down on the arm of the chair, her hand still gripping the handle to stop the mug tumbling to the floor. "He's a lovely man. He wouldn't." She lifted the tea again, and took a careful sip. "Although ..." She peered at Jess in the manner of a stern headmistress seeking an explanation for a playground misdemeanour. She appeared to be about to say one thing, then gave an almost imperceptible shake of her head, and when she spoke, Jess had the distinct impression that the words were not those she had first intended. "He's dying, you know?"

"Yes. That's what convinced me it must be him." Dammit. She'd promised Marcus she wouldn't tell anyone he'd told her. She bit her lower lip, considering how to put her thoughts into words without dropping Marcus in it. She gave herself a mental shake. *It doesn't matter how I know. I don't need to say anything about that.* "It's because he *is* so old, and also sick, that he could do it."

Linda nodded fractionally; another tiny, almost unnoticeable movement. "Yes. I can see why you would come to that conclusion."

Alice tore off another chunk of her rock cake, her face crumpled in thought.

Jess plucked a stray raisin from the edge of her plate. "The only other people it could really have been are Thomas's parents. There is no one else, aside from Anne—Thomas's sister—who could have been there and not been noticed. That's why I said my theory only works if *no one* is lying." She stopped to take a large bite of her bun.

Alice filled the silence. "Because his parents are each other's alibis. Both said they were together in bed, asleep, from about midnight, when Mags told Anne and her friends to quieten down or go somewhere else, until the milk lorry arrived and woke them. And even then, they didn't go out to the yard, because Old Thomas got there first."

Jess swallowed her mouthful and washed it down with a gulp of tea. "And Anne was at her cousin's house, which is backed up by both Lila and Siobhan Docherty. They all said the same thing, without prompting each other or conferring. So unless they'd prepared and practised an alibi ... I suppose that's possible, of course, but I think it's unlikely, because if they lied for each other, then one of them was asking a heck of a lot from her friends ..."

"And none of them seemed awkward or shifty when they said it ..." Alice glanced at her sister, who nodded.

"And everyone else; the farm dogs would've barked."

"And if that were the case, and the dogs *had* barked, why would everyone say they hadn't, not until the milk lorry came?"

Linda followed the parry as Jess and Alice tossed the story from one to the other, each sister effortlessly picking up whenever the other stopped to take a breath, or a bite, or a sip.

"It would be in their better interest to have said the dogs *did* bark, because that would've shifted the suspicion away from the family." Jess nibbled at a torn-off chunk from the crumbly rock bun. "And Old Thomas not only found the body, and called it in, or told his son and daughter-in-law, or whatever—"

"We don't know exactly what he did, but we do know that he—"

"Was up first when the milkman couldn't find Thomas, despite being the oldest and slowest mover in the house—"

"As if he was already awake. Maybe even already dressed? The milk driver might confirm those details. You'll have to ask Marcus to get onto that." Alice smirked at Jess. "He'll be delighted with you." Her words were laden with sarcasm, and Linda rewarded her with a thin smile.

"And he may seem sprightly, for his age," Linda said, still nodding slowly as she digested their words. "But I can tell you for nothing, no one of his age can get out of bed and get their clothes on at any great speed." For a moment her eyes glazed over, and Jess suspected she was wistfully remembering a time when she could still jump out of bed and pull on her socks without aches and pains hindering her every move.

"And," Jess said, "from what we've gleaned, it didn't take him long to find the body, once the milkman had left. Of course, that could be coincidence, but I wonder if it would be usual for Thomas to be in the hay barn at that time of day."

Alice chuckled. "We already established that his *usual* place at that time of day was meeting the milk lorry."

Jess glared at her. "You know what I mean. Anyway ... so he finds his grandson, shot and dead, and then less than a couple of hours later, he strolls to the village shop, chats with Mrs Dunne, buys his paper and his cigarettes, and strolls back to the farm as if it's just another ordinary day. He doesn't show any—"

"He's not a bit *surprised*." Alice finished.

"Even when anyone else heard, even if they wouldn't exactly be surprised that someone would have it in for the man, everyone would still be a bit surprised by *murder*. Everyone's first reaction before they said they weren't surprised, really, was to show surprise. It's the natural reaction, to hearing someone's been murdered, I would have thought." Jess finished her tea and got up to re-boil the kettle. "So what do you think, Linda?" she asked, standing in the doorway between the kitchen and living room while she waited for the water to boil. "Does it work?"

Linda's face was soft and crumpled like a tissue at a funeral, but her eyes were bright and her expression kind and thoughtful. "You know what,

Jess, I think it does. Thomas cares about that farm and his family more than anything. He's loved it since he was a child, and it's broken his heart to see what young Thomas has done to it. It's saddened him that his son never intervened. Never stood up to young Thomas." Linda pushed herself slowly out of the armchair with a soft moan followed by a gentle giggle. "This, girls, is what I mean about us oldies not being able to move in a hurry." She groaned again as she straightened up and moved in an over-exaggerated shuffle to join Jess in the kitchen.

Beyond the French doors, grey rain hid the view and the day was as dark as winter.

"Brr." Linda drew her pale blue cardigan tighter around herself. "You'd not think it was already April, not today." She shivered, although the kitchen was warm. "I don't like to say it, love, but I do think you are going to have to admit to your lovely Marcus that you and your sister have been sleuthing again." She set her tea mug down beside the sink and patted Jess's forearm. "Because, my love, I do believe you are probably correct in your deductions. Old Thomas is dying, and I would bet my hips—if I still had them—that he did what he felt he needed to ensure his family would mind his beloved farm in the way he wanted it minded when he let them take it over. I'm not saying it was right, but I'm not sure I can blame him, to tell the truth. I'm sorry to say that, and I'm not endorsing what he did, but I can see it through his eyes. He may be a decade older than me, but when you're as old as we are, it matters less. Many an hour we've passed, chatting about the good old days. Our Bert respected him, too, Jess, and that says it all, don't you think?" She turned pale, watery eyes on Jess.

"It says a lot." Jess rested her hand on Linda's as the two shared a quiet moment thinking of Bert, and how much they both missed him.

"Now, love, I will brave that weather and take myself home to Hansel and his supper. He'll be wondering where I've got to."

"He will not! Cats don't care."

Linda had adopted the street's feral tomcat after luring it into her home with a trail of salmon, and the cat had proved excellent company for her in the months after Bert's death. "You take a peek out of your window," she told Jess, "and you'll see him there at the kitchen window, waiting for me to get home safely, you mark my words."

"You'll not have another cup of tea first?"

"I won't." Linda shuffled back through the living room, stooping to meet Alice as she half-rose from the sofa to exchange a hug.

Jess, meanwhile, had knelt up on the sofa in the bay window to press her nose against the glass and peer at Number 15 across the street. "I'll have to take your word for it. I can't see that far in all this rain. Will you be all right, now? Don't get washed away."

She walked with Linda to the door and helped her into her coat, pulling it closed and fastening the zip for her elderly friend. "Thank you for the rock cakes. They were the perfect thing for a rainy nostalgic afternoon. You're such a good friend to me. And to Alice, too." She pecked Linda's papery cheek, opened the door, put Linda's umbrella up, and pressed it into her hand. "Go on. I'll watch till you're in."

Chapter Thirty-Nine

Marcus kicked off his shoes, greeted Fletcher with a rub, Jess with a warm hug, and Alice with a friendly peck on the cheek, and yawned widely. He shooed Snowflake and Fletcher into the kitchen and straight out the French doors to continue their exuberant greeting of each other in the garden. The dogs out of the way, he turned once more to Jess. "What have you done now?" He hid another yawn behind his hand and Jess passed him a cup of tea. He sighed heavily and pulled out a chair at the table. "Go on. Out with it. You're looking guilty. But do try to remember that I *cannot* discuss an open murder investigation with you, please?"

"Let's go sit comfortably? You're wrecked."

"But it might be important, if we're right, so we have to say it," Alice added. "Sorry."

Obediently if not happily, he got up and moved to the living room, where he sank down into the armchair Linda had perched on earlier, yawned again, and drank the tea in a few quick mouthfuls. As was his way, he listened carefully as the sisters filled him in on their conclusions, asking few questions but nodding occasionally to show he was paying attention. That he had chosen not to sit beside Jess on the sofa, in what had become his usual seat over the past few months, was enough proof that he was taking their accusations seriously, and when he got to his feet and paced the room, Jess knew he was considering the likelihood of truth in her words.

When she'd finished presenting her jumbled spiel of speculation and evidence, Marcus rubbed his hand over his head, sighed again, and finally sank onto the sofa beside her.

"Let's say for a moment that you are right, and old Mr Docherty did in fact, shoot and poison his grandson, with *deliberate intent*—" He emphasised the words to allow no doubt of the severity of the accusation. "—then I would have to call it in." The tiredness and worry in his eyes caused Jess's heart to flip, and she rubbed his knee softly.

"You would," she agreed. "But you wouldn't have to do it now, would you, because we didn't have this conversation yet." She looked at Alice, who shook her head.

"We didn't have this conversation until, oh, I don't know, breakfast tomorrow? Are you working tomorrow?"

Marcus shook his head, stifling another yawn. "Not until tomorrow evening."

"I am, don't forget. I told you, I'm covering Ella, since there's no college this week."

"Jess is taking me to the station on her way to work. About twelve. We probably had a serious conversation about this over a late, lazy breakfast. We wouldn't bother you with it after a long day, and if we tried, you'd brush us off, tell us not to get involved. You wouldn't listen."

Marcus watched them, his eyes darting from one to the other as they spoke. He said nothing, but as they went on, his face creased into the deep laughter lines Jess loved so much.

She reached up and touched his cheek with her fingertips. "Sorry. You're wrecked. Dinner's almost ready."

"And that, my love, is exactly why I believe your mad notions. You didn't even bribe me into listening by feeding me first. I won't call it in now, because right now, it is nothing but speculation, assumptions, and village gossip. It is also nothing we have not considered in the course of the investigations, and I am quite confident that our Mr Docherty is not going to be any threat to this village tonight. If you are indeed right, we will allow an old man one last night in his own home before he is charged." He tipped his head back against the sofa and closed his eyes. "You might like to know," he said, his eyes flickering open again for a fraction of a second, "that we have reached almost the same conclusion at the station, anyway."

No wonder he was so drained, Jess realised. The idea of jailing a nonagenarian was bad enough, but when he was also respected and loved throughout the parish and had done something that many others must have considered doing, it would be an emotional arrest. She stroked Marcus's face again, drinking him in, a flush of warmth and affection pulsing through her veins and leaving a tingle in her belly. He didn't open his eyes, but smiled, probably guessing she was watching. She kissed his cheek and got up.

In the kitchen, Alice set the table while Jess put the final touches to plates of sausages, mash, green beans and a river of onion-filled gravy.

"You've got it bad." Alice reached past her sister to get glasses from the high cupboard.

"You're wrong," Jess replied, her back to Alice as she spooned beans onto the plates. "I've got it good." She turned, a plate in each hand, her smile so wide it made her cheeks ache. "I love him, Al."

"I know, silly. You should tell him."

"Yes." Jess set down the plates, added the third, and tiptoed back to the living room to call Marcus to the table. "Wake up. Dinner. You can go to bed after."

⁂

They woke up late the next morning, and Marcus, craving a fry-up, drove to the shop to get a packet of bacon. When he returned, somewhat later than Jess would have expected, his face was sombre, his eyes dark, and his forehead creased in a frown.

He set the bacon on the countertop and stared out over the garden. "Mr Docherty didn't pick up his paper this morning," he said without turning. "So I drove on up to the farm. He died in the night. Peacefully, in his bed."

Jess let out a gasp, echoed by Alice's sharp inhalation of breath. "He's dead?" they said, together.

"He's dead." He continued to stare out across the garden, his words heavy and slow. "It was expected. Honestly, that's partly why I ... why I agreed to listen to you last night, and why I didn't act on what you said. When we interviewed him, he told us he'd been told he had days. I'm glad he died peacefully, and not in jail, Jess."

She wrapped her arms around his waist and rested her head on his back. "You're a good man, Marcus. You did the right thing." *I love you.*

"I'll need to go in, after breakfast. He left a letter." He twisted around to return the embrace. "It means I'll be home tonight, though. Silver linings, huh?"

"Home?" She raised her face to meet his eyes. "Or here?"

"I meant here. It feels like home, O'Malley." Then he added softly, so only she could hear, "*You* feel like home."

∞

With the excitement and distraction of Marcus's news, Alice missed another train. Instead, she sat once again in Shay's office, sipping boiled water from a chipped Bart Simpson mug, while Jess served a steady stream of customers in the shop.

At ten to three, she plonked two mugs of tea beside the till, one for Jack and one for Jess. "Shay said you'd be needing another one by now. I need to get to the station. I'll walk, though. You're busy here. Give me the keys so I can get my bag?"

Too busy to argue, Jess handed over the keys, pausing briefly in the middle of helping a customer order a new garden patio set and elaborate water feature for a garden far too small for them.

A moment later, Alice dropped the keys onto the counter. "Here you go. It's locked. Let me know what happens, yeah?"

"About Old Thomas? Of course I will." She stepped around the counter and wrapped Alice in a long, tight hug. "Come again soon, won't you?"

"I will. I'd better say goodbye to Shay. Back in a sec." She parked her bag behind the counter and strode towards the double doors leading to the garden centre yard, only to reappear a moment later with Shay in tow.

"I'll run her to the station; I've to shoot out anyway. Meeting a chap about some stone. Be about an hour, I'd say. Hold the fort. Ready Alice?"

Alice flung her arms around Jess for one last hug, whispering, "Tell him. Marcus, I mean. Tell him how you feel. He's worth it, Jess." She pulled away, still grasping Jess's hands. "And don't forget to let me know about Old Thomas. See you soon."

Shay picked up Alice's bag, and she dove forward for one last peck on Jess's cheek, let go of her hands, and followed Shay out to the carpark.

Chapter Forty

The Dochertys buried Old Thomas on Saturday morning, under a bright blue sky and the warmest day of the year so far. Jess, although she wasn't sure she'd ever met the man, felt compelled to attend the service, and stood at the very back of the church beside Marcus, listening to Father James speak with genuine warmth about the deceased patriarch.

After the mass, she joined the long, long line of well-wishers, and was surprised when first Anne and then Siobhan pulled her into a quick hug as she reached each of them in the receiving line.

Matty, too, seemed happier to see her than she would have expected from someone she barely knew. "Thank you," he whispered, as he grasped her hand between both of his for a brief moment.

What for? She wanted to ask, but the line of mourners ushered her on.

She skipped the graveside ceremonies and walked the short distance to Marcus's cottage with him, hand in hand as they strolled along in the sunshine.

Thomas's last letter to his family had confirmed Jess's theory.

At ninety-six, his own shaky hand-writing was illegible, so by necessity, he had chosen Colm as the keeper and scribe of his final secret. In slow and careful enunciation, two days after he'd shot his grandson, he'd admitted to Colm that he'd killed Thomas to save the farm from destruction and reunite the remaining family, who he tasked with returning the farm to the old ways.

With the culprit dead, and no longer able to be held to account for the murder, Marcus shared the details freely with Jess. By Thursday evening, he'd told her most of the finer details of Thomas's killing, although, as it transpired, they were infinitely less gory than she'd been imagining.

The poison had not, as Jess had envisaged, been rammed into the man's mouth at gunpoint while he writhed in terror, facing his attacker with the dawning realisation he was about to be murdered by one of his family. Nor were his gunshot wounds administered in the same order as those found on the buzzard. He'd been killed quickly, cleanly, with a single shot to the chest; the pellets fired into his shoulder had been a secondary, postmortem addition. Two guns, too. One to kill fast and sure like a mink in a trap; the second to fire a spray of pellets to link the crime to the buzzard. Only then, after closing his dead grandson's eyes, and laying him gently on the hay, had Old Thomas put a single lump of rodent bait into Young Thomas's mouth. The order of injury had been one of the reasons the Gardai had, like Jess, narrowed the suspects down to the very closest members of the younger Thomas's family.

"He wouldn't have known a thing about it, bar the moment he saw the gun in his grandfather's hands," Marcus had said over a second glass of wine after a simple pasta meal on Thursday evening. "He died instantly. Someone went to great efforts to ensure it was as painless and quick as possible, despite initial appearances. He was laid out gently, too."

"A humane killing, like they do with the vermin at the Gun Club." Jess's laugh was dry and brittle and without amusement. "Oh!" She smacked her hand to her mouth. "I might have met him, actually. Old Thomas. Kind of. I bet it was him I saw up at the Gun Club the first day I walked up. There was an ancient man leaning on a cage. I'm sure Billy said he was called Thomas. And there were two border collies, too ... bet it was him."

"He wanted to leave a clear message; a clear motive." Marcus had told Jess. "To leave no doubt as to why he'd killed the boy, and enough pointers that we'd get the right culprit soon enough. In his letter, he said he hoped he'd be dead, too, by the time we joined the dots, but if he wasn't he'd take the repercussions. If we'd have made an arrest—anyone that wasn't him, that is—he'd have spoken up."

"Would he?" Jess had wondered. If push came to shove, would a man who could kill his own flesh and blood care if someone else took the blame for it? She wasn't so sure.

Linda, however, had been quite sure, when Jess discussed it with her afterwards, on Friday morning. "He was a good man," Linda insisted in her soft, gentle way. "He set it up to work out as best it could, given he'd killed a man."

"He mentioned you," Marcus had told Jess as they'd watched the sun go down over Marcus's little garden that Thursday night. "Not by name, but as 'The young one who reported us to the NPWS'. He said you weren't to feel any guilt over his actions. He'd been planning things for a while; needed to ensure that the farm would be properly cared for once he was gone. When Peggy called to the farm, it wasn't so much the final straw—that had been laid on his back long ago, the note said—but it did give him the idea as to *what* to do. He wanted to make a statement so clear that anyone would know why he'd done it."

"But," Jess had argued, "by leaving so clear a message, he almost had the opposite effect to what he'd intended. He can't have counted on Mrs Dunne and Gerry telling the entire village about the poor buzzard!" Their wagging tongues had made the suspect pool so huge it looked like almost anyone in the parish had the knowledge to have done the deed. That knowledge, combined with the widespread bad feelings about what young Thomas had done to the land, both on his own farm, and its knock-on effects to the surrounding land, gave motive to the masses. "I am glad you gave me such a strong alibi, I have to admit. And in more ways than one." At that, she'd given him a look so laden with intent they hadn't talked about the Dochertys any more that evening.

※

After a full week of April sun, the grassy verges had really greened up. The spring flowers on the bog lane, the river road, and the track to the Gun Club spread a cheerful carpet of colour across the parish that made Jess smile wherever she walked. Spring was in the air and in her steps, and she was inching ever-closer to asking Marcus what he'd think about moving in.

Her motives and enthusiasm for walking the dogs along the pub lane had dissipated with the revelation that Old Thomas had shot his grandson, and since then, she'd walked closer to home most days, enjoying the sun on her face and the drier ground underfoot.

The Friday after Old Thomas's funeral, she was moseying along the trail to the Gun Club when a shot rang out, startling her and sending the dogs running to her in panic. She clipped on their leads and rounded the bend, hesitating when she saw Billy White's muddy black pickup parked in front of the gate.

He raised his arm as he saw her cautious approach. "It's okay, come on over."

They met at the gate, and behind Billy, Matty stepped out from behind the bird cages, a gun slung over his shoulder.

He too, lifted his hand in greeting. "Jess," he called as he closed the gap between them and came to a stop beside Billy. "Good to see you." He rested a hand on the top bar of the gate and a foot on the bottom rung. "How's things?"

"I heard a shot?" She gestured to the gun.

"Mink. We got one in the trap. Little feckers."

"Oh. Colm said you have to shoot them."

"Aye. It's the law. Pests, they are. Invasive. Trouble." He shifted his weight to the other foot, and the gun to his other shoulder. "Anne was talking about you, the other day. She said you'd know about hedging and wildflowers and the like?"

Still keeping an eye on the gun, she nodded, then shook her head. "A bit. I work at the garden centre. And I'm on a horticulture course." She named the college, and the two men nodded in recognition. "Why?"

"Granda's will. He asked that any money left after expenses be used to rewild areas of the farm. Within the bounds of sensible farming, of course. Anne said you might be a good person to ask about it."

"Sounds interesting. I'm glad. Tell me what you want to know and I'll try to find out?"

"We're planning to reinstate large areas of woodland; put in a pond or two, let corners of fields go wild, that kind of thing." Matty waved his arm to encompass the rough ground behind them. "Incorporate some preserved areas. Introduce new stocks of game birds."

"Bring back the buzzards." Billy grinned at her; a spark in his eyes that told her he was teasing her. "You'll know all about those."

She smiled back. "Peggy would, for sure—you know, the Parks and Wildlife woman? The one who told everyone I reported it. She'd know exactly what you'd need to do, to encourage them to nest there again."

"Tell you what," Matty said. "You free tonight? Want to meet us at the pub, discuss some ideas? Bring your Peggy one along too, if she's free? More the merrier. Granda would've liked to see a bunch of us young ones putting our heads together for the good of the farm. I'll give Anne a shout, see if she's up for a pint or two." He pulled out a phone, smirked, and added, "She usually is." He grinned at Jess and fired off a text, watching the screen until it lit up again a moment later.

"Told you so. Eight suit you? Bring your policeman, if you like. He's a sound fellow, is Marcus."

⁂

By the time the landlord called last orders, the group had covered several pages with ideas and dreams. Peggy, as Jess had suspected, knew exactly what could be done to encourage the larger prey birds back to the farmland. Not just buzzards, but kestrels, hawks, and owls. Bats, too. She suggested ways they could access grants and funding, and her curls bounced like loose springs as she jiffled with excitement.

Her partner, Julie, tall, dark-blonde, and dryly funny, had tagged along too, and enthused about fish, ponds, and frogspawn more than Jess had ever thought it possible to get excited by slimy jelly and stagnant water.

Anne and Matty, heads bent together over a map of the land, sketched out where to replant hedges, where to plant new trees, where to leave wild.

"We'll seed the front of the house with native wild flowers, like Granny used to have," Anne said, tracing a large square on the map with her fingertip. "Put in beehives?"

Matty quickly, easily, agreed. "I was hoping to add more bees anyway. Be nice to put some on the old land, if there's no more spraying."

"We'll open a nature reserve for the local schools, and call it the Thomas Docherty Nature reserve," Anne said, to guffaws of laughter and much table-slapping.

"Oh God, yes." Lila spluttered into giggles at the suggestion and tipped the last of her Budweiser down her throat. "Your old grandpa would be delighted, and—"

"And only we will know it's for our Thomas, too," Anne said, her smile becoming sad. "He'd forgotten how much he loved it when he was small. He was the one who taught me and Sarah to make daisy chains, you know." She dabbed away threatening tears. "We do miss him, but what we miss most is the kid he used to be before he turned into such a tosser."

"Time, everyone. On you go now." The landlord gathered a trayful of bottles and glasses and nodded at Anne and Matty. "On the house, that last lot; till's locked up now, and good luck with it all. Goodnight."

As they stepped out into the cold, starlit night, an owl called from somewhere behind the pub, and another, further away, called back. Marcus wrapped his arm around Jess's shoulders, and they crossed the road and set off towards his cottage. Behind them, towards the Dochertys' farm, the pair of owls called again, like a pair of creaky gates blowing in the wind.

The End

Acknowledgements

January 28, 2024

As usual, I thank you, the reader, first. Without you, there'd be less incentive to keep writing. I'd do it anyway, of course, because I like it, but knowing **you** are reading my books is a great driving force to keep me at it, and makes me exceedingly happy. Thank you.

My husband, as always, supports and encourages my writing, and affords me the time for it by working his little socks off to pay the mortgage while I sit around writing books. My children, too, have become increasingly supportive as time goes by. They say they might even get around to reading something I write one of these days.

Another big thank you goes to Cindy Cripps-Prawak, who won the opportunity to feature in this book. She has become a larger character than either of us expected, and will probably show up again in the next book! (Look out for future opportunities to feature in books by subscribing to my newsletter—see the *About the Author* section.)

The rest of these acknowledgements are harder than usual. At the front of the book, I promised to explain why I dedicated this book to the people who live in my village, so I'll tackle that first.

Jess O'Malley first came into existence way back in 2017, when I was doing an Open University degree module in Creative Writing. I remember sitting in my car outside my daughter's ballet class in rapidly-fading light, frantically scribbling out what eventually became a complete short story about Jess, Kate, and Bert. The idea for that story grew from a much-loved and respected villager, who attended the local slimming group and suffered a suspected heart attack (from which he fortunately recovered). That short story then grew into a full novel, and became *A Diet of Death*, the first in my Jess O'Malley Irish village mystery series.

As I completed the final draft of *A Wake of Buzzards*, in October 2023, the man who'd triggered the whole idea for that first story, and became 'Bert', died. He was very much the pillar of our community for the first decade or so that we lived here, before ill-health and age finally slowed him down. He will be greatly missed by the whole community, and for me, will be ever-entwined with my notions of what this village is and has been.

Other events or people in the village have inspired many other story ideas, and *A Wake of Buzzards* was born from the time I found a dead buzzard, shot and poisoned, on a farm track not too far from where I live. Peggy, my fictional Parks and Wildlife woman, is probably nothing like the real NPWS woman who came to relieve me of my own dead buzzard—I don't remember her at all! Thomas Docherty, meanwhile, *might* be very loosely based on a particular farmer, who *might* be a little trigger-happy with the weedkiller and decimation of the hedgerows, woodlands, and wildflowers. IMHO.

So, initially, the dedication in this book was to honour the friends, neighbours, and villagers who have slipped into these pages, albeit unknowingly, and to thank them for inspiring the almost-fictional world of Ballyfortnum. This book is still for all of you.

Then, in January 2024, just as I was tackling the edits and preparing to get this book out into the world, two of my dearest friends also died. The community is still reeling in shock and sorrow, and I am writing these acknowledgements just two weeks after we said our goodbyes at their funeral. On one of the many blurry in-between days of the past three weeks, while numbness carries us between their deaths and *now*, I was walking my dogs along the road beside my house. The day was bright, the sky blue, the rain finally stopped for a while. Two buzzards swooped into the road ahead of me, then soared across the fields in the sunlight. A wake of buzzards, for my dear, dear friends. Morag and Paul.

About the Author

For up-to-date news and exclusive content including your own map of Ballyfortnum and extra short stories about the characters in this series, please sign up for Jinny's newsletter by popping over to her website:
www.jinnyalexander.com
Say hello at facebook.com/JinnyAlexanderAuthor
or
instagram.com/jinnyalexanderauthor/
To help other readers discover this series, please leave a review on Amazon and Goodreads. Thank you.

※

Jinny was first published in Horse and Pony magazine at the age of ten. She's striving to achieve equal accolades now she's (allegedly) a grown-up. Jinny has had some publishing success with short story and flash competitions and has been placed in the prestigious Bath Flash Fiction Award, Flash 500 and Writer's Playground contests, published in MsLexia Magazine and Writing Magazine, among other publishing credits. Jinny has recently completed an MA in Creative Writing with the University of Hull, for which she was awarded a Distinction.

Jinny also teaches English as a foreign language to people all over the world and finds her students a constant source of inspiration for both life and stories. Her home, for now, is in rural Ireland, which she shares with her husband and far too many animals. Her two children have grown and flown, but return across the Irish Sea when they can. If you follow her on Facebook, you'll see many photos of the settings of her novels. *A Wake of Buzzards* was inspired by a real incident, where the author found a buzzard a few years ago, much as Jess did, and had to report it to Ireland's National Parks and Wildlife Service.

Also by Jinny Alexander

The fourth and fifth Jess O'Malley mysteries, ***A Deathbed of Roses*** and ***A Snapshot of Murder***, will be coming soon.

Jinny is currently working on more sequels in the Jess O'Malley series, and plotting a new series: Mrs Smith's Suspects.

Jinny also has stories and flash fiction in anthologies and magazines.

A more comprehensive list can be found on her website at

www.JinnyAlexander.com

Dear Isobel (March 2022, Creative James Media) is currently out of print following Jinny's reversion of rights.

Praise for *A Diet of Death*

This is a light-hearted cosy that will delight fans of M C Beaton's Agatha Raisin. […] Highly recommend it to those looking for a frothy, enjoyable read that is low on violence and high on feel-good entertainment!

MAIRI CHONG,
The Dr. Cathy Moreland Mysteries

Well-written and intriguing, this mystery revolving around members of a weight-loss group is one that will keep you turning the pages until the very end.

KELLY YOUNG,
The Travel Writer Cozy Mystery Series

A classic British style whodunnit.
With an engaging and believable heroine - Jess O'Malley - and set in rural Ireland, this is a fun mystery with lots of heart. An enjoyable read leading to a satisfying solution, already looking forward to the next book.

GERALDINE MOORKENS BYRNE
The Caroline Jordan Mystery series and *On the Fiddle! The Music Shop Mysteries*

The whole book was a warm, comforting read for anyone who loves mysteries. Highly suggested for fans of *The Thursday Murder Club*.

ALISON WEATHERBY,
The Secrets Act

Jinny Alexander's outstanding cosy mystery *A Diet Of Death* is a real treat. (And not the kind with calories!)

J. IVANEL JOHNSON,
The JUST (e)STATE Cozy Mysteries

This tale is a homage to those much loved classic detective authors, and is perfect for escaping the worries and stresses of the world.

LOUISE MORRISH,
Operation Moonlight

Jinny Alexander embeds her murder mystery with the satisfying atmosphere of rural Ireland. […] Cozy mystery readers who enjoy stories of friendships and murder possibilities will find *A Diet of Death* unusually strong in its atmosphere, which does equal justice to both the murder mystery component and the entwined lives of a small village […]

MIDWEST BOOK REVIEW

Praise for *A Hover of Trout*

A warm hug of a book; a literary mug of cocoa with a dash of murder for spice. Jinny Alexander once again captures village life with her quirky cast of characters. I'm already looking forward to Jess O'Malley and the gang's next outing.

AMANDA GEARD,
The Midnight House, The Moon Gate

A Hover of Trout is an excellent second book in the Jess O'Malley Mystery series […] as well-written as the first, with intriguing characters, plenty of suspects, and some interesting character dynamics.

KELLY YOUNG,
The Travel Writer Cozy Mystery Series

A Hover of Trout, the second in the Jess O'Malley Mystery series, is an absolute joy for those who love classic detective mysteries. Sprinkled with a little romance along with the comfort and familiarity of Jess's rural Irish village, this expertly-crafted page-turner of a whodunnit had me guessing until the end. An excellent addition to the series!

ALISON WEATHERBY,
The Secrets Act

Fabulous characters and witty dialogue as more mysteries are revealed and solved by Jinny Alexander. I guarantee you will go back and read Book 1 in this charming mystery series.

MIKE MARTIN,
Award Winning Author of the Best Selling Sgt. Windflower Mystery series

The story is satisfyingly twisty with plenty of red herrings, coupled with likeable, believable characters. There's plenty of fun, and a lot of heart. The Jess O'Malley series deserves to become a firm favourite with mysteries lovers everywhere.

GERALDINE MOORKENS BYRNE
The Caroline Jordan Mystery series and *On the Fiddle! The Music Shop Mysteries*

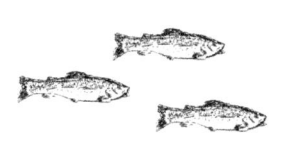

Lyrical, atmospheric, Alexander's words lure you alongside amateur sleuth Jess O'Malley into the tangled webs of Ballyfortnum village. Very soon, you're too caught up to leave, nor do you want to. If you need a cosy weekend escape read, this is your ticket.

DAMYANTI BISWAS,
The Blue Mumbai series

This, the second in Alexander's Jess O'Malley series, is an incredibly satisfying read.

Jess O'Malley is the perfect companion on a wintery evening with the curtains drawn and a steaming mug of hot chocolate! A frothy mystery sprinkled with just the right amount of intrigue and a healthy dollop of romance, what's not to love?

MAIRI CHONG,
The Dr. Cathy Moreland Mysteries

Printed in Great Britain
by Amazon